THE WEATHER DIVINER

THE

WEATHER

DIVINER

A NOVEL

ELIZABETH MURPHY

Breakwater Books
PO Box 2188, St. John's, NL, Canada, A1C 6E6
www.breakwaterbooks.com

**A CIP catalogue record for this book is available
from Library and Archives Canada.**

ISBN 9781778530319 (softcover)
© 2024 Elizabeth Murphy

Laurence Binyon, *For the Fallen*, The Times, 1914. Public domain.
Gerald S. Doyle, "A Noble Fleet of Sealers," *Old-Time Songs and
    Poetry of Newfoundland* (1978). Quote used with permission.
Margaret Duley, *The Caribou Hut: The Story of a Newfoundland
    Hostel* (The Ryerson Press, 1949). Public domain.

We acknowledge the support of the Canada Council for the Arts.
We acknowledge the financial support of the Government of
Canada through the Department of Heritage and the Government
of Newfoundland and Labrador through the Department of
Tourism, Culture, Arts and Recreation for our publishing activities.

Printed and bound in India by Imprint Press.

Breakwater Books is committed to choosing papers and
materials for our books that help to protect our environment.
To this end, this book is printed on a recycled paper and other
sources that are certified by the Forest Stewardship Council®.

 Canada Council   Conseil des Arts
for the Arts   du Canada

 Newfoundland
Labrador

 Canada

For
NEWFOUNDLAND

Loved despite its harshness.

Newfoundland is a country where wind and fire make vicious company, but truly the wind will always make the country one of the "Big Breath." The wind never lets people off. It bends them double, sniffs at them like dogs tempted by a bone; it snatches at the fashionable hat and the new hair-do; and in pioneer days it is recorded that the settlers went out tied together. Once, it is told, that a wrestler came to Newfoundland, and he became so tormented by the wind, that he stopped in the street to fight it.

– Margaret Duley, *The Caribou Hut:*
The Story of a Newfoundland Hostel, 1949

1

The new year surprised us with a white hurricane so fierce, even someone with my skills could not have predicted it. At its peak, I feared the gusts would strip our saltbox house down to its wooden bones, starting with the roof, followed by one plank of spruce clapboard after another. The old house already suffered a slight tilt, shaped by the same prevailing westerlies that deformed the shoreline's evergreens into gnarly tuckamore, or what my father called *krummholz*. As for the stone lighthouse tower and covered passageway to the house, water, not wind, posed the greatest threat. Repeated cycles of freezing and thawing would eventually erode the mortar, destroying them both. I'd be long gone from my windswept home by then, though not by choice.

While the storm raged, we endured rattling windows, creaking walls, and the rumbling drone of swash and backwash on our shingle beach. We dressed in woolen layers, drank scalding hot tea, and fed the cookstove like it was a spoiled pet. We kept the kitchen lanterns glowing, their chimneys polished and wicks neatly trimmed to excite the flame, yellow one minute, blue the next. Neither of us dared venture outside, aware of the risks of losing our way, then accidentally falling over granite cliffs hundreds of millions of years old and seemingly that high in feet.

Finally, the sky cleared, the sun shone, and the snow stopped falling. I donned my one-size-fits-two sealskin parka, sure to keep me warm though too heavy for comfort on my slight frame and awkward for shovelling. With the full force of my body, I rammed the door, fighting against a drift, then squeezed through, shovel in hand. At first, I felt relieved to breathe fresh air without a hint of cookstove smoke. After clearing paths to the well, outhouse, chicken coop, root cellar, woodpile, and shed, I couldn't wait to go back inside, sip on a strong cup of tea, and devour a generous serving of Maryanne's boiled pudding. But I wasn't finished yet.

I used my measuring pole to determine snow depth in six different spots, then mentally calculated the average. No need to check the anemometer except to ensure it hadn't blown off its mount. Frothing whitecaps and spindrift told me the winds were still gale-force. By then, my toes were painfully cold despite two layers of wool socks in my boots. The raw air stung my cheeks, and the sunlight's blinding reflection off the snow made my head ache. I pulled back my sleeve to check my watch. The sun wouldn't set until four thirty and it was only early morning. The remaining chores could wait—topping up the water barrel, disposing of the chamber pots' contents in the outhouse, feeding the chickens, and lugging in wood to replace the extra junks burned.

Warm air gushed past when I opened the door to the kitchen from the porch. With it came an appetizing waft of Demerara rum mixed with Jamaican molasses.

Maryanne stood, clutching her hand-knit shawl to her chest, bits of sage green wool hanging off its tattered ends. "You were gone so long, I thought the fairies took you, Violet," she said, and laughed.

In a hungry, rather than a laughing mood, I bent over, arms extended.

She tugged on the bulky parka, pulled it over my head, and hung it to dry behind the cookstove. "That thing weighs as much as a seal."

I wanted to ask why she seemed out of breath but knew she'd never admit feeling tired or unwell, as if that required an apology. "Rest. I'll take care of the other chores later."

"I'll rest in my grave. Sit down. Tea's hot, pudding's warm."

I leaned back on the chair, its spindles pressing uncomfortably against my muscles, tender after too long bent over at the waist. "Guess how much fell."

She picked up the folded newspaper from the corner of the table. "Enough to cause trouble."

"A month's worth in two days. That's a record. I already decided what I'll write in the weather log. 'January fourth to sixth, 1942, thirty-nine inches of snow. Sustained winds of seventy-five miles per hour. Northeasterlies.

High swells…" I paused to watch her, the newspaper close to her eyes, elbows poking out, a strand of white hair hanging from under her bandana grazing her cheek. "Are you listening, Maryanne?"

"Where's the darn thing?" She flipped between pages, tutting and shaking her head. "I saw it five minutes ago."

"How about I order glasses for you?"

"Forget glasses," she said. "If I had a minute to squander, I'd write to the editor, tell him there's so many ads, he should pay us to read the news, not the other way round."

"I'll do it for you. I know you dislike writing letters."

"Don't waste your ink. You'd have to be a Mister Violet for the editor to pay attention." She smacked the crease, folded the paper into fourths, then laid it between our teacups. "Have a gander under 'help wanted.'"

I pinched a fat raisin from the pudding, chewed on its juicy sweetness, then swallowed it with black tea. I'd been shovelling since dawn and had slept fitfully for the past two nights. The last thing I wanted was to face those ads again, each one a pitiful reminder of my *zugzwang* position—forced to make a move yet certain nothing positive could come of it. In Maryanne's words, caught between a rock and a hard place.

WANTED: *Young housemaid with an understanding of plain cooking, washing, tending babies. Family of 6. $20/month. References required. 7 Hayward Ave.*

WANTED: *Good needle hands. Outport girl preferred. Newfoundland Clothing Company. Phone 3023 W.*

WANTED: *Experienced lady assistant for confectioner's shop. Apply to Box 68, Evening Telegram.*

"This is your best rum-and-molasses pudding yet, Maryanne." I licked my fork, savouring the burnt caramel taste. "The assistant for a confectioner's shop sounds promising. Does a sweet tooth count for qualifications?"

I imagined my father, Vati, joking, "As long as it's a sweet wisdom tooth." Of course, if he'd still been alive, we wouldn't be discussing help-wanted ads. We'd be reviewing the signs that foretold the storm—high humidity, darkening sky, the startling drop in barometric pressure, and the calm before the wind's abrupt shift. I'd be making excuses for why I hadn't pre-dicted winds of such magnitude or precipitation in those amounts. How could I have predicted something record-breaking?

"Not those ads," Maryanne said. "The one from the Yanks. Get in with them while you can. Before you know it, they'll up-anchor and sail away on the high tide. Once they're gone, there'll be no work for women except in service."

She may have had it right about work, but she was wrong about the Americans. They had come to defend the new Gibraltar of America, gate-way to the Gulf of St. Lawrence. Someone had to do it. "I doubt your Yanks would be spending millions of dollars if they planned to leave any-time soon. They've only been here a year and in the war for a month. Their ninety-nine-year lease of bases has a long way ahead of it."

"Ninety-nine?" Maryanne said. "We'll all be in the ground by then or living on the moon."

She tapped the paper with the end tine of her fork. "Read it out loud, Violet, please, so I know you got the right one."

A tiny crumb lay on the page like a misplaced punctuation mark. I flicked it away with my finger, wanting to flick the entire paper in the direction of the cookstove, as if that could change the fact that Vati was gone forever, the new keeper would arrive in a month, and I had nowhere to go and no means to earn a living.

"Wanted: Office girls. Minimum grade 8 diploma required. Apply in person. Fort Pepperrell, St. John's." I'd read it out loud, slowly, pausing after commas and periods, pretending for her sake to be interested. "Even if I wanted to apply, I don't meet the minimum requirements."

"What odds about minimum in a world flipped on its backside with torpedoes and guns? Maximum is what counts, your know-how. It's worth five of their diplomas."

"My keeper's know-how isn't worth anything except at a light station."

"If that's all you see in the mirror, then don't be saying I'm the one needs glasses. And don't be like Dorothy, too blind to see she could go where she wanted. Don't be like the scarecrow either. He had straw between his ears till the wizard gave him a brain."

"I wish the wizard would give me one. Either that or magic shoes."

Maryanne stood, bent over at first, then turned toward me, hands on hips. "You could be a teacher of teachers with everything your father taught you. If you can run a lighthouse, you can spin an office on your little pinkie."

"You're forgetting that the foghorn hasn't worked in months. I haven't got a clue how to fix it. Vati was the magician, I, merely his assistant."

"What do you think an office girl is? An assistant."

I sighed purposely. "Not the kind the Americans want."

"Who's to say what they want? Barrels of money, living high on the hog in cities, none of that makes them any grander than us crowd."

"It has nothing to do with being grander, Maryanne. They simply want proof the girls are educated."

"Their eyes are crossed, thinking a scrap of paper proves anyone's worth. But if that's what they're after, I got just the thing." She stood up from the table.

"A diploma?"

"Something far better. Let me fetch it for you." She left the kitchen, shuffling her feet like they were too heavy to lift, her long skirt sweeping the wooden floor.

What did I care about office girls or diplomas? I cared about having to leave home—the only one I'd ever known—a home ruled by the natural world, by cycles of seasons, tides, sun, and moon, by forces as powerful yet as invisible as gravity. Vati called it the land at earth's edge, surrounded by seas savage one day, docile the next, the tower's light a warning to mariners not to fall over the horizon. Maybe we would have stayed forever at Crag Point. If there hadn't been another war, if politics and power didn't rule and ruin the world, maybe we'd have headed to Europe and visited Vati's childhood home in Berlin.

The steam rose from a pot on the cookstove, enveloping the top cabinet where the windup clock tick-tocked the seconds, the house's steady heartbeat, second after second, season after season, reassuringly predictable. It tick-tocked that way when Vati was alive and now that he was gone. Four months or four hours—what did the clock or calendar know about loss? I still pictured him by my side in the tower, his brown eyes magnified by his spectacles, elfish smile so endearing. I wished I could simply turn to him and say, "Where will I go, Vati? What will I do?" He usually had an answer to my questions. If not, he'd tell me to ask Maryanne. If she didn't have an answer, she'd be quick to invent one.

2

f the ad for the office girl had said to apply in writing, I might have considered doing so. I had extensive experience composing Dear-Sir and To-Whom-It-May-Concern letters, regarding orders damaged, incomplete, or missing and for subscription renewals or cancellations. Though I didn't congratulate myself for it, I was a champion at not receiving replies. A champion too at imagining the readers of my letters—editors, their fingertips blackened with printer's ink, shopkeepers in their aprons, postal clerks with their pencils neatly sharpened.

In this case, I pictured a man at the civilian personnel office, Fort Pepperrell. He's slumped over a desktop cluttered with unopened envelopes—all letters of application for the office girls' position. He rests a hand over his forehead to block the ceiling light's glare and soothe the headache that worsens with each new mail delivery. An envelope catches his eye. "Hm, useful office girl skill," he mumbles to himself, admiring the decorative swirls on the *F* and *P* in Fort Pepperrell. He slides the letter opener into the gummed seal and slices open the envelope. He takes out the letter and unfolds it, impressed by the neatness of the Spencerian script.

January 6, 1942

Dear Sir,

I would like to apply for the office girl position. Though I completed the grade 11 syllabus through independent study, I lack an actual diploma. Who could blame me for not daring to venture from my Crag Point home in Notre Dame Bay to the nearest community, Pine Harbour, to write examinations when I was only seventeen? Picture, if you can, a one-hour dory ride in North Atlantic waters so coldly unforgiving they'd numb you to death in twenty icy minutes. Add to that the threat of rogue waves, bloodthirsty polar bears, and gusts that would blow off your eyebrows.

The man stands up from his desk, hand on the lower part of his back where the stabbing pain originates then radiates down his leg. The large wall map of Newfoundland situates Notre Dame Bay under the shadow of the Northern Peninsula. Crag Point must have escaped the cartographer's attention. The man won't bother searching, not with his patience waning, a new mail delivery expected at noon, and his stomach growling.

Serving as lighthouse keeper's assistant has endowed me with a capacity for challenging tasks and complex problem solving. I credit my late father's dedicated teaching for my knowledge of mathematics, science, and German history, culture, and language. He passed away recently following a head injury after a fall on the tower's stairwell. I, however, am of sound mind and, despite my German ancestry, staunchly loyal to the Empire and its Allies. Tuberculosis consumed my mother before I formed any memories of her. My own health is robust, as I have been well cared for since I was a toddler by our devoted housekeeper, Maryanne.

Glasses off, he rubs his tired eyes, debating whether to read to the end. He breathes onto the lenses and wipes them with a handkerchief. Not one to leave tasks undone, he puts on his glasses, ready to tackle the final paragraph, grateful for its brevity.

Regarding my attitude, I long to play a role in defeating the Nazis. King George VI's 1941 Christmas message praised those who answer the call of duty for the common good. I am ready to answer. The indomitable Winston Churchill called on single women over twenty to serve the Empire. I reached that age two years ago. Your most determined President, F. D. Roosevelt, asked for a commitment of work, will, and life to one's country. Consider me fully committed. "Nothing Matters but Victory!"

~~*Sincerely,*~~ *Patriotically,*
Violet Morgen

The man returns the letter neatly folded into its envelope. He opens the desk's top drawer and rummages around until he finds the rubber stamp with its wooden handle and rectangular block of one-half-inch lettering. He presses it firmly on a pad of crimson red ink and follows with a forceful jab on the envelope. *Unsuitable.* Lips pursed, he blows on the ink and drops the letter in a tray by the corner of his desk alongside the others in that category. He shakes his head, sighs, then selects another letter at random from the pile.

3

Panting like she'd come down the chimney instead of from the other side of it, Maryanne plopped a stack of my old weather journals on the kitchen table next to my plate, licked clean. "That darn closet under the stairs is a tinderbox," she said. "I ought to feed the pile of old newspapers to the stove before the house goes up in a blaze. Not these though. They're proof of your maximum qualifications. Forget this minimum nonsense."

I sneezed.

"Sneeze on a Friday, fry your fish. Sneeze on a Saturday, steal a kiss. Sneeze on a Sunday, make a wish. I forget Monday. What odds! I'm off to feed the chickens."

"Leave it to me, please, Maryanne."

"I'm hungry for fresh air, tired of being cooped up."

She was bundled up and out the door, calling to the chickens, before I could ask what the eight journals had to do with being an office girl. They each had the same marbled, book-board cover and title—*Weather Journal, Crag Point*, followed by the year. On the first page of the 1941 volume was something Vati had once said: *Weather invites us to consider our place in the universe, war, our role in the world.* I knew everything about weather, plenty about the war, and too little about the world and universe. As for my role, I hadn't a clue, though I was certain it had nothing to do with being an office girl.

I flipped through the journal, browsing my short-range forecasts, then turned it sideways to read my musings in the margins. *The Greeks sacrificed animals to the benevolent and the destructive winds. They feared and worshipped the invisible force that powers sails, shapes landscapes, and fuels fires.* At the top of the page, I eyed a rough sketch with the caption: *What can the shapes of snowdrifts reveal about the wind's movements and characteristics?*

My final 1941 entry was for September 8, the day I lost Vati, the day I lost interest in keeping a journal, the day I lost interest in most things. What was the point if I couldn't show him what I'd written, listen to his questions, kind critiques, reminders to think like a scientist, and provide evidence for my claims?

The journals had been his idea. He knew I was bored with maintaining the weather logs—simply observing, measuring, and recording temperature, wind speed, and precipitation amounts.

"Search for patterns in the logs," he'd said. "Analyze and interpret them to predict what's coming. Use your journal to show me what you've learned."

I was studying my sketches of snowdrifts when I heard Maryanne stomp her boots in the porch. The door opened and she plumped down in her usual chair. "The rascal is at it again, trying to get into the chicken coop. I saw his tracks in the path you shovelled. One of these days, I'll nab that darn fox, skin him alive, and drape his furry hide round my neck."

I folded my arms close to my chest to block the draft. "You could use pieces of sea glass for the eyes," I said. "On my next visit to the beach, I'll search for the right colour."

"Don't be teasing." She slid the open journal toward her. "'Adapting the Beaufort Wind Scale and Douglas Sea Scale for local conditions.'" She licked her finger to turn the page. "'Monthly wind speed averages correlated with temperature,' whatever that means." She closed it, then drummed her fingers on top. "Was it you or your father told me forecasts were important for the war?"

"Me. Weather systems, fronts, and storms normally travel left to right, west to east—for example, from Newfoundland to the German-occupied Atlantic coast of France. If the Allies were planning an invasion in those parts, they'd want to consult our forecasts."

"What about for us crowd here on the island?"

"Think of all the aerial surveillance, patrols for U-boats, and convoy protection. Those pilots can't take to the air without accurate measures of wind speed and direction, plenty more besides. Mariners need to know what types of swell they might face, whether there's a risk of having equipment covered in ice." I glanced at her sideways. "Where are you headed with this talk, Maryanne?"

"Where do you think? You're right what the Americans need."

"A journal writer?"

"Never mind your foolishness. An expert forecaster."

"The Americans have their own meteorologists."

"What do they know about the mysteries of weather on this island?" She pulled her shawl tight around her chest. "Most of them haven't suffered a full winter here yet. Wait till they realize the winds got a mind of their own. Watch them shake their heads when the fog's got them drove blind."

"They'll catch on before the game's over."

"Catch on, yes. Catch up, never. You got a head start by twenty years. When you were a youngster, you couldn't be bothered with dolls, knitting and cooking. You'd be outside finding clues in the clouds, weighing the air, measuring, counting."

I remembered lecturing to my doll, Stella, about the number of days needed to count to one million. No wonder her head fell off. Knitting, with its basis in patterns, earned my respect as an observer. Cooking might have interested me if Maryanne paid attention to exact measurements instead of relying on guesses—a cup here, a cup there. "Their forecasters have degrees in science and mathematics. I can't compete with them."

"How can they be any better than a girl who spent her life spying on the weather's secret habits, learning its tricks, understanding its mischief? You heard of Lauchie McDougall at Wreckhouse. The railway company pays him twenty dollars a month to watch for signs, smelling the wind, letting them know if the weather's safe to run its trains. He's like you—a proper weather diviner."

"My senses are very attuned to natural phenomena, and my mind is quick to see and interpret patterns, but my forecasts also rely on science and mathematics."

"And you got the journals to prove it."

"Except they want office girls, not weather diviners or amateur forecasters."

"If you were a man, would you be talking like that?"

"If I was a man, we wouldn't be having this discussion. I'd probably end up staying here as keeper."

"You'd be pounding on the American Army's door, ordering them to hurry up and give you an office."

"I'm certain it doesn't work that way."

"Thinking things already work a certain way is the biggest mistake ever made. Especially for women. Make it work."

I stared through the window, my view somewhere in the offing between shore and horizon, my mind lost in the blank space between now and then, here and there. Predicting weather was possible, especially in the short range—predicting anything to do with my near or far future, impossible. The war didn't help. So much was changing so fast, the best anyone could do was adapt.

"Thanks for the nudge to stop stalling, postponing, avoiding—whatever I've been doing for the last five months. A maid is out of the question. A confectioner's assistant sounds appetizing, but unlikely. An office girl for the American Army might work, though how I'll get from there to being a forecaster is a mystery to me."

"One step at a time, Violet. Get a foot in the door. Before long, the men in the office will be asking you if bad weather's on the horizon. Should they wear rubber boots or leather shoes? Tell their wives to go ahead and hang out the washing? Next thing you know, the captains will be asking if it's a safe day to set sail or take to the skies."

"As you say, 'Never mind your foolishness.'"

"I'm dead serious."

"Not about the diploma, you aren't."

Maryanne tapped on the journal. "You got something better. The war's shaken things up. No need to play by the old rules. Flaunt your know-how. Brag about your skills. Push open doors and see where they lead. Keep going until you get somewhere you want to be."

"Supposing you're right, I can't leave in the dead of winter. The steamer to Lewisporte could be blocked by ice, the train to St. John's by snow at the Gaff Topsails. Worst of all, there's the ride to Pine Harbour in Fred's dory."

"A bit of snow or ice won't trouble the train or steamer. Fred neither. He's been coming to this crag since before you were born, brought your parents here." She rested her hands on the table, her head leaning over them. "He'll get you to Pine Harbour quick and dry."

"You're forgetting those times weather forced him to postpone his delivery, we almost ran out of kerosene or flour and waited on news of the world. Dorothy's cyclone would be safer than the North Atlantic in February or March."

Maryanne folded her arms, the wool flattened on her sleeve from resting her elbows on the table. "Make a deal with the new keeper. Be his helper like you were with your father. Hold onto the rooms upstairs. The room in the base of the tower will do him till you leave after Easter."

"If you came with me, I wouldn't mind the journey."

She opened the oven door and rubbed her hands over the rising heat. "Fifty years ago, I'd be tagging along, smiling. The eighteen nineties are so far gone I barely believe I lived them. Sun, salt, and wind got me whittled down worse than the tuckamore, needles blown off, cracked and brittle."

There'd be no tuckamore in the city, only streets crammed with motor cars, houses, buildings, and with people who'd never seen that type of tree and never thought about natural forces that shape landscapes. "I wish I could bring the tuckamore with me."

"Forget this place, me too. First thing in the city, scrub yourself clean of Crag Point. Buy yourself an outfit like the city girls wear. Tell the hairdresser, 'Cut off my long black braids.' Get a look to show off your eyes, big and brown like a rabbit's. Walk out sparkling new, chin up, chest out, 'America, here I come.' That's what I'd do in your lucky place."

If I'd been lucky, Vati would be alive and I wouldn't be forced to abandon my home in wartime—or ever. In any case, I'd need more than luck in mid-April. That departure date coincided with the thirtieth anniversary of the *Titanic*'s sinking near the Grand Banks of Newfoundland, a tragedy I blamed on the weather. A cold front had brought an Arctic air mass with clear skies and a barely visible moon. The water's surface shone smooth as glass. Without swell or waves, the water didn't break against the iceberg. To the two lookout men, therefore, the mountain of ice remained invisible in the dark. Someone should have warned them of the dangers ahead. Someone like me.

4

By February, I was packed and ready to leave, just in case the new keeper refused to allow me to stay until April. House, tower, cliffs, beach, and most of my belongings—I'd leave them behind. Not my mother's suitcase. She'd travelled with it to Crag Point from Nova Scotia and before that, from Rotterdam. My weather journals, barometer, and the binoculars Vati ordered especially for me would travel in his old camelback, navy blue steamer trunk.

"Got a spot in your trunk or suitcase for this?" Maryanne said, a familiar notebook in her hand.

I stared, surprised to see it after so long.

"It's for you." She passed it to me. "Does it count as a gift if you're the one gave it to me in the first place?"

I ran my fingers over the cover's soft, brown skived leather. "For me? Thank you, Maryanne." I remembered giving it to her in 1940 and feeling disappointed that she didn't want it. Embarrassed too for assuming a purchased notebook was better than her habit of pasting clippings from the newspaper on the pantry walls. A few months earlier, a northeast gale had driven rain in around the room's sole window. Cary Grant's head was covered in water rings. The ads for the movies *Wuthering Heights*, *Rebecca*, and *Dr. Jekyll and Mr. Hyde* were destroyed. All that survived were notices of St. John's entertainment such as *Uncle Tim's Barn Dance*.

For my birthday gift to her, I'd ordered the best quality notebook I could buy and wrapped it in brown paper with a twig of juniper for decoration in the knot on the string and with a note that said, *Enjoy your new scrapbook*. Maryanne wanted nothing to do with the notebook. "The glue will spoil the fine paper," she'd said. "The pantry wall will do me."

I held it to my chest. "I'll cherish it, especially knowing it came from you, Maryanne."

"Fill it up. When we're together again, you'll have something to show me."

"A 1942 weather journal?"

"Weather's not the only thing worth paying attention to. You'll figure that out once you're off this crag."

The notebook lay unopened for days. Once the ink touched the paper, if I didn't like what I'd written, I'd have to strike out the words and ruin the page. I decided against using it as a diary with chronological records. A scrapbook wouldn't do either unless the clippings were written by me. I eventually determined what I wanted, then sat at my desk, the fountain pen tip on the page, feet on the floor, back straight.

EDITOR'S FOREWORD

Welcome to Violet's commonplace book (1942 edition), a compendium of observations and musings on everything from travel, entertainment, and food, to city guides and odd ditties. Enjoy minimal advertising, unlike the newspapers, their pages littered with offers of cod-liver oil, kidney pills, Lestoil, and Dr. Chase's Syrup of Linseed and Turpentine. Dare we mention the photographs of Clark Gable and Vivien Leigh in ardent embrace? They say, "Gone with the Wind." You say, "Gone with the Wisdom." One wonders: Where is the real news? Wonder no more. May your reading be both enlightening and entertaining.

Maryanne stood at the table, flour dusting her apron and her chin. She slapped, punched, and folded the dough.

"What do you think they'll want to know when I apply in person?" I said.

"Your name and where you come from, I suppose."

My pencil rested between my fingers, its tip sharpened, ready to take notes.

"Pretend you're in charge of hiring civilians at the American base."

"Well, that's a promotion in two shakes," she said.

"Ask any question. Not only related to office-girl duties, whatever those are."

"Let's see. What type of girl are you—Cary Grant or Spencer Tracy?"

"Why would they ask that?"

Hands in the dough, she rubbed her chin on her shoulder to scratch it. "The type of man a girl sets her heart on tells tons about her own character."

"Ask me about the war," I said. "For example, 'How might forecasting help us win this Battle of the Atlantic?' You could even throw in a question or two specifically about weather. For example, 'Does the presence of icebergs affect land temperatures?' or 'How do the Labrador Current and Gulf Stream affect the island's weather?'"

She turned to face the stove, sensing whether the temperature felt right for the dough to rise. "Let me sleep on it."

"Anything will do."

"What about this? Have you ever used a typewriter or telephone, Miss Morgen?"

"No, sir, neither. But give me a hygrometer, barometer, anemometer, and thermometer and I'll offer expert advice on their use. I'll even throw in tips on how to get the most out of them."

"Sounds like you've been practicing already."

"Excellent question, Maryanne. Something more general this time, please."

She stopped kneading and stared at the dough. "What's best for winning the war?" She began kneading again. "A brain, a heart, or courage?"

"You can be certain the Americans won't bring Dorothy's friends into any interview. We're a long way from Kansas."

"They'll do whatever suits them," she said. "They're the bosses here now."

"Okay, I give in. All three: intelligence, compassion, confidence."

"It's a good thing you're practicing."

I laid down my pencil and sighed purposely. "Tell me. Which one?"

"You said to ask you questions. Don't expect me to have the answers. What does an old woman like me know about winning the war anyway? My tale was told at birth. Yours is just begun. Add a touch of romance. Make sure it has a happy ending."

"It's St. John's, not Hollywood."

"Hollywood, Holyrood, Botwood, Boston—love carries on, war or no war."

I stood, ready to give up and return to the tower. "I've never even had friends my age, let alone a beau."

"That won't be long changing. Your mother gave her beauty to you. It's from a foreign land, but it'll turn men's heads." She covered the bowl of dough with an old flour sack. "You got your father's mind. It's a sharp one, for sure."

"But?"

She brushed off her hand on her apron and laid it on my cheek, her fingers warm on my skin. "It's foreign too."

"That isn't a very good start, is it?"

"Don't be thinking like that. Set your course and hope for following winds."

"And if I hit headwinds instead?"

"Sure as water is wet, you will. Don't let them knock you off course."

5

So much depended on the new keeper, yet we knew nothing about him beyond his name, Teodoro Russo. Would he be the silent type like Paddy Hayward who came in June to cut our wood for heating and cooking? Or would he be the officious type like Joe Bishop who, on his annual inspections, remained adamant that Mr. Morgen rather than his daughter, Violet, should be responsible for the weather logs?

Would he be anything like Wally, son of Miles, master carpenter, who did repairs to the house? The son was a genius with anything mechanical. Vati used to say, if Wally couldn't fix the machine, he'd build a new one. Wally had once offered me ten cents to show him my breasts, barely developed though they were. I didn't tell on him, too young to understand the implications of his request. After that incident, I made myself scarce when they came, glad they brought a tent rather than bunk in the house. My breasts had grown since then, and I sometimes asked myself what Wally would think if he saw them now.

One thing we did know about Russo was that he wouldn't arrive as the authorities had advised, not with a fierce blizzard raging outside. The visibility remained near-zero, but in the storm's lulls I saw swells capable of devouring a dory in one quick gulp. I pictured the havoc in the city with cars hidden under drifts, people trapped in their homes, unable to open their doors, and roofs caving in under the weight of snow.

We waited a week for the sea to calm down. Its waves lazily lapped the battered shoreline under a sapphire sky against the sparkling brilliance of the whitewashed landscape. I finished shovelling a path down the gentle slope to the beach, then returned to the watch room to scan the waters for signs of Fred's dory. I saw an object, lost sight of it until it rose out of a trough, and, for a nervous instant, thought I'd seen a U-boat. When I spotted it again, I had no doubt what it was. I laid the binoculars on the counter and rushed down the spiral stairwell and through the passageway to the kitchen to alert Maryanne.

We grabbed coats, boots, mitts, and hats and headed to the beach, hands at our foreheads to block the sun's reflection off the snow.

Fred stood alongside the dory, his hand outstretched to Mr. Russo as he stepped on shore. A wave rolled in and swamped Russo to the ankles. He bolted forward, tripped, and fell on his side, at Maryanne's feet. "*Merda!*" he shouted.

Though I didn't know the word, I gleaned the sentiment from his tone.

Maryanne bent over to help him. "We'll sit you right next to the cook-stove to warm your bones."

"No," he said, head hanging, and with what looked like dried vomit on his jacket. "To bed."

I ran ahead to open the doors, glancing back at Maryanne, the poor woman panting, out of breath, helping Russo walk up from the beach.

While she settled the new keeper in the room at the tower's base, I helped Fred unload our supplies. He was eager to be on his way, behind on deliveries because of the storm. He had little to tell about Russo except that he'd huddled under a tarpaulin in the dory, seasick after the ferry crossing from Nova Scotia and the steamer from Lewisporte, repeating, "*Merda.*"

That evening, we waited for Russo, eager to make a good impression on a man who'd come from Canada, and a big city. Maryanne wore a clean apron and bandana. I'd washed my hair and woven two neat braids fastened with clips around my head.

Maryanne was serving the meal and I'd finished fetching water from the barrel in the porch when he entered the kitchen from the passageway. Judging by the pale, smooth skin on his face, he hadn't spent much time outside. The prominent bridge on his nose and his pointed chin reminded me of an Italian painter in my encyclopedia. His black hair looked smothered in squid ink. Once we knew each other better, I'd ask why he wore it like that—high on top, neatly shaven on the sides. I'd ask, too, if all men in Toronto were his height, at least a foot shorter than me. Had he brought other clothes? A tweed blazer, ironed shirt, and creased pants weren't suitable for a keeper's tasks. I would have offered him Vati's shirts and trousers except I wore them myself.

Maryanne and I had already decided she'd be the one to negotiate on my behalf. We were no sooner seated when she raised the subject. "I'll feed you, take care of the house and your clothes. Violet can help with your keeper's duties if you don't mind her holding onto the rooms upstairs. What do you say to that, Mr. Russo?"

"It's a deal," he said, without pausing to think it over. "By the looks of the place, I'll need every speck of help I can get. And call me Teo, please."

Maryanne winked at me and I winked back, surprised at how easy it had been to convince him, relieved not to have to leave Crag Point in winter. "We're going to get along perfectly," I said under my breath.

"Shame your feet got wet on the landwash," Maryanne said. "In all my born days, I never saw such fancy shoes."

"If you or Violet would like a pair of Salvatore Ferragamo shoes, ask me," he said. "I can order them at a special price. The Italians are the best shoemakers in the world. Everyone knows that."

Everyone but Maryanne and me. She came from Pine Harbour, population 103, and had lived at Crag Point for more than two decades where, while my mother was alive, the population peaked at four. Except in my imagination, I hadn't visited anywhere.

"Have you been to Italy?" Maryanne said, leaning toward him over the table.

"Only in my dear mamma's belly." He smiled. "You should meet the woman. The best cook there is in Toronto and the best—"

"What about your house?" I said. "Did you have indoor plumbing? Bathtub? How many electric lamps? Ever ridden in a motor car?"

"Give the man a chance to breathe, Violet," Maryanne said.

"Plumbing and electricity? It may not be a big and great Italian city, but Toronto has everything a person could want—fine restaurants, department stores, mansions, motor cars."

"Tell us about the Eaton's store," Maryanne said. "I saw pages from their catalogue, after the Great War, plastered over a bedroom wall in Pine Harbour."

He talked about modern marvels I could barely imagine—a cafeteria, elevators, and moving stairways. At Christmas, besides a toyland on the fifth floor, the store's main windows featured decorative displays that attracted crowds from miles around the city. Its annual Santa Claus parade included marching bands, bagpipes, drums pounding in unison, clowns, dancers, and horses prancing in formation.

At home, his mother laboured for days in their kitchen preparing holiday delicacies like panettone and tiramisu.

We laughed at my imitation of Teo's pronunciation.

"Not 'Dear I miss you,'" he said. "Teer-ah-me-su."

Teo was an entertainer and had a captive audience to encourage him. If every evening was this much fun, I'd miss his company when I left Crag Point.

"Tell us about your family," Maryanne said.

Teo boasted about an uncle who, before the war, operated a famous diner on Yonge Street, the longest paved street in the world. He described in detail the diner's Sicilian pasta, its spaghetti, cannelloni, and busiate, supposedly the best in the city, possibly even in Canada. Its facilities were the latest, with separate bathrooms for men and women and an outdoor area for year-round dining.

I knew nothing of department stores, could barely picture a parade, and had never seen a restaurant menu, but I was certain open-air dining wasn't a year-round pastime in that part of Canada. "Weather permitting," I said. "In winter, your busiate would turn into icicles. Your spaghetti would taste uncooked. Your cannelloni would explode when its stuffing froze." I thought the images were very funny. Accurate too.

Maryanne nudged me with the tip of her foot under the table.

I looked at her with my eyebrows raised. What was wrong with what I'd said?

"If you'd been to Toronto," he said, "you'd realize that many Italian restaurants have large, open outdoor stone ovens."

I might have dropped the argument if he hadn't insinuated I didn't know what I was talking about. "They must be monstrous ovens. Toronto has a continental, not a maritime climate. Its winter temperatures can reach fifteen or twenty Fahrenheit. Add the wind's chilling effect on top and—"

"I've lived in Toronto my whole life. Nearly thirty years. I don't need a lecture on its weather."

I was tempted to say three decades should be long enough to realize outdoor dining wasn't possible in winter, but I knew Maryanne wouldn't approve. "Yes, of course," I said. "I'd like to clarify, however, that I wasn't lecturing. A lecture would be if I told you about a project I've been working on about the relationship between wind and temper—"

"Leave talk of wind for now, Violet," Maryanne said. "Let Teo tell us what brings a man of the world to this rough old crag. I bet it's got to do with the war."

I was glad she'd asked the question. The more he talked about modern city life with its conveniences and luxuries, the more I wondered what he was doing at the edge if not the end of the world. From a young age, Teo had helped his father in the family's lighting store. The store sold lamps that ran on electricity and illuminated the elegant rooms in some of Toronto's greatest mansions. He'd worked his way up from packing and unpacking boxes to taking responsibility for choosing and ordering stock. As part of his responsibilities, he'd travelled to large American cities to select light fixtures. Chicago was one of them.

We marvelled at his descriptions of a city with opera houses, jazz clubs, skyscrapers, and a river with moveable bridges and drawbridges. I raised my eyebrows at his talk of lakeshore parks where ladies and gentlemen in their finery paraded along paths lined with palm trees. I hadn't been to the city and knew nothing about its marvels or its parks. I did, however, know its weather. Chicago was the Windy City. Its winter wind, nicknamed The Hawk, blew in from Lake Michigan with cold, moist air that preyed on everything in its path.

I chose my words carefully, to avoid upsetting him or Maryanne. "Pardon me, Teo, but I'm certain palm trees couldn't grow in Chicago. A 1930 blizzard dropped nearly two feet of snow on the city. That's a minor weather event by Newfoundland precipitation averages, but not palm-tree weather."

Teo folded his arms against his chest. "Obviously, I was talking about summer."

I shook my head. "Summer or winter, doesn't matter. Palm trees aren't deciduous. They're evergreens, though not coniferous. They don't have cones or—"

"Thank you again for your lecture, but I stand by my description of ladies and men strolling under palm trees."

"Maybe you saw them in a book with photographs from somewhere in South America or Florida."

"Are you accusing me of lying?"

"Of course not. I'm simply saying you must be mistaken because—"

"I'm neither mistaken nor lying."

"I didn't say he was lying, did I, Maryanne?"

She gathered our plates. "Anyone for a drop of tea before bed?"

Teo stood up from the table and put his hands in his pockets. "Well, you may know a lot, but where I come from, we know our manners. Someone needs to learn you them."

I couldn't ignore such an obvious mistake. "Teach. Someone needs to teach you them. Teach *me*, I guess, though I fail to see what—"

He turned his back to me and faced Maryanne. "My mamma would say your cooking is *deliziosa*. *Buona notte*, Maryanne."

She spoke as soon as he was out of earshot. "Men don't look kindly on women showing off their smarts. City people don't expect us crowd from the bay to tell them what to say or how to say it."

"You forgot people who lie, then accuse you of being wrong."

"Don't be calling him a liar."

"I never said he was. I thought it though. How did he get the job if he didn't lie? No experience whatsoever. How will he manage?"

Maryanne topped up the water in the pot on the cookstove. "What do you expect? It's a miracle they got anyone to come here. The local men are gone off to war or working on the bases. They'd be wanting office boys, not girls, at Fort Pepperrell if they could find them. What odds anyway? He'll manage fine. There's barely a boat in these waters anymore. None in winter besides Fred."

"Don't forget maintenance, the logs, plus extra war duties, binoculars at his eyes half the day."

"Help Teo and be thankful you get to hold onto those two rooms upstairs."

"I won't pretend to be a judge of character, but I sense a falseness."

"Show some heart, Violet, dear. Teo's suffered enough. Any man who minds his family like he does deserves a pat on the back."

Something wasn't right about Teo—something Maryanne wouldn't admit and I couldn't yet name. As for a pat on the back, I'd do it my way, with a commonplace book entry.

THE WAR'S INNOCENT VICTIMS

In 1913, Giuseppe Russo sailed across the Atlantic to Canada in search of a better life for his family. After surmounting formidable obstacles, he opened a store selling lamps in Toronto. A story with a happy ending if Italy hadn't allied with Germany and Japan in 1940. Ten months later, Giuseppe and his two Italian-born sons were accused of being fascist sympathizers, interned in a camp in Ontario, and had their bank accounts frozen and a red circle placed in the centre of their shirts. Fortunately, the Canadian-born son, Teo, was willing to work at anything to support his mother and sisters-in-law, even if it meant moving to Newfoundland. Wherever that was.

6

Months before Teo arrived, I'd written to the authorities to announce Vati's passing and to offer recommendations. The new keeper would need to be a jack of all trades. If he wasn't accompanied by a wife, he'd require a housekeeper.

A reply came in the form of a typed letter that merely said, "Our condolences. We will be in contact." Included with the letter was the last of Vati's wages.

In my response, I resisted threatening to withdraw my services if they wouldn't compensate me for the work I did in place of Vati. Likewise, I resisted complaining about their lack of acknowledgement of my contribution to the war effort, watching the ocean for signs of U-boats and the sky for German bombers. The foghorn needed a replacement part along with someone to do the replacement, and while they were at it, did they have a replacement for my father? By November, I hadn't heard back. I wrote another letter beginning with the words "We anxiously await your reply and remind you of…"

A response came near the end of 1941 informing us that a Mr. Teodoro Russo would arrive mid-February, weather permitting. He would require and pay for Maryanne's services. When the war ended, the Crag Point light station would be decommissioned given its need for repair, expense of operation, and the lack of marine traffic in this area. The laconic reply had revealed nothing regarding the new keeper other than his name and approximate arrival date.

By the end of Teo's first week, I could tell he was no jack of any trade, other than a lamp salesman. Worse than his lack of experience was his apparent disinterest in the light station.

Maryanne made excuses for him, that he'd come from far away and had so much to get used to. "Give him a week to rest his head, spinning from the journey. He never saw the sea before."

That week turned into two, those two into three, and he'd already arrived later than expected. He was becoming increasingly reclusive, retiring to his room after meals. I expected any day for him to inform me he'd be leaving with Fred next time he came. What then? Ever since that first evening at the supper table when we'd argued, there'd been a lingering friction between us, evident in his tone and in how he avoided looking directly at me. Was he punishing or avoiding me? Or both?

It was mid-March when he finally joined me in the watch room. He entered the cramped space, bent over, hands on his knees, head hanging, panting.

"Are you all right?" I meant in general. Though I couldn't admit it, I was curious and concerned about why he'd waited so long to start his duties.

"After one hundred steps?" he said, in between breaths.

He'd have known the correct number if it hadn't been his first visit there. "In fact, it's only fifty-two, then another ten rungs on the ladder up to the lantern—"

"*Basta.*" He stood up straight and surveyed the small space, arms folded. "I get it."

What did he get exactly, or did such details bore him? Did he realize he'd be trudging up and down those steps repeatedly every day?

"Here you go," I said. "Notes on the light station operations, all nineteen pages written by yours truly. I hope they're useful." I counted on my fingers, listing the contents. "Daily tasks, emergency procedures, equipment maintenance, weather logs, ice reports, et cetera, et cetera—if the answer to your question isn't in here, there likely isn't one."

He stared at the cover with its title, *Notes for C. P.'s New Keeper*, then flipped through the pages.

I was about to tell him to feel free to write in the margins, but he passed the notes back to me.

He picked up the binoculars and peered out over the water. "We made a deal, didn't we? You care for the light station and enjoy those two comfortable rooms upstairs in the house while I'm stuck in a dingy, damp cave with a leaky wood stove."

Had he misinterpreted our original deal or opted to change its terms? Was it worth risking an argument by questioning him, or was it simply easier to carry on as usual, knowing I'd be gone in a matter of weeks? "A deal, yes. You may, however, need to know a few basics. For example, the anemometer doesn't work well unless you oil it monthly, more if it's been windier than usual. Daily measures, for example, of temperature, wind speed, et cetera, must be taken at the same time each day, then recorded in the logs the same way."

"You're a bit obsessed with weather," he said, binoculars still at his eyes.

Was that an observation or a criticism? "Maryanne calls me a weather diviner. Actually, my forecasts rely on far more than signs, senses, intuition, or instinct. There's analysis of past averages, observations, calculations—"

"Ha! Along with a lot of red skies in the morning." He grinned and laid the binoculars on the counter with a thud.

Vati would have been disappointed by such disregard. Those binoculars had been his second set of eyes, and he'd always treated them with such care.

I picked up the notes. "Let's see. Where should I begin? The light station operates with a revolving lamp on a twenty-second cycle—fourteen of light, six of darkness. In dense fog, the horn's supposed to do the work except it's broken. Light the lamp at sunset, extinguish it at sunrise. Keep wicks well-trimmed and the lens polished. The lamp stays off from December to the beginning of April. Maintaining equipment and the logs and watching for U-boats or German bombers will give you plenty to do. Fred brings supplies, weather permitting. The winch doesn't work so you'll need to help him carry the five-gallon containers of kerosene up from the beach. We used to have a dory for rescues. Just as well it rotted— you'd end up needing the rescue. Careful when out on the gallery, cleaning salt off the windows—the rail's not safe. Regarding communication and a wireless telegraph—"

"Thanks for another lecture, but *che importa*? The minute the war ends, I'll be out of here. If you're smart as you pretend, you will be too."

"I wasn't pretending to be smart. I was simply telling—"

"It's in your notes, isn't it?"

"Yes, I guess."

"If I have an urgent question, I'll ask you."

"Of course I'll be glad to help, for now. As you know, I'm heading to St. John's in less than a month."

"Of course, of course." He laughed. Not with a fake laugh but more of a sincerely amused laugh, from the belly rather than the throat, long, not short. "If the waves don't swallow you in a single gobble, the American soldiers will devour you in tiny Violetta pieces. Weather diviner? Ha! Surely you're joking."

He left the tower before I could respond. What would I have said anyway? He'd have to get used to his new home and role. Either that or hope the war ended sooner rather than later.

WEATHER LORE

Red sky at sunrise: wet & windy weather

Smokey chimney: mild weather

High-flying gulls: fair weather

Fine Candlemas Day: foul weather

Green Christmas: white Easter

Wind on Good Friday: windy summer

Fair August: prosperous fall

Plentiful October berries: rough winter

7

Unlike at the start of the new year when I wanted desperately to remain at Crag Point, by April, I couldn't wait to leave. If Fred proposed a departure for the following day, I'd tell him the sooner the better. Listening to Teo's talk of the world had made me want to see it for myself. St. John's wasn't Toronto, but it offered as much. Dance halls with orchestras, theatres with drama on a giant illuminated screen—I couldn't wait to experience both. Hot running water and electricity—amenities people in the city took for granted would be nothing short of magic for me. At the library, I'd have access to the world's knowledge, encyclopedias, atlases, newspapers from around the globe, books on every topic, possibly a how-to manual for women new to the city. Best of all, I'd be free of the light station responsibilities, free of the burden of a role I wasn't adequately prepared to carry out on my own, and free of a man I didn't trust.

Teo hadn't returned to the watch room since that day. The notes I'd composed for him lay untouched. More worrisome was the fact that he'd almost stopped joining us for meals, eating in his room instead. His hands had a nervous quiver he blamed on the pounding surf and howling winds. He walked hunched over and complained the cold damp air made his joints ache while the short, gloomy days made him want to remain in bed, blankets pulled up over his head.

According to the calendar, winter was over. The weather had improved remarkably, and the snow had melted except where the drifts had been high. I stood outside Teo's room at the bottom of the tower's spiral stairwell in rubber boots, holding my favourite walking stick, determined to help him. He could borrow Vati's boots and follow me through a path in the woods that led to a small inland pond. We might spot a moose, the one-thousand-pound beasts introduced to the island at the turn of the century. I'd once seen Maryanne chase one with a shovel while it munched on cabbage in our garden. With the binoculars, we could scout for eagles. If he was afraid of wolves, I'd reassure him they were as rare as leopards. I'd say nothing about the threat of polar bears wandering down on pack ice from Labrador. We kept a rifle in the pantry. Though it probably wouldn't kill a bear, it might frighten it away.

I knocked on his door, waited, and knocked again.

He peeked out, hair hanging over one eye. "What is it?" His voice, guttural and cracking, sounded like he'd recently woken up.

"The wind is southwest, only seven miles per hour. I can hardly believe it. Usually, it's—"

"How often do I need to tell you I don't want to hear about the weather?" He closed the door.

I heard a cough, then a squeak from the bed.

"A man doesn't need a bad fall like your father's to lose control of his mind," Maryanne said when I told her what happened. "I saw men in the lumber camp before I came here. Either they cared about nothing anymore or cared too much about everything. Both kinds rotted them from the inside out."

"Are you saying there's no hope of him staying? That I won't be able to go to the city and—"

"You'll leave here no matter what. Let me worry about Teo."

"You've already been through—"

"He's good as gold with me."

"What are you saying?"

"If you'd hold off bickering with him, he'd good as gold with you too."

"Surely you're not blaming his behaviour on me, are you?"

"There's no blaming anything on anyone. Help him where you can. I'll do the same."

Easter Sunday fell on April fifth, nine days before I was due to leave. Maryanne made four loaves of her best molasses bread and killed, plucked, stuffed, and cooked our plumpest chicken, Hazel. She mixed the last of our cocoa with butter, molasses, and berries for dessert. "Teo's got nothing but good to say about my grub. I'll give him the best of it. Sometimes, that's the only thing helps a man in his condition—a dash of salt and a dose of kindness."

I'd assumed Teo wouldn't be in the mood for a celebration and was surprised when he joined us for the Easter meal. His face was pale and eyes droopy, but he was animated and cheerful. He entertained us with descriptions of Italy's Easter procession of thousands of hooded penitents and people in costumes depicting the characters from the Passion of Christ. He told us about his mother's special treats—baby lambs made with marzipan and a dove-shaped cake named La Colomba. "I'll learn you how to make it, Maryanne."

After the meal, he asked Maryanne while she was up from the table to bring him the framed photo of his nephew Gino from his room. "I want you to know more about my dear family."

The instant she left the kitchen, he slid his chair next to mine and drew a lace-trimmed handkerchief from his shirt pocket. "My mother's handiwork. I want you to have it."

"How kind." I admired the intricate detail on the linen's trim and scolded myself for not being more caring. "By the way, I think you'll manage quite well. Rely on the notes. Send me a letter if you have any questions. Maryanne can give you my address and—"

"I hate this awful place. I pray I'll wake up in the morning back in civilization with my family. I'd rather be behind bars than here." He eyed the passageway where Maryanne had gone, then turned back to me. Thick black stubble masked the lower half of his face. A small vessel had ruptured into a pool of blood in the corner of his eye. A tear rolled down his cheek, translucent and round.

I dabbed it with the handkerchief, then thought of showing him my commonplace book entry about his family. "Let me know if you'd like me to write to the authorities on your behalf regarding the unfair treatment of your brothers. I could also request a relief keeper, although that might be a waste—"

He grabbed my wrist tightly and pinched the skin. "What if this war drags on? Do I have to stay here forever? How long until they release my brothers and father? You know everything. Tell me."

I tugged my arm loose. "You're hurting me."

He lowered his head and shook it. "I'm truly sorry. It's not your fault. You have helped me a great deal. *Grazie*. Don't leave me here alone, please. I beg you, Violetta."

Before Maryanne returned, Teo moved his chair back. I told her nothing. If I claimed to have hit headwinds, she'd say that was impossible because my journey hadn't yet begun. I stared at the photograph of his nephew. He had Teo's sideways glance and reminded me of the wily fox, so clever with his ruses.

MOOD FORECAST

As winter wanes and the days lengthen, those new to this isle's forsaken shores can expect a brightening of spirits and a diminished sense of doom and gloom. Squalls, gales, gusts, hail, sleet—all will lessen in frequency and intensity. Spring promises periods of hope interspersed with fog, drizzle, rain, and doldrums. Summer sun and gentle breezes, short-lived as they are, will induce instances of bliss, triumph, and courage. The dying of the light in the fall will bring on bouts of irritability and despondency. Expect a repeat of the cycle on a yearly basis.

8

Fred Peckford arrived on the eve of my departure, looking no different than on his last visit, with a belly so big and round I wondered how he manoeuvred the oars around it. His face bore wrinkles that could be mistaken for scars. Only forty-one, he'd lost most of his hair. The ocean breezes had blown it away, so he'd once said. Despite how he sometimes treated me, I looked forward to his visits. Besides staples such as flour and molasses, he brought papers, correspondence, and news of the world. On his last delivery before Christmas, following Vati's passing, he'd kindly given us each an orange and for me, a jigsaw puzzle map of the world.

Fred leaned back on the wooden chair, legs stretched out, sipping on a glass of rum.

From my trouser pocket, I took out a list of questions, opened the four folds carefully, and smoothed them over with strokes of my palm. "With such a long fetch, even moderate winds could cause high swells. If that happens, will you get me to Pine Harbour in time to board the steamer? Also, I assume you have a sail or an extra oar in case you lose one overboard."

"My ducky, I've been navigating this bay since I was a lad, riding every size of wave. Oars? Who needs 'em? See this?" He held out his arm bent at the elbow, the muscle flexed. "Foul or fine, following winds or none, I'll handle what she throws at me." His voice was raspy, his laugh more of a snort.

"I guess it's settled. No need to worry?"

"Ha!" he shouted, loud and fast. "Yawing, rolling, pitching, heaving— when we dock in the harbour, you'll be tottering worse than a rat swished round in a rum barrel."

If Maryanne hadn't been in the pantry, she would have urged me to ignore him—something he tended to do with me, like I was still the child he told to go away while he chatted with Vati.

"Have you heard of any sightings of U-boats anywhere in the bay?"

"If I hear so much as a whisper, I'll tell you on my next breath."

"Any sightings of strange equipment on shore? Canisters or a not-so-strange weathervane?"

He slid his small glass near the rum bottle.

I took his cue and filled it to the brim. "The Nazis will want to set up a weather station along the coastline. They're sure to have thought of it. They'd be poor strategists if they hadn't."

He leaned toward me, elbow resting on the table. "Don't worry. When the bad guys come sniffing around asking if it's a good day to hang out the wash, no one's going to be leaking secrets."

I crumpled the sheet of paper with my questions into a tiny ball and dropped it into the stove where the flames reduced my curiosity to ashes.

VEAL OF THE OCEAN

The delicate texture of the mahogany-coloured flesh due to lack of muscle tone in a young harp seal has earned it the sobriquet *veal of the ocean*. Follow Maryanne's seal flipper (shoulder) pie recipe: Remove blubber. Fry flesh in fatback pork and onion. Add ~~2 tablespoons of sugar~~, 1/2 cup dark rum (to diminish gamey flavour). Bake long and slow. Stoke fire infrequently. Once cooked, transfer into a pie shell with gravy and root vegetables. Top with pastry. Bake until brown. Serve with fresh bread for fond farewell meals. "Tho' Newfoundland is changing fast, some things we must not lose. May we always have our Flipper pie, and Codfish for our brewis."

With patchwork oven mitts protecting her hands, Maryanne laid the flipper pie on a slab of slate in the table's centre. Fred pinched off a piece of pastry and popped it in his mouth.

She smacked his hand. "Hold your oars. I'm saving a piece for Teo."

When Maryanne told me Teo wouldn't attend my farewell meal, I'd felt relieved. After the incident a week earlier, I hoped I never saw him again. I'd spent the morning in the tower, expecting any second to hear the scuff of his shoes on the steps, certain we'd end up quarrelling.

Fred didn't ask about Teo. They'd met only twice at Crag Point. On the first occasion, Teo had boasted about the advanced and modern life in Toronto and how what he'd seen of Newfoundland so far made him think he'd gone back a century. The next time, Fred had come prepared with a lengthy rant in which he bragged about the island's vast lands, abundant resources, and the persevering spirit of its people. There'd been no sign of friendship between them. If Teo's absence meant a larger serving for him, Fred was delighted.

"There's no better flipper pie from here to Labrador," Fred said, a morsel of pastry visible in his mouth. "Flesh is so tender, the knives are confused. Gravy might as well be salted molasses."

After the meal, Maryanne refused my offer of help with the dishes. "It's your last night in your home. Sit back and enjoy it."

Fred picked at his tea-stained teeth with a toothpick. "Your last night and first time leaving here. What are you, twenty?"

"Officially twenty-two this past January."

He pointed the toothpick at me like a commanding baton. "How often I said it, I can't remember—'Send her to board in Pine Harbour, go to church and school, make friends, learn how to behave.' Your father'd say, 'Someday, Frederick.' Never met a soul like him, skittish as a hare in a snare."

What right did he have to judge Vati or criticize how he'd raised his daughter? "If you knew him like I did you'd understand why he was skittish."

Maryanne stood at the table and wiped her hands on her apron. "The man had a heart of gold. Best teacher ever, her father was, better than anything in the Harbour."

Fred folded his arms. "What are you now, Maryanne? The expert on education with your grade 6?"

I should have realized the evening wouldn't go smoothly. As usual, they were crossing swords. They rarely agreed on anything, or if they did, they wouldn't admit it, like two people holding a grudge for so long they forgot the reason behind it.

"My boy Tommy has been the Harbour's teacher for three years," Fred said. "He's twenty now. Got an appetite for adventure. Soon as I find someone to replace him, he's free to go. What do you say, Violet? It's grand work for a woman. It'd be a help to the community."

"Me?" I glanced at Maryanne, reassured to see her rolling her eyes. "I haven't been to school myself. How could I be a teacher?"

Fred shook his head. "There's teacher training in the summer."

"Leave her be, Fred. She'll be an important person in the city, serving important people, doing important things."

"Right. Churchill's personal assistant. Main duty, lighting his cigars."

"He lights them himself, apparently," I said, "using Canadian matches, in London, of course." I was trying to steer the conversation in a different direction. The evening was meant to be a celebration. I'd even prepared a final speech, mostly for and about Maryanne, though with a thank you to Fred. He'd proven himself a loyal friend to Vati in his final months, making special trips to be by his bedside.

Maryanne gazed up at the ceiling. "A young Maryanne in St. John's would die to light his cigar, or a Yank's."

Fred smacked the table, rattling the dishes and my nerves. Maryanne scowled at him for frightening her, hand on her heart.

"A bunch of crooks and swindlers, the Yanks are," he said, "strutting round like cocky corner boys, digging up graveyards if it suits them. What for? To build their bases. We might as well be strangers in our own homes."

"What's that got to do with Violet?" Maryanne said.

"Could we talk about something else, please?" I said. "I want to say a few words—"

"I bet my britches Heinrich wouldn't be too pleased with his daughter traipsing around on her own."

I hated when Fred claimed to have insight into Vati's mind and my relationship with him. "Stop this conversation, please, and stop talking about my father."

"Good for you, Violet, standing up to him."

Fred rested a hand on his belly and burped. "Stand up all you want. They're wolves, the Yanks are. Secret ways, fast-talking, doling out candies, chocolate, and cigarettes, pretending—"

Maryanne smacked the table lightly, without any rattling of nerves. "Give me a Yank over the best in the Harbour." She smacked it again. "Give me the gent on the steamer." She softened her tone. "'Pretty little bird,' he called me. Nicest words were ever said in Pine Harbour."

I'd heard the story before. What fifteen-year-old girl wouldn't have been thrilled at the arrival of the coastal steamer? What girl wouldn't have been flattered when a man working on the steamer told her she reminded him of a pretty little bird? She was being kind and grateful by offering him a ladle of water. He was being friendly by inviting her for a stroll after he finished off-loading. They went to a meadow by the schoolhouse and lay in the uncut hay, where for the first time, a man kissed her and for the last time anyone told her she was pretty.

"What's that got to do with Violet?" Fred said.

"Did I get to live the life I wanted? Did I get a chance to see the city? Meet people from new places—America, Canada, anywhere? Or did I end up the shame of the Harbour with a babe and no husband?" She shook her head. "Don't let yourself be trapped, Violet, dear. Stay free." She raised her hand, fist closed, then opened it to watch the imaginary bird fly away. "Best of luck, my sweet girl!"

I stood and leaned over to hug her, wanting to tell her how much I cared for her, but not in front of Fred.

"Luck won't do you any good," he said. "Sin, not Saint, John's is what they call it. It's not proper or safe, Violet. Don't care how sweet you are."

Vati once said regarding Fred that he was guilty of *schadenfreude*, meaning he derived pleasure from seeing others distressed. I didn't know him well enough to decide if that was true, but he'd left me feeling uneasy about what lay ahead.

9

Maryanne had finished cleaning the dishes and Fred was already snoring on the kitchen daybed.

"See you at cockcrow." She dropped a fat log in the cookstove then went to her bedroom at the bottom of the stairs like it was any night, not our very last together.

If the strip of light under her door hadn't disappeared, I might have knocked. What would I have said? That I bit my nails, imagining everything that could go wrong? That I could barely picture my life without her? That I was sorry Fred had to spoil the evening? I would have liked to hold her hands one last time for, oddly enough, I'd remember her by them, in particular by the decades-old scar on her left thumb where the hatchet had strayed while she split a log for kindling. I'd been shocked at the sight of puddles of blood. She'd comforted me, caring more about my distress than her own injury. Her fingers were long and thin, perfect for weaving braids in my hair, something she did so gently, never tugging, and yet the braids always felt neat and tight. Her hands were an expert tool for kneading bread, filleting and gutting fish, skinning rabbits, and plucking feathers. They were expert at caring for Vati in his final months and would be waving me farewell the next day.

I went upstairs telling myself we'd say our goodbyes in the morning. I sat at the desk in my parents' room, my commonplace book in front of me, the lantern's glow reflected in the windowpane. There'd be no lanterns glowing in my window in St. John's, no wicks to trim or chimneys to polish. A completely different life lay ahead of me in a city I knew only from listening to Maryanne and Fred, neither of whom had ever been there.

CITY OF DREAMS

Twirling my parasol in Bowring Park like a movie star. Partying at the Knights of Columbus Hostel, soldiers and sailors with magazine smiles, ironed uniforms, and polished boots, itching to know my name, filling up my dance card. Dining at the Newfoundland Hotel, a print of my lipstick on my crystal goblet. Relaxing at the Seagoing Officers' Club, my man's eyes doing the talking. Shopping in the grand department stores on Water Street. Jack-easy feeling year-round.

CITY UNDER SIEGE

Drunks prowling streets like hungry hounds, children with rags hanging off their scrawny backs, scrambling over each other for the best scraps from the garbage, mothers crying, fathers gone to war or for another drink. Chimneys spewing coal dust, clotheslines collecting soot, cars and trucks ruling the roads, sirens squealing, horns honking, rows of wooden houses on the verge of an inferno. Be no loss if the Nazis burnt it to the ground.

I stepped across the small landing into my own room, the space comfortably warm with the cookstove's heat rising through the floor vent. I changed into my flannel nightgown and unpinned my braids to hang by my sides. I lowered the lantern's wick and crawled under the eiderdown. It was light but warm, filled with goose feathers and made by Maryanne, yet another favourite item I couldn't take with me. I'd have to get used to sleeping without it and without counting the seconds of light and darkness from the tower's lamp. I closed my eyes…thirteen, fourteen, one, two, three, four, five, six, repeating the cycle over and over, my mind drifting, gradually losing focus, surrendering to sleep.

The bed shook and I opened my eyes as the tower's light swept past. Teo was sitting by my side.

My body stiffened, every muscle taut. "Is it Maryanne? What's wrong?"

He laid his hand on my shoulder. "Nothing. Calm down."

Was I dreaming? "What are you doing here?"

"*Calmati*, I said." He spoke in a hushed voice. "You're not leaving tomorrow, are you? At least ten times, you asked, 'Were you scared?' I told you I thought I would perish in Fred's pathetic excuse for a boat in those monstrous waves. Remember?"

"I don't understand. What's going on? Leave or I'll call Maryanne," I said, knowing I couldn't risk upsetting her or Fred, who, a short while earlier, had claimed the city wasn't safe for a young woman. Evidently, not only the city, but my own bedroom.

"What about Maryanne, anyway?" Teo said. "Are you planning to abandon a woman who cared for you your whole life? Is that the type of person you are? Selfish?" He nudged my hip with his hand. "Is it?"

I tugged on the eiderdown to drag it up over my head, bursting to say everything I'd held back until then, that I didn't trust him, that he was the selfish one, that I looked forward to having him out of my life.

"You don't care about her. What about me? What about our deal? I can't do the work by myself. You know that. When I came here you told me you were my assistant. Did you forget that?" He tugged on the eiderdown and put his hand under my chin to turn my head toward him.

I jerked it back. By then, I didn't care if Maryanne or Fred heard me. "Leave or I'll call out."

"Shush. I'm nearly finished. The war will be over soon. I'll return to my family. You'll go to St. John's, and they can find someone else to waste their life in this godforsaken land."

If he was waiting for me to agree, he'd have to wait forever. There'd be no acknowledgement on my part of his presence or his lies. I'd more than fulfilled my half of the deal. Who'd earned the keeper's salary for the past two months while I tended to the light station? Where was my share?

He tapped my knee. "In the morning, tell Fred and Maryanne you've come to your senses. You've decided to wait until the war ends before you leave this place."

I'd been coming to my senses ever since he'd arrived at Crag Point.

"My apologies for entering your private quarters."

The last sound was of the passageway door closing downstairs. With my heart pounding, I tiptoed across the narrow landing into Vati's room, relieved the door had a lock. I stood at the window in the dark, heeding the light's repetitive warning—beware of shifting tides, reckless gusts, and unpredictable perils in your path.

A FATHER'S PROMISE

Once upon a winter's gale, under the twinkle of the morning star, by earth's edge, at the dawn of a new year, a daughter was born. Named Violet, she was a vibrant hue in a stark and frozen landscape. The father cradled the babe, ran his finger gently over her cheek, and whispered in her ear a promise of a better life in a new world beyond the horizon. But promises come with no guarantee, for winds may shift on a whim, without warning or mercy.

10

Fred had believed me when I woke him an hour earlier than planned to say there'd been a sudden drop in barometric pressure. He'd followed my advice to leave early.

I drank my tea in between dressing and arranging my braids but ate nothing for fear of seasickness. I washed, noting for the last time the scent of Maryanne's soap made with mint leaves. I emptied my chamber pot in the outhouse and refreshed the water in the wash basin. The hardest part was going to the tower to turn off the lamp, terrified I'd meet Teo on the stairs or in the passageway. If he caught me leaving, who knew the trouble he might cause?

I woke Maryanne at the last minute, determined not to complicate my departure by telling her about the intruder in my bedroom.

"You got me scratching my head, Violet," she said. "Yesterday morning, you said we were in for grand weather today. Why the scramble?"

"I'm taking precautions, in case," I said, certain she knew I was lying.

Clouds opened to shine light from the crescent moon. Not that I needed light. I'd walked the route a thousand times along the path from our house down to the narrow shingle beach, the sole shoreline in a twenty-mile stretch of cliffs. On the beach itself, I stepped carefully to avoid tripping over driftwood. If I hadn't been in a hurry, I would have said my goodbyes to memories of happier days—wading in the water at low tide, scooping up kelp and buckets of capelin in June, stoking the bonfire and watching sparks floating up into the sky like shooting stars in reverse.

I wrapped my arms around Maryanne, closed my eyes, and hugged her tightly. "I wish you could come with me. How will I manage without you?"

"You'll manage," she said. "You're a grown woman now."

"I'll write soon as I can."

"Don't waste paper or pennies on me."

"It isn't a waste. Write back, please—"

"Here she comes," Fred said, his voice muffled by the breaking waves, the swash and backwash, and the hollow sound of rocks smacking off each other. He stood in water to the top of his waders, both hands on the dory to steady it in the flood tide, watching the waves. He beckoned with his arm.

I gripped the gunwale yet couldn't pull myself up with my long coat in the way.

"Help her, Maryanne. Wave's breaking. Ready?"

I was almost in, abdomen resting on the gunwale, when she grabbed my feet to give me a boost.

Fred jumped in after me and the dory jerked forward with the thrust of his oars.

I'd seen him launch from shore many times but didn't know how it might feel to be a passenger, rising, falling, tipping to one side, then to the other, expecting any second to be swamped by a wave or tossed overboard. Eventually, the vessel's movements became regular, and I knelt, both hands gripping the gunwale, with a rope tied around my seat on one end, my waist on the other, in case I fell overboard and Fred needed to haul me back in. Sea spray dribbled off my hair. My lips tasted salty. I stared at Crag Point, barely recognizing the hexagonal tower rising up like a cyclopic giant, our house dwarfed by it and the landscape. I waved to Maryanne, hand high above my head. With the sun below the horizon, I couldn't see if she waved back. I shouted her name.

"She can't hear you," Fred said.

The dory fell into a deep trough so quickly, I thought my heart had left my body. If a wave caught the bow, we'd be thrown into the sea. I'd already imagined that fate. The shock of the cold would trigger a gasp, salt water in the lungs, followed by coughing, then choking.

In the twilight, I watched Fred, senses on alert, paying attention to wind and current, eyeing the wave cycle, the distance from rest to crest, the oars tamed to respond to his touch. I closed my eyes and mumbled to myself, "Everything will be all right. Everything will be all right." Once we reached calmer waters, the rocking changed from jarring to soporific. I hugged my knees against my chest and huddled under the tarpaulin for protection from sea spray. Awake all night, I fell willingly and gently into a light but troubled sleep in which I saw Maryanne on shore, about to be swept away by a rogue wave, Teo doing nothing to save her.

DORIS AND HER SKIPPER

With its high sides and long length, the *Doris* was designed for ultimate stability in the sloppy seas of the unpredictable North Atlantic. The dory's pointed bow offers the shape needed to launch into pounding surf, while its flat bottom allows it to rest on the beach or on top of another dory. Its yellow frame and green gunwale make it conveniently visible except in the thickest fog. Experienced skippers like Fred Peckford have the skill to compensate for the dory's limitations in hazardous conditions. He masters the downwind, upwind, tail- and headwind, follows the currents like someone guided by a map, and commands the oars skillfully like a lumberjack with an axe.

"Steady she goes, girl," a man's voice said. "You're on land now. Tell that to your legs."

Fred had been right about how I'd feel after the dory ride. Either that or Pine Harbour was moving. I stood on the shore, surrounded by what must have been the community's entire population. Men stared from under the shade of duck-billed hats, with pipes or cigarettes between their lips. The strangest sight was of multiple Maryannes wearing bandanas made of old flour sacks over their hair. Children with gaping eyes, dirty faces, and tousled hair surrounded me, shouting and squealing like hungry gulls around a dead sculpin.

"My turn," a little girl cried.

"No, it's my turn," another shouted.

The children talked over each other, arguing about who would hold my hands. They told me their names, those of the dogs, their age. They led me up an incline from the beach, along a gravel road, through a narrow lane to a house, and finally into a crowded and noisy kitchen that smelled of the cooked flesh of a wild animal.

A woman introduced herself as Fred's wife, in between shouting "Get outta here," either to the dog, children, or both. She wiped her forehead and pointed to a seat at the table.

Outside, children pressed up against the window, their breath condensing on the pane, their noses flattened, their looks distorted. Fred's black water dog, Oscar, hid under the table. We'd met before at Crag Point. I pushed away his snout sniffing between my legs. At the other end, was a young man who might have been my age, though I couldn't say for sure. What did people my age look like? His eyes were the colour of sea glass, a blue faded by salt, his thick hair the colour of hay after fall frosts.

Next to Fred was a man in a black suit and with bushy black sideburns falling almost to the collar of his shirt, no hair on his chin or around his mouth. What were they talking about, huddled together and glancing my way?

"Time for grace," Fred's wife said. "Thank God. Don't forget to thank me too."

The kitchen was so abruptly quiet I had to tap my ears to make sure my hearing was all right.

Head bowed, eyes closed, fingers interlaced under his chin, the young man spoke. "Lord," he paused, "we thank you for the flesh and fruit of land and water. We ask for a peaceful end to the war. We welcome our special guests, Reverend Peters and Miss Violet Morgen, Pine Harbour's new teacher. Amen."

I'd eaten nothing since my farewell supper and would have welcomed the meal except I'd lost my appetite. Fred wouldn't have dared play such a trick on me if Maryanne had been there. He sat at the other end of the table, avoiding eye contact with me. I waited for the moment to get his attention and shake my head, but it never came, not with Oscar wanting more of my serving of rabbit stew, Mrs. Peckford saying I looked scrawny and urging me to eat, the boys on either side of me arguing over how many pounds they could each lift, and did I want to be a judge later?

After the meal, when Fred got up to go outside with the Reverend, I tried to follow him, but Oscar pounced on me, paws on my chest, slobbering tongue licking my lips.

"He's friendly, same as all hands round here. Fetch the bird, Oscar."

The dog darted off so suddenly he tripped over his paws.

"I'm Thomas, Fred's oldest, and you're Violet."

"Yes, but certainly not the teacher. Why did you say that?"

"Awfully sorry, Violet. Pop ordered me to. *I'm* the teacher." He whispered, "*Was* the teacher. I'm taking off with you on the steamer."

11

OUTPORT TEACHER WANTED

Pine Harbour invites single women to apply for the position of teacher (all grades). Requirements: Must not engage in any amoral activity such as drinking alcohol or accompanying men. Must be active in the community and church. Must provide own books, chalk, and slates. Must start at 8 a.m. to prepare the fire to heat the room. Must expect a salary significantly lower than that of a male teacher performing the same duties. Must devote summer holidays to teacher training at Memorial University College.

I hurried to keep up with Thomas, the children hurried along with me, and barking dogs, including Oscar, hurried after them. The layers of clothes weighed on my back and slowed me down, especially my mother's ankle-length coat, not stylish but practical, except while walking uphill with no free hands to hold it up.

The children asked questions: How high could I count? Was I a strict teacher? How old was I when I finished school? When had my mother last cut my hair? Why was I wearing trousers under my long skirt?

I had my own questions, but they were for Thomas. Why were we heading to the schoolhouse if I wasn't the teacher? What had he meant by "taking off" with me?

Thomas stood at the school's entrance, its clapboard lime-washed white, its black, peaked roof blending with stands of pine behind it. He clapped his hands, an echo followed, and the children hushed. "Head to the wharf while the steamer's docked, eyes and ears open wide. How many barrels of pork and bags of mail were unloaded? How many passengers are there? Hurry."

They ran off, skipping, hopping, squealing.

Thomas opened the door and gestured for me to enter. "Be thankful you aren't the teacher. I love the little urchins except when they're swarming around me like blackflies. I can't even use the outhouse without a pupil knocking, wanting help with homework, or pestering me to come out and play."

We sat side by side on a bench next to the teacher's desk, facing those of the pupils. It was more of a room than a house and surely too small to accommodate the hoard of children I'd seen so far.

"You're here finally," he said. "I can't believe it's you."

I turned toward him, facing the window where a boy appeared, sticking out his tongue, then was gone in a second. "Were you expecting someone else?"

"Just you, Violet. I've been waiting forever to see you in person. I love saying your name. It suits you one hundred per cent. You like numbers. I know that and lots more about you."

In the window, the boy crossed his eyes and poked a finger in his nose.

Thomas turned to glance at the window, but the boy was gone. "Hope I'm not confusing you."

Everything to do with Pine Harbour confused me, especially Thomas acting like we'd already met. "If you'd visited Crag Point, I would have remembered you."

He shook his head. "Sorry. I can explain everything once we're on the steamer. We'll travel together to St. John's, farther if you'll come with me."

"Farther where?"

He squirmed on the bench. "Can I tell you something first?"

I nodded.

"It's about your mail. Pop picked it up one day, delivered it to you a few days or weeks later. What you don't know is—" His shoulders rose as he took in a deep breath. "In between, I opened a few of your packages. Only the books though."

While Thomas explained how few books he'd had growing up, I remembered writing to the city's main post office to complain that someone had tampered with my mail. There'd been a fingerprint on the novel *Storm* and a drop of candle wax on *The Long Winter*. Months later, I received a reply. The clerk said if he was reckless enough to risk his employment, he'd choose more interesting packages than mine. In my second letter, I pointed out that his response proved his guilt. How could he claim they were of no interest if he hadn't opened them? I heard nothing else from him. "It was you, all along," I said.

Thomas slid closer until our hips and shoulders touched. "I should have asked you, meant to, wanted to. I'm hopeless with letters, no good at explaining things either. Disappointed in me?"

The signatures on the correspondence I'd received—advising a subscription was due for renewal or a shipment had been delayed—were each so unique I wished I could meet the person on the other end. "We could have been pen pals."

He cupped my hand in his. "You wouldn't believe how happy that makes me, Violet. I wanted to hide a note in one of your books, signed, 'Your secret admirer,' but didn't dare in case it upset you, you'd tell Pop, and he'd have my hide. You know how he is."

I wasn't interested in listening to his criticisms of Fred, not when my senses were so alert, feeling his skin against mine. Was his whole body that warm? His clothes had a recently washed, peppery smell of lye I usually found irritating, but there was something pleasantly alluring about how it blended with the scent of his skin. What soap had he used, or had he patted his face with aftershave as Vati used to before he grew a beard?

"Pop judges everyone. I've been listening to him my whole life, complaining about you and your father, Heinrich. You spent too much time in the lighthouse tower, Maryanne spoiled you, you had no friends, no religion, no mother, no proper upbringing, your father was so terrified of the Nazis, he wouldn't let you leave—"

I drew back my hand. "Fred's wrong."

"Please don't be cross, Violet. I agree with you. Pop thinks he knows what's best for everyone. I'm supposed to be here now, convincing you to be the teacher. He said you're one of the smartest girls he ever met, smart like your father."

I pictured Vati and Fred after I'd been sent to bed, Fred ranting about the price of saltfish, the disrepair of Pine Harbour's church, the loss of fishermen gone to work at the Boston docks or the Nova Scotian mines. "Our fathers were good friends."

Thomas interlaced his fingers in mine.

I looked down at his hand, mine small compared to his.

"Whenever I see a lone lantern in a window, I picture you, pencil behind your ear, binoculars around your neck, on duty, like a captain sailing through rough waters. I've been doing that for years, dreaming of seeing you in person." He paused like he wanted me to say something. "Do you feel anything for me?"

I could, though without being able to name the feeling. "Yes."

"What I want to say is, if you were interested, I mean if you care for me a bit, would you consider being my girlfriend? You don't have to answer right away. Take a few minutes to think."

For my twentieth birthday, Maryanne had given me a book, *Rebecca*, saying I should start reading novels, in particular, stories featuring the lives of young women. I'd enjoyed the haunting descriptions of the setting but disliked the selfish Rebecca, diabolical Danvers, and the gossipy Mrs. Van Hopper. If real people were anything like those characters, I was glad I lived far from society. I remembered, however, feeling curious about the couple kissing "feverishly, desperately like guilty lovers." Had Thomas read my copy of the novel? Wally, Crag Point's repair man, hadn't asked me to be his girlfriend, only to show him my breasts. Would Thomas want to see them? I glanced down at our hands. "I can be your girlfriend, yes. I assume that involves kissing and—"

Thomas glanced at the window again, then back at me. "Oh Violet, I've been waiting ever since Pop said you were coming this way, heading to the American base in St. John's. More than anything in the whole wide world, I want to kiss you."

"I'm ready," I said, lips puckered.

He stood up off the bench. "Not here. One of the kids might see us." He looked at the window again, then back at me. "Everyone will be wagging their fingers." He pointed to his chest. "At me, the teacher, alone with an unmarried woman in the schoolhouse. Pop will have me whipped."

"Where, then?"

"On the steamer, on the train to St. John's, in the city, then overseas if you want. I wrote to my Aunt Rose. She's in Lewisporte to see her grown son. She'll meet us at the train station. She won't recognize me, but she'll spot you. I told her to watch for a crown of braids. We'll travel, the three of us, to St. John's. I'll stay with her until I head overseas to Scotland. Say hello to Thomas the lumberjack."

While Thomas described his plans to see the world, far from the life of a teacher, from Fred's control and the community's prying eyes, I imagined what it might be like to kiss feverishly and desperately.

He went down on one knee and took my hands in his. "The Women's Timber Corps is hiring lumberjills. With our wages saved, after the war, we could tour France, Italy, even Egypt. What do you say? Want to go together? Come with me, please, Violet."

A FELLAH WHO FELLS

The dangers posed by the *Kriegsmarine* (German Navy) make unfeasible the importation of lumber into Britain. Yet, timber is needed for repair of bombed structures, telegraph poles, railway ties, coffins, crosses on graves, and much more. Britain has the forests but lacks the manpower to harvest the trees. Young men like Thomas Peckford, willing to work as lumberjacks in the Newfoundland Overseas Forestry Unit, can avail of free transatlantic passage and pay of $12 per week, $6 of which will automatically be sent to his family. When asked about the risks, including broken bones from bolting horses, bronchitis from sawdust inhalation, or amputated hands, Thomas said he wouldn't worry as long as his girlfriend was close by.

12

The SS *Clyde*'s whistle blew as it glided out of the harbour, retreating from the shore with the people on the wharf waving, gradually shrinking from view, the children's squeals and laughter fading to whispers. There beyond the harbour with its fishing rooms, beyond the densely packed homes with smoke billowing from chimneys, there by the dense pine forest stood the schoolhouse. Nowhere did I see Thomas, though I searched and searched. We'd been on the wharf, waiting to load my trunk. He'd said if I wanted to kiss once we set sail, he'd be more than happy to do so. But first, he had to say goodbye to his mother and grab his bag, packed and hidden under his bed.

WELCOME WARNINGS
Unlike some of her sister vessels in the Alphabet Fleet, the bay boat SS *Clyde*, is not equipped with ice-breaking capacity. Passengers are advised to prepare for extended delays due to ice. Winds commonly reach moderate to severe gale force and may back or veer suddenly. Dress appropriately. U-boat attacks are possible given Lewisporte's important role as a transportation hub for oil, aviation fuel, and lumber. Patrol by gunners and aircraft is limited to the town and its harbour. Passengers should report any sightings of periscopes, not to be confused with the long necks of cormorants.

"Miss Violet?"

Maryanne had cautioned me about strangers, especially men, who might attempt to trick me out of my money. This was no man. Taller than me, yes, but more of a boy. He stood facing me on the deck, his eyes a striking green in contrast to his pitch-black hair and the reddish freckles covering his cheeks. "Are you Violet?"

"How do you know my name?"

He laid a hand over his mouth, hiding a smile. "Some fair-haired fellah told me to watch for a girl with braids and a *V* glued on her suitcase and trunk. *V* for Violet. I'm an *E*, after King Edward. I won't change it to Albert or George on account of him marrying that American—don't care what Mom says. Edward Cuff at your service. All hands call me Cuff."

"Hello, Cuff. Do you know Thomas Peckford?"

Finger and thumb on his chin, head cocked forward, he said, "No, miss. We got no Peckfords up our way in Gull Cove. First time I ever saw Pine Harbour."

"This fair-haired fellow, did he have blue eyes?"

He scratched his head and looked down at the deck. "Don't remember, miss."

"Could you help me find him?"

"If he's on the *Clyde*, Cuff's the one to find him—cross my heart, hope to die—supposing I got to pester every single crewman, stokers in the boiler room, skipper, the whole gang."

Why wouldn't Thomas be on board? Had I misunderstood?

"You seasick already, miss? Want water? Tea's brewing in the diner."

"Thank you. Tired, that's all. I booked a cabin. Could you please take me there, Cuff?"

He picked up my trunk and told me to follow him below deck. He talked over his shoulder while we navigated through a narrow corridor. "Water on deck, mind your neck. Briny smell, expect a swell." At last, he stopped, then slid open a door to a cabin the size of a tomb.

I felt the vessel sway and sat on the bunk. "Thank you for your help. What do I owe you?"

"Not a copper, miss. My job's helping passengers. In three months when I'm seventeen, I'll sign on with the British Merchant Navy."

"Seventeen seems young to be heading to war."

"No matter there, miss. Mom wouldn't have me fighting. The last war killed her brother. Uncle Jack got me this spot on the *Clyde* till I find my sea legs. I'll be a seaman first, one day earn my mate's certificate, be serving on ships, maybe even on the *Caribou*."

"That's very brave of you. Not afraid of German U-boats, the *Unterseeboot?*"

"Don't know no German words, miss. Never heard tell of them kind of boats. Anyway, I'm off. If you're one for dancing, there'll be a scuff later."

He raised his right hand to his temple, palm down, saluted, and was gone.

JOIN THE MERCHANT NAVY

Merchant seamen may serve on any of the hundreds of ships leaving Newfoundland ports each week heading across the Atlantic to Britain, transporting tons of supplies: food, tanks, guns, motorcycles, aircraft engines, trucks, medical supplies, steel, and whatever else is needed. If you're between the ages of 14 and 70, take advantage of the opportunity to serve the Empire as a civilian alongside citizens of the Commonwealth representing a diverse range of classes and religions. Women are also invited to sign up and can work on passenger vessels. Join today!

Noises from the corridor woke me—a woman's shriek of laughter, a man's voice saying, "Slow down, Joey," and a child's croup cough.

If I hadn't been wearing my boots, I might have slept through the night and not merely through supper. I headed up to the main deck where I took in deep breaths of the cool air like I was quenching my thirst. The blackout made walking on deck tricky. One wrong step and I could fall overboard or bump into another passenger. I gripped the rail as I walked, then stopped when I found a spot out of the wind and the path of soot from the smokestack.

No lighthouse flash interfered with my view. No moon dimmed the stars' brilliance. I gazed out over the water, my eyes struggling to adjust to the darkness. Was a U-boat cruising opposite us on the same course? Was its captain's hand on the knob, controlling the periscope's height, determining the angle of the target, ready to turn, then launch, releasing the steam-powered pressure to propel the torpedo? I imagined the German sailors, hearts beating faster, anticipating the strike, the *Hurra!* to follow, to celebrate that one small step closer to victory. They were only human after all, praying they survived until the conflict ended, longing to return to their loved ones. Surely, no sensible U-boat captain would squander a valuable weapon on a vessel filled with mothers, fathers, children, young women heading to a new future in the city, and young men dreaming of a life at sea.

Looking up at the sky, I thought about what Vati had said, that war invites us to consider our role in the world, weather our place in the universe. I was working on my role. As for the universe, I stared at the Milky Way where the sun's light reflected off the moon, the two controlling the tides, tides partnered with currents, currents driven by winds, winds driven by a spinning earth. There were forces in the universe more powerful than all of man's weapons combined. Understanding them and protecting ourselves against the destructive ones would be key to our survival. How unfortunate that we fought among ourselves, blind to the more serious and significant threats faced by us all.

"There you are," a man's voice said.

I turned my gaze away from the sky. By my side was the Reverend, dressed entirely in black with black hair and mutton chops, barely visible. If I hadn't seen him in Fred's house, I might have been frightened. Instead, I was happy to see someone who knew Thomas.

"I've been searching for you."

"For me? Do you need help, Reverend?"

He gripped the rail with one hand, a cane with the other. "Thank you, but only the Lord God could be of assistance at this point in my life's journey. You're the one in need of help, here on your own."

"Thomas Peckford was supposed to be with me." I explained how he'd gone home to fetch his bag and never returned. "I don't understand what happened."

The Reverend fixed his gaze ahead. "It's quite simple, Miss Morgen. The fact is, no unmarried woman should be travelling alone with a man."

"I won't be alone. His Aunt Rose is meeting us, in Lewisporte. Me, I guess. I hope."

He tapped his cane on the deck like a gavel ordering me to be silent. "My dear girl, learn not to contradict your elders, especially a man of the cloth. You're not in my parish. From what I understand, you aren't in anyone's parish. No father to set you on the right path either. Be it known I tried to help you." He tapped his cane again. "Rose Peckford is an unsuitable companion. Mrs. Gibbons is the name she should be using. Regardless of how she lives her life, she's still married. Twice your age, ten times your experience. Straight into temptation is where she'll lead you. Choose your company based on their moral virtues." He let go of the rail and leaned on his cane. "I've said what I had to say. I'm retiring to my cabin. You should go to yours."

"Are you certain I can't help you?"

He turned his whole body toward me, as though he couldn't turn his head alone. "Help yourself. Pray for the SS *Clyde*'s safe passage. Pray that God in his mercy will forgive you your sins and save you from perishing in these cursed waters." He walked away with a limp, sliding his left leg behind him without flexing the knee.

I shivered and pulled my collar tight around my neck. My sins? Lying to Maryanne about my early departure—was that a sin? Did such sins come with punishment? I headed back to my cabin. Along the way, I heard unfamiliar sounds and, at first, imagined a mysterious sea creature calling from the depths. I followed the sounds to the common room, then opened the door. Inside, people were laughing, shouting, and dancing to music played on fiddles and an accordion. I jostled for space until I got closer to the dancers and musicians. I only planned to watch except, in an instant, a man, shirt sleeves rolled up past the elbows, grabbed me by the waist.

With a smile that revealed a missing front tooth, he said, "Let's have us a scuff." He dragged me onto the packed dance floor before I could shout, "I don't know how!" He twirled me around, hopped, and stomped, held me tightly, especially around the torso, then relaxed his hold and moved his hand down my spine. Once it reached below the waist, I jerked loose.

Plenty of hands helped me remove my coat, then passed it overhead to rest on a table by the wall. I wished I could shed my skirt and dance in Vati's trousers, but none of the other women wore them. The pace of the music picked up and another man invited me onto the floor for a dance filled with energetic turns and swings. That dance was followed by another, then another, and another, with so much twirling and turning,

I wasn't even sure if it was with the same partner. Best of all was Cuff, so patient and encouraging, teaching me to square dance. "You can do it, miss." One thing was for certain—I'd never had so much fun. By the time the entertainment ended, my voice was hoarse from laughing and singing along with the others on the refrains. I would have danced all the way to my cabin except I needed one hand for the rail and another to hold my collar around my neck. In a matter of hours, that kind southwest wind had backed to the southeast. I knew what that meant. East, then northeast. Not a reassuring move.

Back in my cabin I opened my trunk and held up my barometer. Did it need to be calibrated or was the extreme drop in pressure accurate? Luckily, I'd noted the locations of the life rafts. As a keeper's assistant, I paid attention to reports of marine disasters. I knew the fate of other vessels in the Alphabet Fleet. The SS *Dundee* had gone aground in slob ice and heavy seas. The carcasses of the SS *Ethie*, *Fife*, and *Invermore* lay under water, playgrounds for lobster and other bottom feeders. Not even the most powerful vessels could survive a fierce storm in Newfoundland's waters.

DEADLY BLIZZARD AT SEA

On a stormy mid-February night in 1942, three US ships travelled en route to the Argentia naval base on Newfoundland's southwest coast. Almost zero visibility caused by a raging blizzard interfered with light signals between vessels and made star sightings impossible for navigation while they sailed in a zigzag pattern to make it harder for U-boats to track them. Decks and radio equipment became covered in sleet. Ice blocked signals, making communication difficult. Gale-force winds and strong currents drove the vessels onto jagged rocks at the bottom of 250-foot-high cliffs. The destroyer USS *Wilkes* reached its destination. The supply ship USS *Pollux* and destroyer USS *Truxtun* took 203 men to a deep, dark, and cold grave.

13

The rain fell in horizontal sheets powered by gusts that would blow leaves off trees if there were any. With my head down and collar raised, I observed little from the dock to the nearby Lewisporte train station. Cuff carried my trunk and had to move slowly. When he finally joined me, his shirt, jacket, and pants were soaked. I insisted he return to the steamer to change.

"Not until I got you squared away," he said.

We stood at the station's entrance where Thomas's Aunt Rose could spot me unless she, too, failed to show.

We hadn't been waiting long when a woman laid down her suitcases in front of me. "Violet? Is that you?" She stared at my hair and clothes, probably thinking I looked very dull and unsophisticated compared to her.

I nodded. Did St. John's women usually wear that much jewellery—pendulous earrings, pearl necklace, four rings on one hand, two on the other, bracelets on both arms? Were ruby lips and matching red nails a common style in the city? As for her short blond hair, I wondered if the colour was her own.

"Rose Peckford. Where's my Tommy? Haven't seen him in eons."

"He wasn't on the steamer, ma'am," Cuff said. "I guarantee it."

"Well hello to you, too," Rose said. "You her boyfriend?"

"No, ma'am. Edward Cuff at your service." He jerked to attention, body rigid, then added a salute.

Rose shrieked with laughter, so quick and loud she startled me. "Aren't you the cutest, wettest boy I ever laid my beautiful, dry eyes on? Bet you were raised on bottles of molasses. Change your name to Ernest, better yet Ernie, why don't you?"

Cuff lowered his head to hide his red face.

Maryanne had sewn a deep pocket into my skirt, covered with a two-button flap to keep my money hidden. I reached under my coat into the pocket, grabbed a fifty-cent coin, and offered it to him. "For service beyond the call of duty."

He stared at his wet shoes, saying "no" as he turned his head in one direction, "miss" in the other, moving side to side steadily like a clapper striking a bell's rim. "Can't be taking gifts from passengers. Only doing my job, miss."

Rose plucked the coin out of my hand. "What's all the fuss? I'm no steamer passenger. Last trip I took on water, I was tempted to jump overboard, best cure there is for seasickness. Hold your head up, Ernie. Don't be afraid of anyone, especially not bossy women like me, ready to right the world." She held it out on her palm. "Here you go. Take it."

He waved rather than saluting. "Best of the best of luck, Miss Violet. You too, ma'am." He ran off, bent over at the waist, rain pounding his back.

Rose dropped the coin into her handbag. "Consider that a small favour paid in advance. Tell me, what happened to Tommy?"

"I wish I knew," I said, puzzled as much about the disappearance of the coin as I was about Thomas.

"I bet the money in that deep pocket of yours my brother Freddy blocked his way. He tried his almighty best to do the same with me years ago. I won't have a husband, brother, father, or son bossing me around. I go where and do what I want."

I was starting to get used to Rose and had a feeling she could help me. "Thomas said we'd travel together, the three of us. Is that true?"

"True it is except there's only two now. Two's better than one. Girls need to stick together. Life can be lousy as today's weather, doing its darndest to crush our spirits. We can't be having that, can we? Let's find some place friendly and dry."

We crammed into the station along with everyone else sheltering from the deluge. The stench of oilskin and wet wool tickled my nose. People pushed against me, stepped on my toes, and poked me with their elbows. Fortunately, Cuff had arranged for my trunk to be loaded onto the train. I had one case, unlike Rose with one at either side. They didn't slow her down or stop her from occasionally standing on her toes to glance around the station. Her efforts paid off when she claimed a bench the instant it came free. We laid our suitcases on the floor and sighed in unison as we sat down.

Rose took out a cigarette, lit it with a lighter, and talked between puffs. "Heading to the city, chasing fame and fortune or soldiers and sailors?"

"They're hiring office girls at the American base. They don't accept applications by mail. I did write to them, then burned the letter in the end. The office-girl work is temporary. I'm going to be a weather forecaster eventually. I'm merely an amateur but my short-range forecasts are remarkably accurate despite my lack of formal training."

She tapped her finger on her cigarette. Ash fell on her shoes. "Good for you, but you know, honey, no guy or gal makes a penny in the weather business in these wicked parts—might as well wear a fur coat year-round. Summer's okay if you can squeeze four weeks out of the season. Rest of the year, it's nothing but snow, sleet, hail, hurricanes, leaks, ruined hair, and blotched mascara. Who wants to hear there's another week of fog? The only people care about forecasts are the gluttons for punishment." She drew on her cigarette and the smoke flowed out magically from her nose.

"I'm not doing it for the money."

"If that's the case, be glad you met Rose Peckford. I'll set you straight right away. If any woman knows how to milk a dollar out of a dime, it's me. Four or five years ago, I never dreamed I'd have enough money to make it worth owning a wallet. Nowadays, there's more money trading pockets in St. John's than you ever imagined, my pockets included. Women like us need to take advantage of these special times."

Women like us? How was I like her?

Smoke came out in a stream through her pursed lips. "Anyone who tells you money doesn't grow on trees is a lousy liar. There's money all right. Oodles. Figure out how to pick it and it's yours. Lots of lads did that. Women are another story. They're too darn busy saying, 'I do,' feeding hungry mouths, and cleaning babies' bums."

What had the Reverend meant when he'd said she'd lead me into temptation?

She pointed to a woman, hunched over and with a limp, peddling sandwiches displayed on a slab of wood. "Picture those big boys in their uniforms on the train with appetites would put a mutt to shame. Empty stomachs and wallets full of American and Canadian dollars. How much do you think they'd pay for a sandwich sold by an exotic-looking gal?"

"I've no idea. I haven't tasted the sandwiches, and I'm full from breakfast."

"Got four and a half dollars? In Yankee talk, bucks. We'll buy twenty sandwiches from that woman there, sell them on the train, and triple our money."

"Her sign says twenty cents each."

"What's the point of getting rich if you can't be generous? That poor woman could use a bit of generosity, probably trudging over these floors sunrise to set, now till kingdom come." She beckoned with an outreached arm for the woman to join us. "Rest for a spell," Rose said. "Head home early, make yourself a pot of strong tea, and apologize to your feet for making them work so hard." She handed her the money I'd given her along with my fifty-cent coin from her purse.

The woman, Elsie, thanked Rose, then shared our bench for as long as it took to explain why she had to be on her busy way. The last thing she said before she left us was, "Keep the sandwiches cool. You don't want them going off."

PROFILE OF AN ENTERPRISING WOMAN

Elsie rises at dawn, rain or shine, snow or sleet, walks five miles to the Lewisporte train station to sell sandwiches, then arrives back home in time to cook supper and tend to her used-to-be-lumberjack husband laid up with a bad back and to the youngest of nine offspring, twins of 18 months, tugging at her breasts. At day's end, she makes another batch of sandwiches, then falls asleep until one of her brood cries out, needing Mommy. Let Elsie's hard-working spirit be an inspiration to all enterprising women.

Rose licked her fingers and wiped them on her handkerchief. "I'm dying to know what's in the sauce. The bread would be a waste of a chew without it."

The remaining nineteen sandwiches were wrapped in a brown paper bag in my suitcase. I was certain I'd made a mistake paying for them, though I could hardly avoid it with everything moving so fast, decisions needing to be made on the fly, not carefully measured and considered. I'd remained awake much of the night, attentive to the steamer's rolling and pitching, and didn't feel like myself. "I'm sorry if I don't understand. You want us to peddle the sandwiches on the train?"

"Not us," Rose said. "You. Those boys want to see a fresh face, not one with powder to hide wrinkles." She patted her cheek.

"Me? I don't know how to sell sandwiches."

She nudged me with her shoulder. "What kind of attitude is that? A smart girl never says, 'I don't know how.'"

"I meant I'd prefer not to."

"I suppose you're rich and don't need to earn a week's salary in a half-hour? Maybe you don't understand that money buys a gal freedom. Tell me anything else that can buy it and I'll give up smoking here and now."

Vati's savings would do for a while if I was careful, but extra dollars could help pay for a new wardrobe. "How do I make a profit on nineteen sandwiches?"

"Sell them for eighty cents. The soldier will hand you a dollar. Pretend you can't find the change. That shouldn't be too hard. He'll say, 'Keep the change.'"

"Why don't I simply sell them for one dollar?"

"I'll need to start charging for the advice." She laid her hand on my head. "This much is free. They're not hiring Rapunzels on the base or anywhere. I'd say let down your braids to dry, but the servicemen would be swinging you around by them. Pay a visit to the beauty parlour in St. John's. Get yourself a couple of victory rolls. These days, what's a gal got besides her looks?" She pulled my skirt up above the knee. "Women don't wear trousers under skirts, over them, or on their own. Trust me—Rose knows. I've been working at Ayre and Sons for a decade, plus I'm old enough to be your mammy."

I pulled down my skirt to hide my trousers. I wasn't used to wearing a skirt, though it had kept me warm in the dory and on the steamer. "Thanks for the advice."

Rose bent over and tapped on her suitcase. "You're in luck today, Violet. Guess what I got a whole suitcase full of."

"Skirts?"

"The most in-demand commodity there is—Kayser seamed-back, copper-tone, silk stockings with a reinforced knit-in, no-need-for-a-garter, stretch top." She tapped again. "Plenty of gorgeous gals would pay a ransom for them. On sale for a dollar twenty-five. One dollar each if you buy two. How many would you like?"

A year's subscription to the *Evening Telegram* cost six dollars and the *Newfoundland Quarterly*, eighty cents for one year. "That seems expensive. How much do they typically cost?"

"Don't go expecting anything typical during wartime. Seventy-five cents, and I'll give you forty per cent of the sandwich profits. How's that for a steal?"

The fair price of stockings was a mystery to me, but when it came to percentages, I knew, in this case, the higher the number, the better. "Fifty per cent."

Rose patted my leg. "You're catching on, Violet. My influence is paying off. Fifty per cent for the stockings too."

"Stockings?"

"Those sandwiches will be gone in minutes. Sell the stockings next. You'll make a killing, believe me. 'Be on guard, lads. Violet's got a deal for you.'" She leaned forward, grabbed her suitcase, and slid it next to mine. "Here you go. The whole suitcase is yours to sell. Soon as we're on the train, ditch the trousers, don a pair of Kaysers. You're a city girl now. Time to dress and act the part."

ROSE'S ADVICE FOR WOMEN

Always look glamorous to boost troops' morale. Beauty is duty.
Mascara's a must. Never use boot polish to darken the lashes.
Beetroot juice makes an affordable and attractive option for lips.
Learn their language: baby doll, broad, cookie, dolly.
Avoid braids, trousers, and dazed eyes.
Be bold and fearless.

14

By the time we left Notre Dame Junction, I'd sold all the sandwiches. My pockets were stuffed with notes, George Washington on most, others with Thomas Jefferson, so many I suspected the men were aiming to be rid of them. No amount of money was worth the pats on my derrière. I couldn't ask a simple question, such as "Which way to the dining car?" without a chorus of "This way, babe." No matter how often or loudly I said "Stop" to those on the floor playing craps, they poked at the bottom of my skirt and peeped underneath, saying "Lemme in," or "Gimme a taste." I regretted changing into stockings and couldn't return to the sleeping car to put on trousers. Rose had some type of train sickness and didn't want to be disturbed.

IRONY ON THE RAILS
The branch line of the Overland Route will stop in Lewisporte to take on freight, lumber, and passengers including Misses Violet and Rose. From there, the train will travel east to the Riverhead Station in St. John's. American servicemen like to call the train The Newfie Bullet because of its slowness on the narrow-gauge Newfoundland Railway. Passengers can purchase cigars in the lounge after enjoying a meal in the dining car, served on white tablecloths with silverware and fine china. Unaccompanied women may rest assured that the train's authorities do not tolerate harassment by men.

If a steward hadn't come by, I might have screamed.
"Sorry, miss. On your own?"
"For now, yes, but—"

"You can't be loitering here, teasing the men. Follow me to the diner." He outstretched his arms to shuffle the men to the sides. "Move over, gents. Hands to yourself or walk to St. John's from the next station."

I stayed close behind the man, head down, brushing off the occasional hand on my thigh or my chest, thinking about the word *teasing*, something Maryanne sometimes accused me of doing with her. I couldn't recall doing anything like that on the train. They'd teased me—that was for sure.

When we reached the diner, he stopped to get a woman's attention. She wasn't anything like Rose. In fact, her style was exactly what I wanted—a suit jacket that flattered the figure without any frills or gaudiness. Her straight brown hair was simple, yet framed her round face in a way that appealed to me.

"Mind looking out for her?" he said to the woman, then was gone.

"I'm Ida."

"Violet."

"Let me finish chatting with this sergeant," she said. "Be right with you."

I felt a tap on my shoulder and turned around ready to shout, "Leave me alone!"

Standing before me was a man who could have been George VI, tall, slim, and distinguished, with perfectly proportioned features and a thin nose. We were so close, I had to look up to see his face.

He rested his arm on the wall to steady himself against the train's sway, his brown leather jacket open, showing its sheep's-wool lining. "I couldn't help overhearing. You're Violet. Allow me to introduce myself. Captain Philip Campbell, Royal Air Force. Heading to the city?"

I nodded, transfixed by the attention in his gaze, curious about his accent, too shy to comment on it.

"Visiting family and friends?"

I shook my head, unsure of what to say.

"Staying there for long?"

I nodded again, wondering if I should tell him I planned to stay there forever or if that would be revealing too much.

"Aren't you a silent one," he said. "I noticed your sweet smile earlier. May I see it once more, please?"

I was trying to decide if his eyes were green or grey, but the train swayed and I fell forward against him.

He held his arms around me for what couldn't have been more than seconds, yet long enough for me to want it to happen again, to feel my body against his.

"Pardon me. I'm not acting fresh. You lost your balance."

I leaned back on the wall of the railcar. "Thank you. Are you from there? St. John's, I mean."

"There's your voice. Delightfully fresh, like you. Not with my Ulster accent I can't be. I'm on leave from the British Overseas Airways Corporation and signed on recently with the RAF. These days, I'm back and forth to St. John's, between the Gander and Torbay air bases, practicing landing and taking off on runways instead of on lakes, rivers, or the sea. Training a few of our new recruits, the airmen. I came here for the first time just before the war started, in Botwood, last stop before crossing the Atlantic in a seaplane. Perhaps you've heard of the Yankee Clipper? North America one day, Great Britain the next?"

I shook my head. I'd never imagined meeting a pilot, one of the few who'd ever flown across the Atlantic, who, before the war, piloted seaplanes. I'd read about heroic men like him in a special *Who's Who* volume of my encyclopedia provided free with the purchase of books *A* to *Z*, men who travelled the world, fearless and daring, able to take to the sky, fully aware of the risk to their lives.

"Anyway, those were the fabulous days," he said, "crossing the Atlantic in style, for leisure and pleasure. Nothing compared to what we're facing in the skies these days. The world has certainly changed since this ridiculous mess started. But enough about me. What about you?"

After listening to him talk about luxury travel, celebrities, and flying planes, I wouldn't dare introduce the unschooled girl from an insignificant crag. I didn't want him to laugh or take me for someone with straw between my ears. "You're the first pilot I've met, but I enjoy reading about Amelia Earhart. She was here ten years ago, in Harbour Grace before she crossed the Atlantic. Did you ever meet her?"

He shook his head.

"What do you think happened? Did strong headwinds force her to burn so much fuel she crashed into the ocean and drowned, or did the

Japanese capture her, believing she was a spy?" If he blamed the wind, we could have a long and interesting discussion about aviation and weather.

"Good God." His laugh resonated between the railcar walls. "What have you been reading?"

Why did people laugh when I least expected it? I felt the blood rush to my head and pretended to be looking at my feet. "Newspaper reports. They're not to be trusted I guess."

"Show me those bewitching eyes again. I say, they must be from somewhere far off." He paused and I wondered if it was a cue to tell him where I came from.

"Forgive me for laughing," he said. "To answer your question, an aviatrix trying to set world records—well, it's merely for show, isn't it? That or a hobby for rich women striving to make a name for them—"

"Table for two ladies," a man called out.

Ida turned around to face me. "Two lovely ladies we are."

"See you again, Violet, I hope," the pilot said.

I raised my hand to wave goodbye. When I dropped it by my side, his fingers grazed mine. Had he done it on purpose? Did it feel as exciting for him as it had for me?

I followed Ida to the rear of the dining car where I sat facing her and the wall while she faced the rest of the diner.

The waiter handed us menus. Ida chose lamb and I ordered the same.

"Lucky you," she said. "I barely got a hello out of that pilot. You had him soaring over you."

She laughed and I pretended to laugh back. "You mean you think he likes me?"

"You'll have to ask him. One thing's for sure, he's very dapper in that jacket, belongs in a shop window. It's not often you see someone with a suntanned face this time of year, not unless they've been up above the fog and clouds. I suppose he keeps that head of hair slicked back for flying."

The waiter served us each a crystal bowl of tiny pieces of fruit.

I hadn't eaten since breakfast and devoured the sweets in three mouthfuls.

Ida leaned to the side, watching the other diners. "Nice to see a girl eat dessert before the main meal. You got your priorities straight."

Maryanne only ever served dessert at the end of the meal. Why had the waiter brought the fruit first if it was meant to be eaten last? At least I hadn't made that mistake in front of the pilot.

"Ever been off the island?" she said.

"No, but I heard they have large department stores in Toronto. You?"

"I wish. Farthest I ever got was on this trip to the Royal Stores in Grand Falls. One of these days, I'll travel to the end of this route, board the ferry, and sail across to Canada. Nova Scotia first. Montreal next."

"They speak French there, don't they?"

"*Oui.* I'll have to practice my *Ooh là là!* Talk about style. For now, I'm at our store on Water Street, in St. John's. Been working there forever."

The waiter brought our order and invited us to enjoy the meal.

Ida picked at her food, talking rather than eating, describing department stores as a land of managers to be obeyed, timecards to be punched, and customers expecting discounts. "And you? Montreal? Halifax? Want to go there someday?"

"As long as it's not by boat. The base in St. John's is hiring office girls. Know it?"

She laid down her fork over her half-eaten meal. "Who doesn't? What girl isn't applying to work there? Every one of them is dressed like the Andrews Sisters with curls and rolls, in the same outfits—button-up shirt-waist dresses."

"If not like them, how?"

"Pop by the Royal Stores when you're in the city. Ask for Miss Fitzgerald. I'll outfit you in the latest style."

"That's so kind of you. If it's anything like your style, it will suit me."

"Why, thank you. I'm like Earhart, designing my own clothes."

"Coincidence. I was just talking about her."

"I overheard you. She was more than a fearless woman buzzing around in an aeroplane, smashing aviation records. Like me, she designed and made her own clothes. Practical wear for active women. Wrinkle-free too. I hope she's relaxing on a sandy beach, in a swimsuit, Nivea cream slathered over her long legs. She had her own Amelia Earhart label. Mine will be Fitz Original. What do you think?"

"I think you're incredible."

"Thanks for the encouragement. I've been told more than once to give up the idea."

"What I said about being an office girl isn't quite true. It's merely a stepping stone. I want to answer Churchill's call to serve the Empire. I'm going to be a weather forecaster with the Americans."

Unlike Rose, Ida paid attention while I explained about the role of weather in the war and how Maryanne had convinced me I could actually help fight the enemy.

"The world needs more women who got it in their minds that they can do something great, something they'll be remembered or even recognized for. I don't care how long it takes me. I'm determined to get there."

"You remind me of Rose Peckford. Do you know her?" I slid my legs out from under the table, pulled up my skirt to the knee, then ran my fingers down my calf to show her the Kayser silkiness. "She claims there's a fortune to be made selling stockings like these to the servicemen."

Ida stood, her coat draped over her arm. "Sure, I know Rose. I admire lots about her, but in your place, I wouldn't get mixed up in her black-market business or any of her other schemes to make a quick dollar. Maybe she'll be rich someday, or maybe they'll lock her up for not paying duty and import taxes."

"Actually, I wasn't planning to sell them anyway," I said. That was true, except my decision had nothing to do with Rose and everything to do with the annoying servicemen.

Ida slid her untouched goblet of fruit across the table. "Here you go. For a girl with your slim figure, you've got the appetite of a whale. Glad I met you, Violet. See you in St. John's. If you need a place to hang your bonnet, visit my friend's boarding house. Twelve Chapel Street. Theresa Power. We grew up together. She may be small, but she's tough. Don't let her scare you away."

I said goodbye, thanked her for the recommendation, but didn't mention I already had a boarding house in mind, on Goose Hill. Maryanne's grand-daughter had recommended it in a letter. She'd described it as luxurious, with three bathrooms and eight furnished bedrooms, each with a fireplace.

"Anything else, miss?" a man's voice said, as I was finishing Ida's dessert.

I glanced up at the waiter. "Anything else?"

He closed his eyes, then opened them again, and I wondered if I'd done something wrong.

"Would you care to order something else from the menu, miss?"

"Oh, I see. No, thank you. Sorry."

He held up his hand, a small can of fruit cocktail resting on his palm. "We pride ourselves on our care of passengers, especially foreign girls. I noticed you enjoyed dessert. This is for you. Welcome to Newfoundland."

15

I was squeezing the can of fruit cocktail into my handbag and preparing to leave the diner when a soldier came to my table. I stared at his khaki uniform, its colour sure to stand out in snowy landscapes, its woollen fabric ideal for sponging up the rain and attracting drafts.

He stood to attention and spoke without looking directly at me. "You the one peddling sandwiches?"

"Sold out, sorry. I didn't taste them, but I'm certain the diner's sandwiches would be far better. For dessert, I'd recommend the fruit—"

He tugged on the back of my chair like he was prepared to pull it out from under me if I didn't hurry. "Follow me, please, miss."

My coat was heavy and bulky in my arms. With everyone staring as I left the diner, I was tempted to drape it over my head, especially while passing by the pilot, still in line.

"What's happening?" he said.

Whatever it was, it seemed urgent, but I didn't get to tell him that. There were no whistles or groping while we walked through the narrow railcars, though the men lining the route made a combined *oooh* sound. Had I done something wrong? We passed through three crowded railcars with a gauntlet of stares before the soldier stopped, opened a compartment door, and gestured with an outstretched arm for me to enter.

I sat opposite a man in a beige shirt and matching tie, his uniform jacket hanging from a wall hook. On the small table between us lay a sandwich, teeth marks in the bread, a sliver of egg yolk sticking out between the slices.

He puffed on a cigar. "You the one sold this to my men?"

With one hand, I fanned myself. With the other, I pinched my nose to block the sour smell of eggs gone bad, mixed with the sickly-sweet stench from his cigar. My stomach sent me reminders of the dory ride and the two servings of fruit cocktail. "Yes, sir."

He stood, slid open the door, gave the sandwich to the soldier, then closed the door. "Don't appreciate my cigar?" He held it in front of him, pinched between two fingers and a thumb, the end saturated with saliva. "Direct from the world's cigar capital, Tampo, Florida."

"Tampa." With my fingers pinching my nose, my voice sounded nasally. If I hadn't felt nauseous, I might have remembered not to correct him. I said nothing about the ash smeared on his shirt collar.

He puffed on his cigar, cheeks hollowed. When he blew the smoke at me, I responded with a torrent of sneezing.

"I took you for an innocent girl got herself in a tangle. Now I see you're a smart aleck can't hold her tongue."

"Sorry, sir. The 1921 Tampa Bay hurricane winds reached 140 miles per hour with a twelve-foot storm surge. I wouldn't forget records like that. The closest we've ever come to those wind speeds is with the August Gales, most recently—"

"We got fourteen American GIs out of commission in the sleeper car. Just so happens, every one ate a sandwich or two you sold them."

He might as well have been slicing onions. My eyes burned. "Sorry they're ill. I had a similar experience yesterday on a dory—"

"Roll up your flaps, missy. How come you're not sick?"

His face was so near my own, I could see the blackheads on his stubby nose, the chip in his bottom tooth, the pointed edges of his haircut, and the creases in his chapped lips. His breath smelled of rotted potatoes.

"I planned to save one for later but ended up selling them. My friend had the idea. She ate one. She's sick too. Blame it on the eggs or hens, I guess. Actually, I'm not feeling too well either."

Someone knocked.

"Heck! What now?" the man said.

The door opened and Ida entered the compartment, the pilot behind her. I'd been looking forward to seeing him again, though under other circumstances.

Ida sat next to me and leaned forward to shake the man's hand. "Ida Fitzgerald. Head of ladies' wear at the Royal Stores, St. John's. I went for a puff, came back by the diner, and her friend, Captain Campbell, with the RAF, said Violet had run into a problem."

"You the other one peddling sandwiches?"

"No, sir. That's Rose Peckford."

"Well, then, we only got this one to blame for making the GIs sick."

Obviously, I hadn't done it on purpose and wasn't a saboteur. I was about to say that in my defence, but Ida spoke first.

"I can assure you, Violet's done nothing wrong. Not intentionally, I mean. Less than an hour ago, she was praising Churchill. Any more patriotic and she'd have the Union Jack tattooed on her forehead. The Captain and I can vouch for her." She opened a silver cigarette case. "Got a light?" With the cigarette between her lips, she lit it off the man's cigar. She pointed to the doorway. "You may be interested in chatting with the Captain. I bet he's got barrels of stories about piloting flying boats across the Atlantic."

The man stood to face him, his head reaching to the height of the Captain's chest. "Flying boats? Jesus! Grab a seat."

Ida whispered in my ear, "Skedaddle."

The man pointed at me, cigar stub in fingers stained a rusty orange. "Give the soldier your address, name, father's name, and whatever else he asks for."

Ida laid her hand on my back as she ushered me out of the compartment.

"Missy," the man called out.

I stopped in my tracks, my head lowered so the pilot couldn't see my fiery-red face.

"We got eyes and ears on you. Your story's not over yet."

TRANSATLANTIC TRAVEL IN A FLYING BOAT

Interested in travelling from North America to England when the war ends? Leave one day, cruise at a speed of up to 200 miles per hour, and arrive the next. Yes, readers, it is possible. How? In one of the world's largest seaplanes. The Yankee Clipper flies from New York, stopping in Shediac, New Brunswick; Botwood, Newfoundland; Foynes, Ireland;

and finally, Southampton. Enjoy overnight accommodations and five-course meals in a grand dining room with full waiter service. Do not be deterred by the noise, vibration, or turbulence that occur naturally during each flight. Trust pilots like the intrepid Captain Campbell to guide you safely to your destination.

16

'd imagined that arriving in St. John's would be like walking onto a stage with bright lights and an audience craving an encore. In reality, the audience had vacated their seats, curtains were drawn, and if lights were on, they'd be in fierce competition with the fog and blackout measures. I thought of sending Maryanne a postcard of the train station: "Arrived safely. Roaring crowd. Momentous moment. Wish you were here." At least the last sentence would have been true.

I stood on the Riverhead Station's platform, alone except for the rat chasing a cat on the tracks. A foghorn sounded and my heart skipped a beat. Its pattern wasn't like Crag Point's horn, yet it had a familiar groan. Nothing else seemed familiar. I might as well have landed on another planet. Maybe the city would better match my expectations after I had a soak in a bathtub, then curled up in a bed by the fireplace. Anything would be an improvement over the last hours spent in the sleeping car berth, Rose snoring, vomit on the floor, and the stink of cigar smoke on my clothes. I'd fallen asleep eventually, pen and commonplace book still in hand. Neither Rose, Ida, nor the pilot had alerted me that we'd arrived. They'd disappeared like characters shifting out of the scene in a vivid but strange dream, one best forgotten.

A HARBOUR CITY

Picture a harbour surrounded by steep hills and landlocked except for a narrow opening to the North Atlantic. Picture that mile-long sheltered body of water as the last refuge before heading east to the European continent. Picture it as the first point of entry to North America. Indigenous peoples, early explorers, and fishermen were drawn to this natural fortress that offered protection from waves, winds, pirates, and enemies. From the harbour grew a settlement fanning north uphill, then west along the Waterford and Freshwater Valleys. Welcome to St. John's, a city defined by its harbour, a place of refuge and of opportunity for young ladies new to society.

A porter carried my trunk to the road where a taxi waited.

"Where you off to?" the driver said.

"Fifteen Goose Hill, please."

He turned around, hands on the wheel, face barely visible. "Goose Hill?"

"Apparently, they always have spare rooms for women new to the city."

"Sure you meant Goose Hill?"

Had Maryanne said Goose Street?

"Hurry up, miss. You're my last ride."

Hurry? At ten p.m., new to the city, without having combed my hair or changed my clothes for nearly two days? "Yes. I'm certain it's Goose Hill."

"They only rent by the hour."

"That will do, assuming it isn't too expensive. It comes highly recommended, multiple bathrooms with—"

"You don't get it, do you?"

My assumptions about taxi drivers were wrong. They didn't simply take passengers where they wanted to go. "Pardon me, but I don't understand what you mean. Get what?"

He sighed. "It's not respectable."

"Respectable? How?"

"If it wasn't the end of my shift, I'd ask my wife to explain it to you. Got any other friends you can stay with?"

Of course I didn't have friends to stay with. The closest I had was Rose or Ida. I knew where they worked, but the stores would be closed. "What about twelve Chapel Street? A boarding house run by Theresa Power. Do you know her?"

"I know plenty of Theresas and Powers, no Theresa Power. Chapel Street will do. Off we go."

He asked if this was my first time in the city. I told him yes without admitting it was my first time in a motor car. Everything I'd read described the ride's smoothness. They couldn't have been referring to taxi drivers on St. John's roads under blackout rules, in fog, swerving and swearing at every bump, eyes fixed on the passenger in the rearview mirror instead of on what lay ahead.

"Shame you didn't come here before the war," he said. "You could walk the streets night or day. No worries besides a few mutts. It's not the locals breaking into houses, smashing downtown windows, speeding. It's them from away. You're not a foreigner, are you?"

I wasn't, though absolutely everything seemed foreign—motor cars, trains, roads. "I'm from Notre Dame Bay."

"Don't know no one from out those parts. Once upon a time, you'd stroll down Water Street and you'd know half the people by name. You'd be related to the other half. Nowadays, it's nothing but strangers. Boarding houses everywhere, filled to the rafters. You got no clue who you're living next to."

I'd never lived near anyone and barely understood what it meant. "Is Chapel Street safe?"

"Yes, love. Churches, convents, and cathedrals everywhere. You'll be on holy ground."

When we arrived and I stepped out of the taxi, I didn't sense anything holy. Chapel Hill was more appropriate than Street. A hill with a row of ten houses on one side, four on the other, along with a church. Not merely any church—one that dwarfed the houses. Its size alone would have been enough to distinguish it. A green leading light shone from the spire. I'd read about such lights designed to help mariners establish bearings as they entered the harbour.

The driver rolled down his window. "Get on with it, miss. The wife won't go to bed till she hears me pulling up in front of our home."

If I hadn't needed his help, I would have gladly told him to leave. The last time I'd knocked on someone's door it was Teo's, and that had not gone well. I took off my glove, knocked, then stepped back, eyeing the small three-storey house attached to another on one side and with weatherworn clapboard.

"Harder," the driver called from behind the wheel.

Either their blackout curtains were one hundred per cent effective, or everyone had gone to bed. If that was the case, I'd need to pound with my foot to get their attention. I knocked again, not much harder, but for longer.

The driver shut off the engine, stepped out of his taxi, then marched up to the house, head leading. "By the Jesus, I knew I should have packed it in at ten." He pounded with such force, the sound echoed off the church.

A dog's bark came across clearly, bullhorn-amplified in the night's stillness. Someone roared, "Shut up, Pete."

"My name's Andy." His fist was in the air, ready to clobber the door when it flew open and he nearly fell forward.

A woman stood in the doorway, the height and stature of a child. She wore curlers in her rusty-coloured hair, a wool coat draped over her shoulders, and a flannel dressing gown underneath. "What's wrong with the likes of you? The neighbours will be blaming us for the ruckus. What do you want?" Her voice cut through the air loud as a siren.

The foghorn sounded and the barking changed to howls.

I stepped forward so she could see me better. "Sorry, miss. Are you Theresa Power?" I said it in my most polite and quiet voice, so she wouldn't blame me for the disturbance.

She folded her arms, leaning on the door frame. "Depends who's asking."

"I'm Violet. Violet Morgen. I met Ida Fitzgerald on the train. We had a delicious meal together," I said, making friendly conversation. "She works at the Royal Stores. She offered to outfit me in a new—"

"Cripes," the driver said. "I've been behind the wheel since seven thirty this morning, driving over roads not fit for a beast. Hurry up, miss."

I didn't appreciate being rushed. I needed to think about what to say. "I'm sorry to hold you up, Andy and Theresa. I'll try to go faster. Ida, Miss Fitzgerald, told me Theresa Power took in boarders. At least I think she—"

"I'm Theresa Power all right. Not the one taking in boarders." She tutted. "The nerve of Ida. We're already two to a room. Besides, this is Mrs. Doyle's house, not mine. Good night." She stepped back, ready to close the door.

The driver raised his hand against it. "Tell your Mrs. Doyle to come talk to me."

She tapped her foot on the doorstep, hand on hip. "Well, well. While I'm at it would you like cream and sugar with your tea? Besides a pile of other problems, Mrs. Doyle's stricken with rheumatism. She hardly ever leaves her room except on special occasions. The only thing special here is a ruffian's making a racket on my doorstep."

"Tell the woman my shift's over, the wife's waiting, and I won't abandon this young one alone with God knows who prowling the streets. Put her on your daybed. I'm sure you got one if your Mrs. Doyle's weak on her feet."

Theresa spoke over the noise of the foghorn and Pete's howls. "How would *you* feel with a stranger banging on *your* door, waking you from *your* sleep, riling up *your* neighbourhood dogs? I'll be up at six making tea and porridge for the girls. I've got to be at the base by eight thirty. Some of us can't afford taxis these days with the prices you're overcharging, asking thirty cents more per ride during blackout hours. Don't go complaining to me about your troubles. Put her on your own daybed. I'm sure you got one if you're on shifts."

Pete howled. Someone shouted, "Shut up" repeatedly while the taxi driver looked ready to charge past Theresa.

I remembered Ida's advice not to let Theresa scare me. I stepped forward, prepared to brush Andy aside if necessary. "Did you say the base? I also plan to work there. I have excellent forecasting skills, based on my background in science and mathematics, which is at least college level, possibly even—"

"All right. All right." She pointed at the driver. "Mister, you wait outside. You, Violet, stand in the hall. I'll warn you, Mrs. Doyle's fierce as they come." She paused like she was reconsidering her offer. "What are you waiting for?"

I was determined not to spend the night on the street or in the house of a taxi driver. I stepped inside, telling myself I'd manage Mrs. Doyle, no matter how fierce.

While Theresa was in the front room, Andy unloaded my trunk and suitcase, setting them in the hall.

"What are you doing?"

"It's past my wife's bedtime and I won't keep her up, worrying after me."

I reached into my pocket, then handed him one dollar. "What if Mrs. Doyle says no?"

"You're on your own now, miss. Hold onto the dollar for good luck."

17

The fact that the house stood on holy ground must have been its sole redeeming feature. The hall was dimly lit by a bulb without a globe and dangling off a wire from the ceiling. The wallpaper's seam had come loose, exposing layers of paper and glue over lath and plaster. The floral motif on the canvas flooring had been scuffed off. The air hinted at a blend of body odour, fried cod, and a pungent mix of mint, menthol, and turpentine.

Theresa eyed me head to toe when she came back to the hall. "Say the Hail Mary."

Before leaving Crag Point, I'd prepared notes on St. John's, organized into categories—weather, transportation, major roads, etc. Nothing on Hail Marys. "I could possibly say it if I understood the context."

"Context? Ha ha. This is a Catholic area of the city. We're in the shadow of the Roman Catholic Cathedral. Mrs. Doyle runs a Catholic boarding house. How many times did I say Catholic? You're good at math so you should know. Go on in, sit in the chair facing her by the fireplace, do whatever she says, and don't waste your pride arguing."

Barely able to see, I entered the room slowly. The sole source of light was a grate filled with coal embers. I stared, transfixed by the spectrum of orange, red, and yellow, unlike the lavender blue of driftwood bonfires and without the crackle and pop of spruce junks. Compared to the Crag Point cookstove, the fire's heat radiated with more intensity and comfort. In contrast, there was nothing comforting about the nauseating stench of menthol. It blended with the odour of the embers, reminding me of the cigar smoke from the train.

I sat, swallowed in an armchair with broken springs, facing a silver-haired woman in slippers and housecoat. More frail than fierce, with pale, flattened cheeks and sagging jowls, she squinted, head leaning forward to see me better. She picked up an amber glass bottle from her side table, *Wintergreen Leaf Oil* on the label, and rubbed some onto her hands, knuckles swollen, fingers sausage-pudgy.

"What are you up to, banging on strangers' doors, waking the dead, boiling the blood of a half-asleep invalid? I can't make head nor tail of you. It's not Christmas, I know that much. You're not a mummer." The tone of her voice matched Theresa's—unfriendly and accusing.

"Pleased to meet you, Mrs. Doyle. I'm extremely sorry if I woke you. Your lovely home here comes recommended by a woman I met on the train. Ida, that's her name—"

She raised her hand, the edge of a handkerchief in her grip. "I got no strength for listening. Who's your parish priest? When was your last confession? What do you give up at Lent?"

The Reverend had reminded me I wasn't in anyone's parish. As for confession and Lent, what could I say? I turned away from the glow of the embers to face her. "I'm intruding. I apologize. Normally, I wouldn't disturb anyone, but the train arrived late. I'm not used to the city, motor cars, or boarding houses. I planned to go to a house on Goose Hill. I'd assumed I'd be able to get a room, but the driver said they rented by the hour and it wasn't—"

Mrs. Doyle coughed, eyes bulging, mouth wide open. Was she choking? I stood to call Theresa just as she opened the door and rushed in.

"Breathe wide, breathe deep, in slow, out slow," she said, patting Mrs. Doyle's back.

The poor woman had a final cough, then told Theresa to wait outside.

She whispered in my ear, "I need to get my beauty rest. Tell her the truth."

"What's Theresa whispering for?" Mrs. Doyle tutted. "Sit back down out of it. I'm an old woman past my bedtime. I could be dead by the end of your next sentence. Quit flannelling. Where are your parents from? One word or two, that's all you're allowed."

"They came here from Canada."

"That's more than two. What trade was your father in?"

"The lighthouse trade."

"Where?"

"In Notre Dame Bay. I was born there."

She draped her handkerchief over her mouth like she was hiding her surprise. "It's all English Protestants up that way. Go right to the truth or right out of this house."

Ready to raise a white flag, I recalled Rose's advice to act like a city girl. That meant being unafraid to be heard regardless of what I had to say.

IN MEMORIAM

Morgenstern, H. (1883–1941). Born in Berlin, Germany, Heinrich fled the anti-Semitism of his homeland following conscripted service in the Great War. Although an engineer, after immigrating to Canada following the armistice, he worked as a machinist at the Sydney Steel Plant in Nova Scotia. One year later, he moved with his pregnant wife to Newfoundland to serve as a lighthouse keeper, a role and life that suited him well until his premature death.

Willemsen, T. (1899–1922). Born in Rotterdam, Holland, Tineke immigrated to Nova Scotia in 1919 after her parents succumbed to influenza. Following a brief courtship, she married Heinrich and accompanied him to Crag Point. Shortly after the birth of their daughter, she was admitted to the sanitorium for tuberculosis patients where she took her last breaths. Tineke will be remembered for her crown of braids.

Mrs. Doyle's coughing started again, each cough stronger than the last. I stood and patted her back, as Theresa had, nervous I'd do it wrong.

She dabbed her brow with her handkerchief, then ordered me to sit. "I don't care that your father was German. At least he had the mind to flee. Religion is a different kettle of fish. Pope Pius in the picture on the wall, he'd tell you same as me. Stick with your own people. There's plenty of your father's kind. They own half of Water Street. Go bang on their doors." She picked up a set of black beads from her side table.

There was no such thing as my own people. There was this house where one of the boarders worked at the base. I joined my palms in a praying position, my best imitation of an angelic pose. "I'm willing to do everything Catholics do. Besides that, you might be interested to learn that forecasts are my specialty. I can tell you if it's a good day to hang out your washing. I can even predict which wind direction will give you the best draw in your chimney. I—"

"Virgin Mary help me. What's wrong with you, blabbering baloney? Weather? Sure, what do I care? Theresa puts out the washing. The chimney does what I say, same as everybody round here. Be off and let a miserable old woman rest." She turned toward the fire, eyes half-closed.

I could have told her the truth, that, as with Theresa, I found her unfriendly and unkind, her house disappointed me, and I'd already decided I disliked the city. I lowered my head, desperate to close my eyes and feel like my journey was finally over. What did I need to do to convince her to give me a chance? I stared at the bulge in my handbag, shadowed on my lap.

She glared sideways at me as I reached into my pocket for a ten-dollar note, then into my handbag for the small can of fruit. I laid them both on her table, hopeful for a sign of approval.

She picked up the can and read the label, holding it close, almost touching her nose. "Open the door and let some air in. You're after taking every bit, saying so many words. Save them for your prayers. Go to the kitchen, empty the can in a bowl. Bring it here."

"Right away, Mrs. Doyle." I left the room and turned to the end of a short hall. The kitchen light shone so brightly, I had to squint.

Theresa stood at the counter, opener in hand. She opened the can, peeled back the lid, and emptied the contents into a bowl. She ran her finger along the inside, licked it, then dropped the can in the garbage. "Best of luck."

I returned with the bowl in one hand, spoon in the other, terrified I'd do something to upset the old woman. "I prefer to save the cherries till last. I counted four. Consider yourself lucky, I—"

"Shush, girl, and who told you I wanted a spoon?" She brought the bowl to her lips, tilted back her head, and swallowed its contents. She wiped her mouth on the sleeve of her housecoat and handed me the empty bowl. "You can sleep on the kitchen daybed for the night. Tell Theresa to come see me when she's got you settled. I'll let you know after my morning tea if you can stay."

A COCKTAIL LIKE NO OTHER

Looking for a special dessert to serve your guests? Choose Del Monte's new product, fruit cocktail, not to be confused with the fruit salad served in alcohol and popular before America's prohibition. The cocktail includes halved grapes, diced pears, peaches, pineapple, and every gal's favourite, sweet, red cherries. Available in a range of light to heavy sugary syrup, this modern invention will save housewives time while providing nutrition. Serve it alongside Jell-O, tapioca, custard, or butterscotch pudding. Enjoy it, alcohol-free, with friends, old and new.

18

I lay on the kitchen daybed, huddled under a quilt Theresa lent me, my coat folded under my head for a pillow. Since my nightgown would have been too cold, I stayed in my blouse, cardigan, skirt, and new stockings, my legs cuddled tight to my chest, missing the warmth of my trousers. I counted Pete's forlorn howls, their duration, and the intervals of silence in between until a man hollered, "Go to sleep, Pete."

The dog howled again, the man roared, "Shut up, Pete!" and the dog was silent.

I fell asleep eventually, picturing the green beam across the street, counting the foghorn's pattern, imitating Maryanne's optimism, and reminding myself there was no going back.

In the morning, I awoke anxious about meeting the others and terrified of facing the house's owner again.

A woman's voice sang, "I'm dreaming of a white Christmas."

I turned away from the wall, then sat up, a hand over my forehead to block the glare of the ceiling light, so harsh compared to a lantern.

Theresa stood at the stove. She turned to smile at me when I coughed to get her attention. "Morning," she said. "Hope you had a decent night, what there was of it."

I yawned, barely awake. "Did I sleep until December?"

She stirred a pot with one hand, the other resting on her waist, elbow bent. "I'm sick of winter but Mrs. Doyle loves Christmas songs in the morning. It helps her mood. I got in the habit of singing them even if she's not around. I should be singing 'Over the Rainbow.' On stage. Please God, I will someday soon. Judy Garland's my idol."

I moved to a chair at the table. Had she heard from Mrs. Doyle? "Last night, you mentioned the base. You meant Fort Pepperrell, is that right?"

"Yup. On the switchboard all day, all week, all year, saying over and over, 'Number, please. Hold the line, please.' I'll be shouting it from my grave, ruining my singing voice." She placed a pot of tea on the table. "Help yourself. I've had my share. My niece Ellen will be the last one down. Give her five cups and she'll still be like she stayed awake all night."

"She must be young to be your niece."

"If you're offering compliments, I'll take them. Sixteen, same as Princess Lilibet except she figures she's a queen and thirty, my spinster age. Poor girl's working as a maid, for now. My nerves are worn raw worrying about her getting hooked up and you-know-what with a gent in uniform, trading compliments for a cuddle."

Theresa didn't look spinsterish to me. I admired her hair, darker than the orange of witch hazel leaves in fall, brighter than red dulse, the top half straight, the bottom, interlaced curls.

She laid bowls for each of us at the table and spooned porridge into them with a thin glaze of molasses on top.

I gazed through the window at naked trees and the rear of houses with their unpainted clapboard, planks missing in places, yards littered with scraps of metal, wood, and broken bottles. The house, what I'd seen of it so far, seemed as shabby—stains on the tablecloth, makeshift blackout curtains, one longer than the other, and an L-shaped counter littered with dishes, jars, and cans of food.

"It's very quiet." I caught myself before I added "except for Pete's howling," a comment she may have interpreted as a complaint about the neighbourhood.

"Enjoy the calm while it lasts," Theresa said. "When Brigid and Noreen get going, there's no stopping them, fighting for the last word. They got along tickety-boo until Brigid's Danny came on the scene and she started worshipping everything American. Now, she can't wait to move to a big-shot city in the US, lose her Newfoundland accent, and make like she never heard tell of this place. In the other corner is Noreen, waving our flag, no sign of a Union Jack or Stars and Stripes, you can be sure of that. She's got convictions, I'll give her credit there. It's a shame she can't see past them."

Mrs. Doyle's approval was one thing, the boarders' approval another. What if Noreen didn't welcome me, someone aiming to work with the Americans? "Is Brigid working at the base?"

"No. The Caribou Hut, down the hill, by the harbour. Noreen's a factory worker in the west end."

I wrapped my fingers around my cup. Their tea wasn't my usual Ceylon brand and would take getting used to like everything else. "What about Mrs. Doyle?" I dreaded facing her again, dreaded she'd order me back to my people, whoever they were.

"We're both hard on the outside, mushy underneath." Theresa winked. "Go along with what she says and you'll get more of the mush." She blew on her porridge. "Let her know you can offer something besides fruit cocktail."

The porridge was mushy, Mrs. Doyle was mean. I could learn to tolerate the mush, though her meanness unnerved me. "I offered forecasts, but she wasn't interested."

"Forecasts? We'll chat later about what you got to offer. For now, finish breakfast, wash your dishes, and go see her."

At the sink, I turned on the tap and felt the water gush over my fingers. I closed my eyes and tried to imagine a bath so hot that steam clouded the mirror.

"Better hurry up," Theresa said. "Before you can blink, she'll be banging on her coal bucket, hollering at the top of her clogged-up lungs, using up every ounce of patience she never had in the first place."

I headed down the short hall, carrying a cup of hot tea instead of a bowl of canned fruit. I opened the door quietly, then tiptoed into the sombre front room, guided by the embers' orange glow. I was grateful the floor didn't creak, even more grateful to find Mrs. Doyle in her chair, eyes closed, chin to her chest, asleep. I laid the cup on her table carefully, watching her, then went to the window to peep outside.

I saw only fog and drizzle. The horn was silent and the light from the spire extinguished. This was St. John's, a city on guard, a garrison town. Like the Allies, the Nazis recognized the island's strategic importance. Control of the harbour and airports could put an end to the transatlantic transport of essential supplies and personnel, resources vital to winning the war. The island would be a perfect springboard for them to conquer the St. Lawrence, the Great Lakes, and the whole continent. If they couldn't control us, there was always the next best thing—destroy us. Would blackout rules, air-raid sirens, and America's strength be enough to stop them?

The radio played a slow, soft tune that made me want to turn my thoughts away from the war. I pictured dancing in the arms of the pilot and swayed back and forth to the music until a loud, quick clang of metal on metal startled me. I grabbed the curtains, almost pulling them off the rod. I turned around in time to see Mrs. Doyle smack the coal bucket with a hand shovel.

"Who asked you to open the curtains?" She pointed to the chair. "Sit down."

I did as she ordered, not daring to turn away from her or the shovel.

She put it back in the bucket, picked up the teacup, poured some into her saucer, and drank slowly. "Just because I squint doesn't mean I'm blind. No one pulls any wool over my eyes. I see everything goes on in this house and more besides." She turned to face the embers.

I did the same, sneaking glances at her.

While the music played, she hummed along, in between sipping tea from the saucer. "I'd be dead without my Golden Pheasant Tea. Dead without *The Barrelman*, my dessert after supper on VONF." She poured more tea from her cup onto the saucer. "Do you listen to Margot Davies and her *Calling to Newfoundland from Britain*? What's your favourite, 'Dream a Little Dream of Me' or 'The White Cliffs of Dover'?"

The change in her tone encouraged me, but I remained on guard, not wanting to say anything to aggravate her. How would she react if I revealed we had no radio reception at Crag Point and my father seemed to prefer it that way? "I like both."

She hummed along until the song ended, then pointed at the window. "Go over there and let me see the girl begging to board in my full house."

Is that what I was doing, begging? I brushed my hands over my braids and tucked a loose strand behind my ear. I opened the curtain on the window opposite her and was ready to open the other one when she shouted.

"For mercy's sake, don't blind me." She squinted. "What's that nest on your head? You'll have birds confused and you'll draw everyone's eyes away from the altar at Mass. Get Theresa to fix you up."

I interlaced my fingers and squeezed them tightly. "Does that mean I can stay?"

She fidgeted with the string of beads while she talked. "You can sleep on the kitchen daybed with Theresa's company at sunrise, making porridge and boiling water for our tea. Don't be surprised if one of the girls turns on the light at three in the morning because she's thirsty for a cup of tea to calm her nerves."

What if the other boarders didn't appreciate their kitchen doubling as my bedroom? "Could I sleep upstairs?"

She waved a hand like someone swatting a pesky fly. "That you can't. Theresa and Ellen are sardined in the room above me. Noreen and Brigid got single beds over the kitchen. The way they fight, you'd swear they shared a board to sleep on."

I pointed at the ceiling. "What about the third floor? Outside, last night, I noticed two dormer windows up there. How about that?"

"How about what? Don't be asking, 'How about that?' The third floor's not fit. Cold as the grave in winter. Summer, it's practice for hell. A fire trap year-round. If you haven't heard of the blaze that destroyed this city and street when I was around your age, you got catching up to do."

"Thank you, Mrs. Doyle. Could you please tell me the house rules? I want to do my utmost to fit in smoothly in your home and get along with the other girls, Ellen, Nor—"

She waved her handkerchief. "Don't be saying so much. Say, 'What's the rules?' My ears are worn out listening to you. You got my eyes burnt out with the curtains open. What's your name again?"

"Violet."

"I don't know any Violets, and I met plenty of girls and women." She tutted. "Whatever your name, rules are rules. Mass Sunday mornings. No gentlemen callers except Brigid's man, Danny. New ones pass by me. I won't have any hanky-panky going on under my roof." She wagged a finger. "Board's due first of the month. Borrow from the other girls if you're short. And one more thing. Don't be known around town. Be a model of a holy Catholic girl." She coughed persistently like the night before.

I stood, ready to pat her on the back. "Should I call Theresa?"

She held a handkerchief around her mouth, then pointed at the coal bucket.

I scooped up a shovelful and sprinkled it evenly on the embers.

"I nearly forgot," she said, You're no more a Catholic than I'm a Protestant. You can stay till we see if you'll do." She pointed at the door. "Go on. Help poor Theresa with Ellen. Help her in the kitchen too. God help the lot of us."

CITY OF FIRES

May the upcoming golden anniversary of the city's devastating 1892 fire alert us to the dangers faced by citizens of this wooden city, including Mrs. Doyle and her boarders. The plague of infernos in 1816, 1817, and 1819 makes evident the conflagration was not the first. Yet again, in 1846, dry conditions and high winds fed flames leaving thousands homeless and destroying or damaging some of the city's finest buildings. Are we due for another inferno in 1942? Watch for flames and flankers, arsonists, and saboteurs.

19

Afraid a draft might catch it, making a noisy bang, I closed Mrs. Doyle's door cautiously. I stood in the hall and looked up at the underside of the third-floor stairs. Not wanting to surprise anyone on their way down, I headed up there hesitantly, then stopped and turned around when I overheard voices from the kitchen. I stepped closer to the door and might have gone in there except I heard my name.

"Violet's not Catholic," Theresa said.

"I work with a Protestant girl at the Hut. We get along well."

"Who mentioned Protestant?" Theresa said.

"Catholic or Protestant, what's she doing gallivanting around in silk stockings when half the women at the factory can't afford a meal of fish and spuds?"

"I regret mentioning the stockings. Be nice to her. She's a sweet girl. Strange-looking, handsome too. Big black braids."

"More stupid than sweet if she wants to live here. Any night now, the Nazis will bomb the harbour, us with it. Mrs. Barrow's house won't be touched. I hate working for her."

"Don't be using that word, Ellen," Theresa said.

"Last week, she called me a fool, said she wouldn't give me a reference."

"Danny would never allow anyone to disrespect me like that."

"Oh, to catch a bucko in an American uniform, have him bowing at your feet. I wonder what you're giving him in exchange."

"I'm telling him you said that."

"Go ahead. Yankee Danny will say, 'Oh, Bridgy girly, gimme more.'"

"You're disgusting, Noreen."

"What's disgusting is you drooling over the Yanks."

"You're jealous because they don't approve of your kind."

"Translation?"

"Commie, lezzie, God save the King."

"Nationalist and socialist, not communist. Nothing wrong with liking girls, and who said anything about the King? In fact—"

"Noreen, make yourself useful," Theresa said. "Help me move her trunk into the pantry. Shove it next to the sack of potatoes."

"Bet you want to rummage through it."

"I tried to move it by myself last night. I thought she stuffed a body in there. I had a peep inside. A barometer, binoculars, and handwritten books full of talk of wind, fog, and ice. Let's move the trunk now, Nor—" Theresa gasped, hand on her heart like someone pledging a promise. "Jeepers." She'd rounded the corner and almost run into me. "I took you for a drunkard wandered in off the street. I warned Mrs. Doyle—we need a lock on the front door. What did she say? Can you stay?"

I wanted to explain the stockings, braids, and barometer, but that would mean admitting I'd eavesdropped and knew she'd opened my trunk. Was that usual behaviour in boarding houses? "Can I stay? More or less." I didn't add that I was there on a trial basis. What had the woman meant by "We'll see if you'll do?"

Theresa grabbed me by the arm and led me into the kitchen. "Come meet the other beauties."

I stood next to Theresa, looking at her to avoid having to face the others, knowing they didn't approve of me.

"That's Ellen there in the corner, elbows on the table, leaning on her hand. Her head would fall off if she wasn't holding it up. Her long red hair's gorgeous except when it's clogging up the bathroom sink or teasing the broom."

Ellen gazed at the small crop of leg visible above my ankles where one stocking had fallen. "Love your stockings. Not sure about your hair."

I was tired of hearing remarks about my braids and couldn't wait to chop them off.

Theresa tutted. "She wasn't raised to be saucy."

"Don't need anyone to raise me," Ellen said. "Can I see your barometer? Theresa told us you—"

"Don't mind her," Theresa said. "She makes up stories."

"No, I don't. It's true. You—"

"That's Noreen, by Ellen. The way she's hunched over her bowl, you'd swear she was reading the porridge instead of eating it. She's a smart one. Dead serious about everything."

"Including breakfast," Noreen said. "Work hard, eat hard. Lovely hair, Violet. Practical and elegant."

I smoothed my hand over my braids and smiled. They could be beautiful for all I cared. I'd get rid of them at the first opportunity.

"Brigid's the one with the fresh curls, dolled up, belle of the ball for her pal, Danny. Isn't she gorgeous with that pale blue ribbon in a bow, matching her eyes?"

I nodded, thinking maybe Theresa had been right to say I was strange-looking.

"Boyfriend, not pal," Brigid said. "Danny's a draftsman in the US Army, just won a promotion to a class-five technician for helping build the base barracks."

Noreen stood, dishes in hand. She was even taller than my five-foot-seven and wore what I assumed were factory coveralls. Her chestnut brown hair was cut short over her ears and with a bang. Somewhere in between her practical style and Brigid's glamour, was there a look that would suit me?

"Base?" Noreen said. "More like little America. We're under siege in case you weren't aware, Violet."

"Don't mind Noreen," Brigid said. "She's got nothing good to say about the Americans. I'm next for the bathroom. See you tonight, Violet."

Noreen rinsed her dishes, then left them on the counter to dry. "Nothing any good to be said about the Yanks. Right, Violet?"

I pretended to laugh, not daring to admit I thought the exact opposite. The Americans were our defenders, powerful ones at that. Without them we were doomed.

"I'm sure you agree," Noreen said. "Anyway, nice to see an original hairdo for a change. I'm sick of the assembly-line, make-'em-all-the-same style. Catch you later. You can show me your binoc—"

"Pick up a half dozen India Pale Ale on your way home, Noreen," Theresa said. "We'll have a peaceful supper together, give Violet a chance to see how well we get along."

Noreen saluted. "Yes, Sergeant. If you say so, Sergeant. I'll slide your trunk into the little room here next to the kitchen, Violet. See ya."

She was gone before I could thank her.

Arms limp by her sides, Ellen stood up. "Ugh. I got to go to Mrs. Barrow's house, change into that awful uniform, and listen to her sermon. 'I want everything spicky-spanny for my pawtee this Sawturday.' Nice to meet you, Viola, oops, Violet."

"Come straight home from work," Theresa said.

Ellen's groan echoed down the hall.

Theresa pushed hard on the broom as if she was scrubbing the floor instead of sweeping it. "Take your turn in the bathroom after Ellen."

I sat in Brigid's empty chair. "I didn't notice a bathtub last night. It was very dark so I might have missed it."

"You needn't worry about your eyesight. The closest we got to a bath is Ellen raving about the giant porcelain tub at Mrs. Barrow's mansion. Toilet and sink—that's our whole kit and caboodle. Be thankful we're not on the honey bucket like in certain parts of the city. Nothing worse than lugging a pail of private waste out of your house into the street, dumping it into a filthy truck in the dark because it's too shameful for light of day."

As someone who took charge of an outhouse, spreading lime, cleaning, and stocking it with strips of newspaper, I saw nothing shameful about a honey bucket, not with such a sweet name. The lack of a bath disappointed me, mainly because I'd come to think of soaking in a tub with indoor plumbing and hot water as a hallmark of modern city life. "A sink will do," I said. "Something to freshen up for my visit to the base. Could I go with you this morning?"

Theresa bent down to sweep up the dust. "Tomorrow's better. Today, pay a visit to the Royal Stores, take up Ida's offer to outfit you. Warn her—send me any more boarders, I'll deliver them directly to her home, supposing I have to pay for the taxi myself." She glanced at my hair. "Beauty parlour's around the corner on Gower Street. There's entertainment at the Caribou Hut, Saturday night. I'm meeting friends there. Tag along if you want."

I had difficulty reconciling the helpful Theresa with the hostile woman guarding the entrance to 12 Chapel Street. Could I expect a similar transformation of Mrs. Doyle's attitude? "The Caribou Hut would be wonderful. Thank you for that, for everything. I'd like to contribute something to tonight's meal—something Mrs. Doyle might appreciate."

On her toes to reach the top shelf, she stored dishes in the cupboard. "Bread. The fancy, sliced, factory kind. Mrs. Doyle adores it smothered in marmalade. Ellen too. Grab a loaf at Clarke's store, bottom of the street. Can't miss it. Introduce yourself to Mrs. Clarke. She'll be asking about your story. Better have one ready."

HAIRSTYLES FOR VICTORY

Wartime calls for women to step into action with hairstyles suited to the circumstances and occupation. Those serving in the armed forces should maintain hair above the collar. Long locks are considered impractical and are discouraged due to hazards posed when operating machinery. Use of a crochet snood or hairnet can secure hair in place while women perform important duties. The preferred style is the victory roll symbolizing the celebratory corkscrew, aerobatic manoeuvres of pilots following a victory. Let us not forget our loved ones on battlefields in the sky, on land, or at sea.

20

St. John's was a city of hills and valleys with a safe and secluded harbour for a heart. I caught a glimpse of that harbour once I rounded the corner onto Prescott Street. I stared, amazed vehicles could drive up the steep hill, even more amazed picturing them coming down the icy slope in winter. With a row of attached wooden houses on either side, I might as well have been walking through a tunnel, competing for space with everything from horse-drawn carriages to US Army trucks. Some were loaded with supplies, others with throngs of soldiers who waved and whistled at the new girl in the city.

"What's wrong, lady?" A tiny girl tugged on my coat. Her head was covered in a matted mess, her eyelids red with sties.

"Nothing. Do you know where the beauty parlour—"

"Thataway, lady. After the butcher's. Gimme a copper and I'll take you there meself."

The smallest coin I had was a dime. I held it out on my palm. She snatched it in an instant, then ran off.

I put my hands back in my pocket, raised my head, and walked as if I knew exactly where I was headed. Trucks backfiring, horns blaring, dogs barking, voices shouting—these were sounds city people lived with daily. I wouldn't be startled by them. The distinct briny smell of a harbour, the whiff of chimney smoke mixed with burning fuel from vehicles, dust everywhere—I'd get used to it all or walk the streets with a handkerchief over my nose.

The parlour was easy to find with *House of Beauty* written in lipstick on the front window. The sign said *Open*. Was that a command or a condition? I took a chance on both and stepped into a warm, humid room, its walls plastered with magazine clippings of women's impeccable hairdos and with barely space for me and the two other customers.

With her crimson red lips and what must have been victory rolls, the hairdresser said she'd try to fit me in, but she was short on help. "The girls got better to do besides working in a beauty parlour. They're at the base, the factory, or run off with the Yanks."

The lady under the drying hood called out, "Speak up. I can't hear a word."

I sat on a chair, my coat resting on my lap, glove to my nose, holding back a typhoon of sneezing while the hairdresser applied hairspray to a woman's hairdo.

After a short wait, she invited me to take a seat in front of the mirror on a chair that swivelled when she turned it.

The hairdresser listed her promotions while she undid my crown of braids. "Keep-Your-Beauty-on-Duty will get you a cut and style plus Parisian red nail polish, Victory Red lipstick, and Maybelline eyeshadow. The We're-Worth-Fighting-For promotion includes a perm, but I'd say you'd be wasting your money. Your hair's already got tons of wave."

"How about victory rolls?"

"That's the Wash-Cut-n'-Roll, comes with a free bottle of Coca-Cola—normal price, five cents and guaranteed to deliver five dollars' worth of energy."

"I'll take it, thank you."

"Ready to say goodbye to those pigtails?"

I was glad she hadn't asked, "Why the braids?" or "Why wear them in a crown around your head?" That was a long story to do with Maryanne encouraging me to imitate my mother's hairstyle as a tribute to her memory. In his last days, with his mind playing tricks on him, Vati sometimes mistook me for her. "Tineke," he'd say, "are you feeling better? Home for good, finally?" At least he died believing she'd come back from the sanitorium, cured.

I looked down at my braids, reaching to my waist. "City girls don't wear their hair this way, do they?"

"Not unless they're Little Bo-Peep."

"Chop them off, please."

She swivelled my chair around, shiny, sharp scissors in hand. Two chops and they were gone. It felt like I'd lifted off a helmet. They lay on the floor, wool ties on one end, frayed on the other. Maryanne would have gasped, then congratulated me. I deserved congratulations. I'd not only transformed my looks, I'd outsmarted Teo and Fred, survived the servicemen and interrogation on the train, and persuaded Mrs. Doyle to let me stay in her Catholic boarding house. The base would be a minor challenge in comparison.

The hairdresser combed what remained of my hair and began trimming. Next, she washed it at a sink. I revelled in the feel of warm water flowing over my head and her strong hands massaging my scalp. Once she'd finished, she had me switch places with the woman under the drying hood. I'd seen hoods pictured in advertising but hadn't realized how intense the heat might be. My scalp felt like it was burning. Surely it wasn't supposed to be so hot. I was grateful when she finally turned it off and I moved back to the swivel chair.

She lit a cigarette, took one long draw, then rested it in an ashtray, the odour of burning tobacco on top of the perfume of beauty products.

"I can't believe you kept this beautiful mane hidden in those braids. Ever had a man who loves to run his hands through your hair, bury his face in it?"

"I've never had a man." Thomas didn't count. As for the pilot, after the incident on the train, if he saw me again, he'd probably pretend not to know me.

"Well now. You won't be saying that for long. Welcome to St. John's, young lady. Take your pick of men."

"Really? Any man at all? Do you have any advice?"

"What hairdresser doesn't? For Fridays and Saturdays, get yourself a good dancer, someone who holds you in his arms like you're precious. For Sundays, pick a gent who doesn't mind hiring a taxi to take you on a Bowring Park picnic. For the rest of the week, you'll want a couple of nights out in a fancy restaurant on his tab. That'll keep you entertained."

"Does it matter where they're from?"

"Anywhere but here. Don't blame women for dreaming of better than what their mothers had."

"How about men from Ireland?"

"They're too much like our fellahs."

"And the Americans?" I said, thinking of Noreen and Brigid arguing.

"Now you're talking." She took another draw on her cigarette, laid it back in the ashtray, and picked up bobby pins to hold my victory rolls in place. "They're in a class of their own. No baggy pants like the Canadians. Nicer teeth too. I'm already taken, but I'd marry one if I had a second chance." She crushed her cigarette in the ashtray overflowing with butts and wads of pink gum. "I present to you Claudette Colbert playing Cleopatra without bangs. Claudette had men chasing after her. Cleopatra had men too. She ruled over them."

In the mirror was a woman with victory rolls resting on her head like a second set of ears. The style didn't appeal to me, but if it helped me get hired at the base, it would be worth it, even if Noreen accused me of pandering to American tastes.

A TALE OF TWO SISTERS

Marilyn fell head over heels for a Yank, packed up, and moved to Florida. She visits the beauty parlour twice a week, perfume-fresh round the clock, leaving a ruby kiss print on her handsome hubby's cheek each morning. He comes home early from the office, waltzes her around, her curls bouncing up and down in time to "Tuxedo Junction." The Chevy's parked out front, swimming pool's out back. Life's so grand, no need to stop and smell the roses.

Marilyn's twin hitched up with Donnie from down the gut. Scrub board's worn the skin off her fingers. Their shack's near the landwash, salt spray blocking the view, wind messing with her hair inside or out. A couple of spuds and a slice of turnip at every meal, except in the hungry month of March when it's leftover peels, a couple of fish heads on the side. Three kids in four years, another bun in the oven, her back killing her, lying down or standing up. Life's so rough and tough, roses smell like dandelions.

My next stop should have been the harbour to view the destroyers, corvettes, merchant ships, and whatever other vessels were anchored there. However, it was jammed with throngs of sailors and longshoremen, two of whom pleaded for a date with the woman who resembled Claudette Colbert. Judging by the flapping flags, the wind speed was no less than forty miles per hour, and I had no hat, long underwear, or trousers.

I turned onto Water Street, its cobblestones crowded with streetcars, sidewalks crammed with service personnel in uniform, showing rank and country. I'd arrived at the core of Maryanne's fantasies about St. John's. Water Street—where the city's magic happened, where the sun glistened off the Yankee smiles, where ladies bought their party dresses and Sunday bonnets, where Violets, new to the city, marvelled at the buildings like they were the world's eighth wonder.

The Royal Stores' name was blazoned above windows displaying colourful dresses for the upcoming summer season. I'd seen the store's advertising in the newspaper with its slogan, "The House for Value." I opened the front door slowly, unsure if I should knock. Inside was a mesmerizing collection of goods displayed on floor-to-ceiling shelves and in glass cases under counters.

A saleswoman asked whether I'd come for their day-long special on Houbigant, La Rose France perfume.

"I'm here to see Ida Fitzgerald. Ida offered to outfit me in a new wardrobe. Do you know her?"

The woman nodded.

"I'm Violet. What's your name and can I shop here without buying the perfume?"

I didn't catch her name because she said it too quickly. She told me to wait while she went to find Ida.

When Ida saw me, she held out her arms. "Welcome to St. John's and the Royal Stores, Violet. Theresa called from the base, said you were dropping by." She stared at my hair. "Did the Water Street gusts blow off your crown of braids?"

I smiled to be polite. I'd hoped my new hairstyle would get rid of that kind of attention.

"Nothing lost there unless you're dying to look like every other girl new to the city. That's not what you want, is it?"

"I'm afraid I don't exactly know what I want—something suitable for the base, for Sunday Mass, and for the Caribou Hut. Have you heard of it?"

Ida laughed but not in a way that disarmed me. "Been there a dozen times. Follow me, Violet."

She led me to a change room where she gave me clothes to try and advice on which items suited me, advice I trusted if it would help me look like her.

"We've got rubber girdles with breathing holes, new in stock, received the last shipment a week ago. That's it now until the war's over. They're so desperate for rubber, they're coming after our girdles. What next?"

"I've seen them advertised but never worn one. They wouldn't have been very comfortable standing for hours in the tower or climbing its steps."

She crossed her arms. "You're not at Lighthouse Point anymore. Throw away your long johns along with those sandwiches."

Was she hinting at her help on the train? "Crag Point."

"Picture the Hut, packed with servicemen, barely a wrinkle in their uniforms, a button missing, or a speck on polished shoes. You're dancing in that pilot's arms. He rests his big strong hands on your waist and squeezes a roll. No girl would want that."

I remembered dancing on the steamer with a man who tried to squeeze more than rolls, then later, the pilot holding me against him when the train swayed. "I'm not sure I have any of those rolls, and I doubt if I'll ever see the pilot again."

"Be prepared for anything and everything these days."

I didn't care that Theresa had insisted I ask for a discount. I paid full price for all items, including the too-tight, top-of-the-line girdle. Ida had proven her value as a friend, and I wouldn't haggle with friends.

She offered to deliver my purchases to Chapel Street, minus the new dress, blouse, and sweater I was wearing. "Visit the tailor on Duckworth Street. He'll chop decades off your coat in minutes."

I had a final glance in the mirror at the new city girl, in stockings, a red dress with white polka dots, and shoes with two-inch heels. "Do I seem more like I'm from here?"

"'Here' means nothing anymore. We're fighting a war. The lot of us together—Yanks, Canucks, Brits, Newfoundlanders."

Vati would have said wartime was the best, not the worst time to move to the city. As the taxi driver had pointed out, nobody knows anyone. "I'm a stranger like everyone else. That should make it easier to blend in."

"Why bother?" Ida said. "The world doesn't need more of the same. Be yourself, original, the one-and-only Violet."

LADIES' FASHION

Modern 1942 fashion reflects the changing role of women, their contribution to the war effort, and their growing confidence in the world. Shoulder pads stuffed with sheep's wool add a touch of sophistication characteristic of contemporary fashion. Minor frills including ribbons like those worn by the lovely Brigid may be added to convey hope and happiness. Shorter lengths reflect wartime exigencies that frequently require women to spring into action. Skirts and dresses may be tailored to highlight the woman's figure but must reflect modesty.

21

April 16, 1942

Dear Maryanne,

*Let the bells ring out. I made it! Goose Hill was full. I'm on Chapel St.—
one of many north-south veins between east-west arteries like Queen's Rd.
and Water St. Outside, from the top of the street, facing the harbour, I see the
Southside Hills with patches of fir and spruce, land being cleared for construction by the Royal Canadian Navy, a reminder we are a nation at war.
Cabot Tower on Signal Hill overlooking the Narrows is a munchkin compared to Crag Point's giant tower. Across the street is a church with a green
leading light outfitted with a metal cap to prevent it from being spotted by
German bombers. Blackout rules mean it's usually only shining while a
ship's entering the harbour. Lucky for me that I saw it the first night I arrived.*

*The boarding house belongs to the irascible Mrs. Doyle, a woman I can
barely believe is two years younger than you. She's in poor health and lives
mostly in the ground-floor front room with a single bed pushed up against
the wall and three armchairs circling a coal-burning fireplace. She glares at
it, eyes unblinking, rosary beads in one hand, handkerchief in the other. On
her side table is a photograph of her son, Timmy, about whom I know zilch.
I have a peculiar feeling she's only allowed me to stay because one of the
boarders, Theresa, convinced her to. I'm hoping Mrs. D. will soften toward
me, as has Theresa, unfriendly at first, very hospitable now. Helpful too. She
works at the base and offered to take me there tomorrow.*

*T. manages the house for Mrs. D. and manages her niece Ellen, too.
("Don't talk to the soldiers or sailors.") Poor Ellen, nails chewed to the quick,
asks when the war's going to end (as if anyone knows). She should be in*

school rather than a chambermaid in a wealthy widow's home. She shares T.'s colouring (reddish hair, pale skin). The resemblance stops there. T. has the physique of a child, Ellen, that of a mature woman. Her voice is also mature and shockingly bold. T.'s voice is very deep, the opposite of what you'd expect given her size. She was the house's first boarder, arrived from Bell Island more than a decade ago when Mrs. D. began accepting boarders after her husband absconded and left her penniless.

Brigid (21) serves in the canteen at a hostel for servicemen. She's determined to rise in her personal and social life, starting with her boyfriend, Yankee Danny, as Noreen calls him. Noreen (24 or 25) has been managing the women workers at the clothing factory since the war started and is aiming for forelady. Her father's a foreman at the pulp and paper mill in Corner Brook and is active in the Nfld Federation of Labour. You claim the Americans are the big bosses and can do as they please. Noreen would likely say, "Not if we don't let them." Also, she believes women in service should have a labour union. Good idea?

A welcoming supper tonight (how kind) almost ended in a brawl. Noreen and Fred must be reading the same letters to the editor or else writing them. "Americans think they're Nfld's owners. They're our tenants," Noreen said. She didn't stop there. Nor did Danny and Brigid. Both sides shouted over each other, Ellen shrieked with laughter, while Mrs. D. said she didn't understand the fuss and couldn't we simply get along?

T. saved the evening with "Tickle Cove Pond," a touching tune about the near loss of a mare while hauling wood on thin April ice. She sang the low notes as well as the high and carried the melody like she had a full orchestra behind her. Brigid and Danny waltzed. Mrs. D. and Ellen held hands. Noreen and I rocked side to side together. Ellen demanded an encore and T. sang it again. I pretended to be cheerful. In fact, the tune made me feel terribly homesick. That's normal, I assume. A good night's sleep will improve my spirits.

Tomorrow, I'm heading to the United States of America in Nfld, my 1941 weather journal in hand, you on one side, saying, "Let nothing or no one stop you!" Vati on the other, saying, "Teach them a thing or three," Noreen behind my back saying, "You're a fool wanting to work for the Yanks." T. said Fort Pepperrell's hiring Nflders by the thousands. She says office-girl duties involve mostly filing papers, answering the telephone, and making tea.

I have a new office-girl look. Brigid said I should have saved my chopped-off braids as a souvenir. Noreen shook her head and tutted at first, then said I was beautiful with or without them. T. said I should have demanded a partial refund from the parlour because my victory rolls didn't last an hour, blown to smithereens by the wind. Mrs. D. claimed the hairdresser should have trimmed the two black moustaches over my eyes. I'm not ready to part with my bushy eyebrows unless they grow long enough to be braided. I'm getting used to having hair that falls just below my shoulders, not to my waist, and framing my cheeks instead of in a crown on my head.

I'll wear my new yellow dress under my mother's coat with its hem shortened to a 1942 length. What do you think of lipstick? It's supposedly good for morale, though I doubt Noreen would agree. She says the Beauty-is-Duty slogan suggests men serve their country while being served by women. The Führer forbids German women from wearing makeup. For now, I'll play it safe by imitating the majority and trust that Noreen won't judge me too severely.

Here's hoping the neighbourhood dog (Pete) will show mercy and not howl through the night. If I thought a bribe would work, I'd buy him a steak. One for Pete's owners too if they'd allow him to sleep indoors.

Yours till Niagara falls,

Violet

PS: Expect a commonplace book entry with each letter.

CITY OF DISTRICTS

Let Violet Morgen be your guide on a tour of a city some claim is North America's oldest. At the harbour's west end is the industrial district with the railway station, dockyard, factories, foundries, and more. The commercial district is centred on Water Street with its grand department stores, their warehouses, and finger piers. The civic centre features the courthouse, museum, library, and Memorial University College. The ecclesiastical district boasts cathedrals, churches, schools, and convents. In the residential area directly north of the grounds of Government House are the stately manors of the merchant class, while many of the row houses running north of the harbour are occupied by the working classes such as Mrs. Doyle's boarders.

22

Mrs. Doyle gave me an enthusiastic send-off on Friday morning as I headed to the base, office-girl position in my sights. She also gave me a warning. Working for the Americans was fine as long as I didn't change my ways and complain like Brigid that she had it no better on Chapel Street than at the Belvedere Orphanage where she grew up.

"Do what Theresa tells you," Mrs. Doyle said. "If it wasn't for her, you'd be banging on the door of a boarding house in the city's slums, praying they don't rent by the hour."

LITTLE AMERICA

The command centre for US military operations in Newfoundland and Greenland, Fort Pepperrell is surrounded by cliffs that shield against enemy attack and is strategically situated near a Canadian-run naval base in a sheltered harbour and an air base in Torbay. When construction is complete, it will host a hospital, recreational buildings, fire station, theatre, bakery, chapel, mess hall, warehouses, training quarters, offices, and more. Fort Pepperrell's layout of roads symbolically forms a cowboy hat. Remember to drive on the right. Listen to the latest American hits from the base's radio station, Voice of the United States (VOUS).

"This is officially American territory for ninety-nine years," Theresa said. She pointed to labourers clearing land and constructing buildings. "They're part of the gang said, 'Shag my job at the paper mill, or my job at the mine, or my fishin' boat, I'm headin' to the gold rush in St. John's.' At least I can work here until the war ends, longer I hope. What happens to them once construction's finished? They'll spend the winter on the bottle and the dole. God help the lot of them." She made the sign of the cross, then pointed. "Over there. Tell whoever's on the desk you're friends with Theresa on the switchboard."

I found the building easily, followed the signs to the personnel office, and knocked gently.

A voice called out, "It's open," in a tone that suggested I should have known that like any sensible city person. A young, pretty woman sat at a desk piled high with papers and folders. She balanced a telephone handset between ear and shoulder. The hairdresser would have been impressed with her victory rolls. Ida might have asked where she bought her bright red dress with puffed sleeves.

She laid the handset in its cradle using two fingers as if it was a soiled object. "Those calls drive me bananas. The Americans want to know more about people applying to work at its bases than I know about my own relatives. What's the point of a teacher's reference for a youngster they taught a century ago? Be with you in a second. Have a peep at the posters on the walls while I write down what the lady told me on the telephone."

The posters were all variations on one theme. A drowning soldier reaching up out of the water and pointing: *Someone talked.* Another featured a woman's face with the words *Wanted! For murder. Her careless talk cost lives. Remember—the enemy is listening.*

"The Nazis are everywhere," she said. "They come ashore at night in their dinghies for a meal or a good time with the girls. Anything's better than being stuck in a sub. Don't be fooled if a Kraut pretends he's Spanish or French. They're quick at making excuses for their strange accents, saying—"

The telephone rang.

"Darn. Noisy ringer, couldn't wait till I finished. Looking for work?"

I nodded.

She handed me a sheet of paper pinched between two fingers. "Doesn't matter what job you're after at the base, make sure you got everything on this list." She picked up the handset. "Civilian personnel office. Hello."

The paper listed the documents required to receive clearance to work as a civilian at the base.

Birth certificate.

Names and addresses of previous employers.
List of schools attended and diplomas earned.
Three character and two work references.
Name checked against a civilian unsuitability list.

I closed the door gently, then stood in the narrow hallway. In the office across the hall, a woman sat at a typewriter, steel types striking paper, a ring at the end of each line, the zip of the carriage return, and silence while her fingers paused on the keys. I walked slowly to the corridor's end, stepped outside into a recessed porch, and sat on the steps. In my mind, I shouted at Maryanne, one minute asking why she'd claimed everything would be easy, the next, pleading with her to help get me back to Crag Point where I'd do my best to ignore Teo's and Fred's I-told-you-so's.

I fixed my gaze straight ahead at the long, narrow Quidi Vidi Lake that bordered the base and flowed into the gut and from there to the North Atlantic where the winds ran wild, driving the waves, their fetch unobstructed. If I'd had an opportunity, I would have told the Americans that my knowledge of local weather was as good or better than any of their men's and that winds were my specialty. "Ask me anything," I'd say, "even the names of the gods of winds, Greek or Roman. Let me tell you facts about the local winds you won't find in any book. Want to know about the December wind, near the solstice, and how it affects storm surges? Allow me to explain how sound travels in wind, like when someone's calling your name."

"Violet? Is that you?"

On the train, I'd only seen him up close. Standing there on the sidewalk, the pilot seemed taller, slimmer too in his greyish-blue RAF uniform with its belted jacket. I stood up off the steps. "Of course. I didn't get a chance to thank you for your help on the train, Captain Campbell."

He removed his cap. "Philip, please. Thank your friend Ida."

"Both of you."

"My sincere compliments. I barely recognized you. I was walking past, couldn't help noticing a pretty face, then said to myself, 'I know her from somewhere.'" He stepped closer. "You were gazing at the sky. Anything wrong?"

What would he say if I told him the truth? That I had straw for brains, no idea how the world worked, and didn't belong anywhere? That the only thing made any sense to me was the weather? "I'm observing the clouds. They're moving west to east." I pointed to the sky. "The wind's blowing in the opposite direction, as you can see from the flapping flag here in front of the building. Expect heavy rain and northeasterly gusts this afternoon."

He gazed at the sky, then put his cap back on. "Aye. It's chilly, I admit. I've seen plenty worse weather in this place—awful for flying."

"Particularly so today."

"I'll take your word for it since you seem quite confident. April showers and all that."

In St. John's, May's rather than April's showers brought June flowers, but I wouldn't correct him. "My barometer showed an extreme change in pressure this morning."

"A girl with a barometer—there's a first. Does owning one improve the weather?"

Why had he asked such a silly question? Or did it seem silly because I was in a critical mood, angry at the world, at myself? "Not unless it's a magical barometer."

He laughed. "I've got an hour before my meeting. The officers' mess is around the corner. I'd be honoured if you'd join me for tea. Something to bring a smile to your face?"

"Thank you, yes," I said, but couldn't force a smile.

As we walked to the mess hall, he asked what I was doing at the base, then talked about the incident on the train, something I preferred to forget. I half listened, relieved not to have to tell him about myself, distracted, thinking about references, employers, diplomas, and unsuitability lists. We were in a war—a war I could help win in my small way. But how, if no one would give me a chance to show what I was capable of?

"The chap kept me there for an hour in that tiny space filled with cigar smoke, firing off questions about seaplanes, takeoffs and landings, float planes versus flying boats. He wouldn't believe I'd met Glenn Miller. Do you like Miller?"

Statesman? Actor? "Of course," I said.

"Who doesn't? Wish I could listen to him when flying. It's terribly noisy up there, lonely too. But back to the train, how did you get mixed up in that sandwich incident?"

"Helping a friend." What was one more lie?

"Generous of you. Can I call on you if I need a favour?" He laughed and playfully nudged his shoulder against mine.

I would have gladly held his hand, let him hold me in his arms, or even let him bury his face in my hair.

At the mess hall, he chose a table for two, then went to the counter to order rather than wait for us to be served. I laid my coat on the back of my chair and sat on my weather journal. I considered making an excuse to leave rather than fumble through a conversation in which I said the wrong thing. I couldn't hide the fact that I felt awkwardly self-conscious, exposed, as if everyone could tell I was cluelessly new to the city.

The hairdresser had sold me Victory Red lipstick. "Courage, confidence, and optimism, in one tube," she'd said when she showed me how to apply it. I reached into my handbag, pulled out the tube, and applied it to my lips.

Philip returned with a metal teapot and two large porcelain cups and laid them on the table. "Here I am again, apologizing for laughing." He held one hand on the side of my head, then wiped the edge of my lips with his handkerchief. "Hardly anything amuses me these days. Flying's serious business, deadly serious these days. You've brightened my week enormously. There. I've fixed where it was smeared."

I should have been mortified at my clumsiness and crimson with embarrassment. Instead, I thought about his fingers on my face. Did it feel the same for him as for me?

"You said you were looking for office-girl work. What will that girl, new to the city, do for fun on her days off?"

Visit the library, walk up Signal Hill for a panoramic view, get to know the city, re-establish bearings, and regain my balance—I had nothing but days off. "I'm going to the Caribou Hut tomorrow."

"Reading my mind, were you? The Hut's wonderful on a Saturday night. Entertainment helps me forget flying in wartime skies. Do you enjoy dancing?"

I recalled dancing with Cuff on the steamer. "You mean a square dance?"

He laughed in a pitch higher than his usual voice. "You're delightful. You know what they say," he paused, "entertainment is good for morale. Would you dance with me there? The orchestra plays Miller hits."

What did Miller hits sound like?

"I'm sorry," he said. "I may be jumping the gun. An attractive girl like you must have a full dance card. You're probably already going there with someone."

"Only my new friend Theresa. She's meeting her other pals there. I'm just tagging along."

"Wonderful! What do you say, young lady? Is it a date?"

"Aye, aye, Captain."

When the hour was up, Philip headed to his meeting, I back to Chapel Street. The waters of Quidi Vidi Lake were a glossy black under a brooding sky. The wind had veered to the northeast and the water's ripples had switched direction. No eagles, gulls, osprey, or crows were in sight. The air smelled of thawing moist earth and bog, the decay of fallen leaves, of plants and insects. A raindrop hit my cheek, another my head. Although the drops fell steadily, I didn't bother to shelter my weather journal. The rain could reduce it to papier mâché for all I cared. Vati had left me a small sum and I'd earned a profit on the sale of the sandwiches. That would have to do me until I devised a better plan. In the meantime, I had a busy city to discover and a date to daydream about.

23

My first Saturday night in the city, first date, first visit to the Caribou Hut—enough firsts to distract me from the previous day's disappointment, mud from the American base fresh on my shoes. Theresa led the way through narrow streets and alleyways, under a moonless sky with blackout rules in full effect—streetlights off, shields on headlights, red tail lights painted white, speed limits of fifteen miles per hour, poles and fire alarm boxes with a white stripe, and houses with improvised coverings to shutter windows.

"Keep an eye on the ground for dirty French safes. You don't want to turn up at the Hut with one stuck to your heel."

An air-raid warden sauntered past and nodded. "Evening, ladies. Mind your step and your backs."

I was tempted to stop him, to ask if what Theresa said was true or exaggerated.

"The Yanks and Canucks are driving round in trucks made for the wrong side of the road," Theresa said. "They can't tell left from right. At least here in the side streets, we won't need to watch for drunks behind the wheel. With beer so cheap on the base, it's a wonder the Yanks aren't drinking in their sleep. Taxi drivers are just as bad. Bad like Mister King of the Castle pounding on our door, ordering Mrs. Doyle to come talk to him. Be thankful she let you stay after the racket he made."

"Luckily, I had a can of fruit cocktail." I couldn't imagine what might have happened without it, grateful too for the driver's help and free fare.

"What's that got to do with the price of tea in Ceylon? You said, 'I'm good at mathematics.' I told myself, she's exactly what I need to get Ellen out of service and into school. I explained everything to Mrs. Doyle. She said she'd allow you to board in her house if I promised you'd do it."

"Do what?"

"Get Ellen through grade 10 math."

A HUT AWAY FROM HOME

Opened in December 1940, in a former hostel for fishermen, the Caribou Hut on Water Street offers more than accommodations for airmen and servicemen on furlough or sailors on shore. Where else can one find a building with a canteen, cinema, bowling alley, rooms for hobbies, reading, and writing, and an indoor swimming pool? Entertainment options include singsongs, movies, and games nights to help curb the hooliganism, fighting, and drinking in the streets of Newfyjohn (naval slang). Visit the Hut on a Saturday night for a dance with a live orchestra. The energetic crowds and lively tunes are guaranteed to distract from the awkwardness of first dates.

We sat, backs to the wall, sipping on Coca-Cola. Theresa surveyed the room, waving now and then at a familiar face. "See you soon, on the dance floor," she called out to a woman in the crowd.

I stared at my half empty glass, puzzled by the promotion to math tutor. I hadn't even gone to school. How could I help Ellen? What if I tried my hardest, but she simply couldn't learn? Would Mrs. Doyle tell me to leave? After only three days, I was beginning to like it there.

"If I can't help Ellen, I don't know who can," I said. "My last mathematics book was university level. I completed the entire syllabus for grade 11, I simply couldn't write—"

"I'm not asking to get her into university or grade 11. I want her to finish at Mrs. Barrow's and start grade 10 in September. She's a smart girl, but she got it in her head that she can't do math. She'll manage the other subjects."

"Count on me. I'll be a dedicated tutor. A co-operative boarder too."

"In that case, keep a few things in mind. In this city, you're either English Protestant or Irish Catholic. You don't look English or Irish. That's fine. If you want to board in Mrs. Doyle's house, you got to be either Catholic or Catholic."

"I'll do my most Catholic best."

"If anyone asks about your parents—and they will—say they're from Nova Scotia. War's got people on edge and suspicious. Rightfully so. Our neighbours are already busybodies. Don't give them an excuse to set eyes and ears on number twelve or its new boarder."

Vati would have advised me to avoid unnecessary attention, especially while we were at war. "Do you think I blend in more now? Less foreign looking?"

"I'll be honest, when I saw you Wednesday night with your hair and those clothes, I had my doubts. I told myself, maybe that's what girls good at math look like. A day later with a visit to the parlour and the shops and you're like something out of a magazine."

"A good magazine?"

"Dunno. You're looking good. Now start sounding it."

"You mean my accent?" I'd been asked too often where I was from, as if I couldn't possibly be from St. John's.

"It's not how you say things, it's what you say. When you're with that pilot friend, follow his lead, like with dancing. If he says it's a grand evening, don't give him the temperature and wind speed or direction. Repeat his words if you don't know what to say. 'Grand evening.' Weather-wise, leave it at 'some foggy,' or 'blowin' a gale.' Don't mention the time you thought your barometer had to be collaborated but it turned out to be a major storm. All the same, I don't mind you warning us like you did yesterday. Glad I didn't hang out the washing. Our clothes would be kites soaring over Signal Hill."

"Calibrated."

"That's what I said."

"You said collaborated."

"What's the difference? On second thought, never mind. I don't want to know."

"If there's anything else I can do, please tell me."

"I can't be hovering over you, explaining how to behave. Ellen keeps me busy enough at that. Do what you can to help out, not just with Ellen— Mrs. Doyle too. Besides that, stay out of trouble. Be careful too. The city's changed since the war started. It's not safe for women."

As someone new to the city, drunks, drivers, and especially those two combined required me to be on guard, but they weren't the greatest threat. "Do you ever worry about fire, especially now, during a war? There must be hundreds of servicemen in this building. What a perfect target! Why waste a torpedo when a box of Eddys will do?"

She put down her glass and turned to face me, whispering, "Are you off your rocker?"

"No. I'm thinking like the enemy. What's to stop them? A lit match thrown into a closet filled with rags or an office with piles of old paper could kill and maim as many as a torpedo. Even a child could commit such an act."

"Well, thank God there's only adults here tonight. For the record, you better not repeat that in front of Mrs. Doyle or Ellen. And good luck landing a job with the Americans, sounding like you're on the enemy's side."

Her tone reminded me of the Theresa standing guard in the doorway. "I thought you said there was no hope for me at the base."

"Without a diploma, no hope from here to Timbuktu. Autodidact? Is that the word you used? Never heard of it. Whatever it is, I'm pretty sure it's not something you need to work at the base. Figure out how to write your grade 11 exams. I don't know anyone who wrote them without going to school, but I'm sure there's a way. I'll do what I can to help, but Brigid's the one with the school smarts. Ask her to—" She pointed to the door. "That him, there, by any chance? Laurence Olivier without a moustache?"

I turned to see Philip standing in the doorway in his sheepskin jacket. I waved and smiled.

He grabbed a chair and sat at our table. "Good evening, ladies." He reached forward to shake Theresa's hand. "How do you do? Captain Philip Campbell."

"Theresa. Did I connect a call for you at the base one day this week? I'd recognize your accent anywhere. Say 'How now brown cow.'"

Philip didn't seem to mind when she asked him to pronounce particular words, then compared them with local pronunciation. She was talented at imitating accents, especially howdy-doody, hot-diggity-dog, cowboy accents she'd heard on the base. Philip laughed and smiled as she entertained us. I laughed too, especially at her imitation of Churchill's "Never, never, never, never." I was glad when her friends arrived and she left us to chat. I wanted him to pay attention to me, not her.

"See you two cutie-pies later," she said and headed into the crowd, straw between her lips, blowing tiny air bubbles into the puddle of cola in her glass.

He laughed. "Don't judge a girl by her size. She's clever." He reached across the table and touched my hand as if to get my attention—something he already had entirely. "What a coincidence running into you yesterday. Meant to be, surely."

"Surely."

"You were spot-on with that nor'easter."

"Spot-on."

"You Newfoundlanders certainly know your weather."

"Some foggy today."

I couldn't have continued talking like that for long, so I was grateful when a man spoke into a microphone.

"Coming up—Glenn Miller's hit from last year, 'In the Mood.' Grab your partner and get in the mood."

"Shall we dance the war away?" Philip said.

On the dance floor, he rested one hand on the small of my back and held the other arm out to the side, our fingers interlaced. I felt my chest against his, my right cheek against his shoulder. I closed my eyes, my sense of smell on alert, breathing in the scent of his cologne. I should have been nervous about dancing and apologizing for stepping on his toes. Instead, he led and I followed, trusting his moves. "Moonlight Serenade" played next, horns filling the air with a soothing lullaby that could lull U-boats into a stupor. I wasn't a Spencer Tracy, Cary Grant, or even a Thomas Peckford type girl. I was a Captain Philip Campbell type girl, willing and ready to be swept off her feet.

DANCE HALL DIPLOMACY

Stoicism and sacrifice contribute to the war effort, but so too does morale. An evening of dancing can not only lighten the spirits of troops preparing to cross the dangerous Atlantic—it promotes solidarity and understanding between the locals and the various nationalities brought together by the war. We must be defiant in the face of danger, yet gleeful on the dance floor. Whether it's a jig, step, or square dance, waltz or foxtrot, put on your dancing shoes and give our servicemen, especially our pilots, a taste of Newfoundland hospitality.

24

When Mrs. Doyle eventually learned of my failed attempt at getting hired at the base, including that I didn't even have a diploma, she was ready to send me knocking on the door of someone else's boarding house. "You can't help Ellen if you never went to school. If you can't help Ellen, I don't know why you're here. I got more troubles than prayers to spare with four girls, not one over thirty. You show up with a tale thicker than the Bible and a false promise to help us out." She blew her nose into a handkerchief. "You had Theresa worked up, thinking her problem was solved, her dream come true—Ellen was going back to school, and one day she'd be sitting on a comfortable chair in a nice office with a window, typing letters and answering the phone for important men."

I pictured myself standing outside the house, suitcase and trunk at my feet, waiting on a taxi. "I can definitely help—"

"What's nine times nine?" Mrs. Doyle said.

"In exponential notation, a number multiplied by itself is called squaring—"

"There you go again with too many words." She wiped her brow. "Eighty-nine is what I want to hear. I left school at ten, but I can recite my tables all the same. Two twos are four, three threes are nine, four fours are whatever. You can't expect to teach math if you don't know your times table."

"Nine times itself is, in fact, eighty-one. Eighty-one times itself is—" I gazed at the ceiling. "Six thousand, five hundred, sixty-one. Want me to explain how I calculated—"

The conversation ended there. Mrs. Doyle said listening to me was worse than the radio tuned in between stations, garbled and making no sense. "Start teaching Ellen right away and find yourself a respectable job or I'll give that room to a Catholic girl who already earned her diploma."

I went directly to Theresa for reassurance that Mrs. Doyle didn't mean what she'd said, that she'd simply had a bad night's sleep.

"I told you the instant I laid eyes on you, she wasn't taking any boarders," Theresa said. "She only let you stay because I convinced her you could help Ellen. It's been over three weeks now and I haven't seen you teaching her math."

"She helped me measure the walls and calculate the cost of wallpaper for the third floor. I even brought in a little geometry with the corners and—"

"Teaching. Not wallpapering. At a table with pencil, paper, and a grade 10 math book, like in school. Sunday's her day off. Start tutoring her this week. You can't be lazing around while the rest of us are struggling to earn a living. Next thing I know, Ellen will be lazing too."

"I'm following your advice to write exams in June. I have to study at the library."

"I'll call Ida Monday morning. You could be a shopgirl at the Royal Stores in a week or two."

"A shopgirl? Bit of a waste of my ability, don't you think?"

"Ability?" she said, like she didn't know the word's meaning. "What good is that? A woman can't even go into service without references, personal character references on top. Where are you going to find them? I didn't mosey in off the ferry from Bell Island and have someone hand me a telephone, tell me, 'Here, lady, we got this respectable position for you.' I worked at every kind of job before I landed where I am today. In this city, a good work reference is worth its weight in sunshine."

RETAIL REALITIES

No other option available to you such as working at the American base? Interested in working in a downtown department store? If yes, you can serve the war and the store. Water Street merchants are proud to offer incentives to encourage employees to volunteer for war service. They also provide bonuses, dances, and card parties to celebrate the return of overseas servicemen and women. Prospective employees should be aware that the city's major department stores may consider an individual's religion when hiring.

Though I didn't admit it to Theresa, I crossed my fingers Ida wouldn't hire me. I hadn't come to the city to sell ladies' wear and could more easily solve a complex equation than advise women on fashion. It had been almost a month since I'd seen Ida. Instead of on the shop floor and as a customer, I met her in an upstairs room the size of the Chapel Street kitchen, used for storage and new inventory. In the corner was a sewing machine and a rack of dresses, with a sheet of paper, *Fitz Originals* written on it.

She invited me in and gave me a seat at a table with bolts of fabric piled on top. "Theresa said you had a big disappointment at the base. Sorry to hear that."

"I blame myself for being uninformed."

"Nonsense. Let's see who gets there first—the clothing designer or weather forecaster."

We laughed and I remembered how comfortable I'd felt with her the moment we met on the train and, like I did now. "Theresa told you I'm looking for work. I'm excellent with numbers. I'd be good at bookkeeping."

Ida laughed again. "I forgot. You're the girl eats dessert first. How does four days a week in footwear sound? Five or six if one of the girls is off sick."

I imagined Maryanne's reaction if I revealed that, instead of working at the American base, I sold shoes on Water Street. Not magic or even Salvatore Ferragamo shoes. Plain old oxfords. "Could I decide later? I want to explore another possibility."

"Sorry to say it, but without experience, references, or schooling, you'll have a hard time finding work shining shoes, let alone selling them."

"I'm grateful but I haven't seen Rose since I arrived here. She might have something for me."

Ida leaned forward, shaking her head. "Up to you, but I may not be there to bail you out like on the train. I warned you back then about her, remember?"

"I don't blame Rose for the sandwiches. My nose is highly sensitive, and I didn't smell anything bad."

"If it's not sandwiches, it'll be something else. Rose takes advantage of people like you."

"Like me?"

"New. Innocent enough to be convinced to peddle sandwiches to servicemen. Children hawk candies and colas. Respectable women don't hawk anything."

"I would never do such a thing now. The past month has taught me an encyclopedia's worth. When you and I ate together in the diner, that was the first menu I'd ever seen. Rose knows where I'm from. She'd understand."

"Good luck to you, then. Keep in mind, the city's a small town as far as a girl's reputation is concerned."

I thanked Ida for her advice and for the job offer—one I hoped I wouldn't need to accept. I headed to Ayre's, thinking how different Water Street seemed compared to when I'd first seen it, with shoppers in a hurry, jostling for space on the narrow sidewalk, and blank stares on their anonymous faces. Not one among them knew who I was, where I'd come from, what I was capable of, and the role I could play in the fight for victory. At least Rose knew Fred and Fred knew Maryanne and Vati. That had to count for something.

I found Rose on the store's second floor adjusting a mannequin's wide-brimmed hat.

"Well, hello there, little Miss Violet without a halo of braids."

Unsure whether to mention the incident on the train, I said, "Without sandwiches either."

"Is that a Royal Stores frock I see under your coat? Spent your profits there, did you?"

"Actually, yes, but I appreciate that you let me hold on to all the money." I was being gracious. Except for coming up with the idea and falling ill after eating one, Rose hadn't paid for the sandwiches. Nor was she the one who'd sold them to the hungry soldiers, then been accused of sabotage. "Sorry, I couldn't sell the stockings. You weren't awake—"

"I heard it all from Ida."

I fiddled with cold coins in my pocket, regretting I'd gone there, even more that I'd mentioned the sandwiches. "Ida helped me on the train and also found me a place to stay. I thought you were going to—"

"Die? Almost. *You* were dead to the world when I left the berth. Now, I'm recovered from food poisoning and you're awake and wide-eyed. I won't be able to eat eggs for the rest of my life." She finished with the mannequin, leftover pins in the palm of her hand. "Is this a friendly new-gal-in-town visit?"

"A looking-for-a-job and nice-to-see-you-again visit." Would she think I was trying to sound cleverer than her? "Numbers are my speciality, not sizes and prices. Bookkeeping, for example."

She leaned toward me with her eyebrows raised. "Sorry to tell you, honey, but we got our own people for that. They all wear a tie. I could do some bookkeeping myself if they'd let me. I'm a Jill of all trades—typing, inventory, clothing displays, you name it."

"Would you have anything for me?"

"You don't have any shopgirl experience. From what I recall, you don't have experience with anything except advising me whether I should bring a rain bonnet."

"Well, it's certainly more complex than—"

She waved her hand. "Come upstairs for a chit-chat. Now that you mention it, I might have something."

I turned to look at the store's entrance, considered leaving, then remembered that my other option involved selling footwear.

"Rest your legs, there," she said after I followed her up the stairs into a small office. "The edge of the desk will do me for a seat. The worst isn't the size of this room, a closet. I can't have a puff whenever I friggin' need it. They want us to stop smoking in the building—something to do with insurance rates."

"They say the city's due for another fire very soon."

"Is that so? Well, with cigarettes, if you feel the urge, you got to satisfy it. Satisfying the urges—that's what everything comes down to. I can get you a good deal on a carton if you're interested."

"My mother died of TB."

Rose held up a lit lighter until it flickered and she turned it off. "Where'd you hear you'll get consumption from cigarettes? Same people told you we're due for a fire? You catch it from a sick person. A bright girl like you should know that."

"Bright but without references, experience, or—"

"Join the club, the one filled with girls, fresh from the bay, expecting a land of milk and money, discovering the milk's sour and the money's in men's wallets."

"If you want me to sell Kayser stockings, I'll tell you right away, I'm not interested."

"What's the Royal Stores peddling these days besides pretty dresses for pretty girls? Whatever it is, I want some if it gives me your new bravado. Last I checked, I didn't say anything about stockings."

"Sorry, yes. I didn't give you a chance."

"There's the Violet from Crag Point that I like—honest and innocent. A bit fixated in her thinking, but her cheekbones, smooth skin, and those gorgeous locks make up for her conversation. Plenty of men new to the island would love the company of a rare blossom like you. Gentlemen who don't know from one minute to the next if they'll be sent overseas to their death. Homesick, lonely, down in the dumps, hanging around twiddling their thumbs while George Washington's burning a hole in their wallets."

"This doesn't sound like anything to do with bookkeeping."

"Loosen up your mind a bit, let some other ideas in there, Violet. You'll be counting tips and gifts. Lots of girls made a fortune escorting fine gentleman, all officers. I've got a trustworthy connection at Fort Pepperrell. You did say you wanted to work there, didn't you?"

I leaned forward, encouraged, eager to hear what she had to say. "More than anything, yes."

"Who knows? One of those officers might be needing a secretary."

For an instant, I'd been hopeful. Now, I was simply glad to have an excuse to decline her offer. "My boyfriend wouldn't want me dining with other men. Captain Philip Campbell. Do you know him?"

"My, my! The little weather gal who lassoed a powerful tornado."

"Tornado?"

She gazed up, eyebrows raised. "Baby doll, if I gotta spell it out, no point saying diddly, except 'watch out.'"

"With Philip? We're dating while he's here for training."

"Training? What's he training you for?"

"I meant he's being trained and training new airmen to—"

She shook her head. "I get what you meant," Rose said. "He's old enough to be your father."

"Thirty-one minus twenty-two is a nine-year difference. That's insignificant."

"It's a difference in experience. Take it from me. He's well-known in certain circles. He swaggers into a room like he's on stage, a girl on each arm, playing the hero."

"When he finishes training, he'll be ferrying planes across the Atlantic in support of victory—that's heroic. And the only girl by his side right now is me, I'm certain."

She put her unlit cigarette back into a case. "Don't get too tangled up with him. Be careful."

I leaned toward her. "Not to get pregnant?"

"That's not your only risk in this city these days. By the way, you do know he's divorced, do you?"

THE OTHER BIG V

The great *V* is neither Violet nor Victory. It is none other than Venereal Disease. The authorities report that delinquents, persons of low repute, and moral incorrigibles both male and female have become infected. In order to limit further spread, the US administration urges infected servicemen to report the females who have given them the disease. Free treatment is available at American bases. There will be no victory if our men are infected with the big *V*. There can be no big *V* if women take due care.

25

May 24, 1942

Dear Maryanne,

Happy birthday, Queen Victoria. I celebrated the Empire Day holiday in Bowring Park under resplendent skies with well-behaved winds and temperatures. It's early in the season for parasols, yet I saw ladies in stylish clothing. Someday, in the summer with the flowers in bloom, I'll visit it with you—fifty acres, playground, swimming pool (in the Waterford River), and tennis courts.

In my company was the charming Captain Philip Campbell, Royal Air Force pilot (eight dates so far). I never imagined with a population of 35–40,000 that I'd run into him after meeting him on the train. I'm in awe. Flying may be modern, but it remains a dangerous activity. A recent funeral reminded us of that—eight Canadian airmen, victims of a crash at the RCAF Torbay air base. What protection do goggles, oxygen mask, and leather helmet offer when a pilot's trapped in a cyclone, facing equipment failure, suffering freezing temperatures, or chased by the Luftwaffe? Then there's the landing and takeoff from a location that's a magnet for fog. No wonder he loves to dance. And I adore dancing with him.

The last time I felt this happy was one evening long ago, listening to Vati's silly jokes. I don't want that happiness to be spoiled by something as unimportant as a divorce, especially given that it happened years ago—1939. P. has the papers from the Northern Ireland courts. Married for seven years and separated for five of them. T. was quick to inform me that neither the Catholic Church nor Nfld courts recognize divorce, which means P. is technically still married. She said I was asking for trouble because Mrs. D.

was sure to find out. I should have anticipated her reaction and not told her. What do you think? Divorce has been legal in Germany since the turn of the century.

Your news. I received your letter two days ago. You wrote that Teo was all right, nothing more. Was he angry that I'd left? Did he say anything about my early departure? Why did you say you won't be able to write, that you have nothing to report? Forget about you? Impossible! And please don't apologize for your printing or spelling. You know I'd never judge you for that or for anything. Besides that, I'm sorry to learn that the fox got into the coop. Fred can easily replace the birds with Pine Harbour chickens, but I know you've grown attached to them. Maybe it's best to avoid giving names to the new ones. Sorry too about the pantry leak. Again! Any clippings damaged? Did you ask Fred to arrange for Miles to come fix it? He could bring his son to repair the foghorn.

St. John's. What a modern, active city. Who needs lanterns? Flick a switch or tug on a cord and voilà—let there be light! Forget hauling buckets of water from a well. With a sleight of hand, clean, clear water flows into a basin. No more emptying chamber pots or spreading lime in the outhouse. Not in this neighbourhood. A quick jerk on a pull-chain, the toilet flushes, and your waste flows into the North Atlantic (via the harbour). There's golf, curling, hockey, football, baseball, billiards, roller skating, basketball (Yanks vs. St. Bon's boys' school), darts, bowling, and likely many activities I've never heard of. I could fly to Moncton, Canada, in five hours along with thirteen other passengers on Trans-Canada Air Lines. Another four hours to Montreal. What movie shall I see tonight? The Wizard of Oz, Citizen Kane, or Gone with the Wind? Wartime morale must remain high. Clubs are common as corner stores. P. promises to take me to a different one on each date.

Chapel St. I ought to appreciate the opportunity to listen to the radio in Mrs. D.'s room except the coal dust makes me want to sneeze. You'd say, "Sneeze on a Monday..." She'd say, "Control yourself, girl." She asks me to read the Daily News to her (her eyesight is poor) with barely any light. I suggested opening at least one of the curtains during the day. "Do it for Queen Victoria," I said. She said "Victoria" was more patriotic than "Violet." I agreed to have her call me by that name if she'd allow me to open them. She told me it was her house, her windows, her curtains, so she didn't need to make deals with Victorias, Violets, or anyone.

T. convinced her to let me use the third floor (rafters, bare wooden walls) for my bedroom and helped me move my trunk and the daybed up there. Unlike in the second-floor bedrooms, there's no fireplace. I've bought a heavy quilt. If it's terribly cold in winter, I may have to go back to sleeping in the kitchen. Meanwhile, the steep pitch on the roof means I can't stand up at the front or back of my bedroom without hitting my head. I miss the white flash sweeping across the water and shores at Crag Point, but there's something otherworldly about the fixed green beam from the church spire. I wish it could be on every night.

My suspicion about T. convincing Mrs. D. to let me stay was spot on. I am now her niece's (Ellen's) mathematics tutor. Reluctantly. The stakes are serious. Her drive's not lacking. She's already decided, after grade 10, she'll enrol in the commercial program to become a typist. She's nimble at arguing, outspoken too, with a don't-get-in-my-way confidence I secretly admire. T. blames Noreen for having a bad influence on Ellen by preaching "equal pay, say, and may (rights) for women." Noreen denies any responsibility, then says, "You know I'm right, don't you, Violet?" T.'s wrong to blame Noreen, but I wouldn't dream of interfering.

<u>Work.</u> Sound the trumpets! I'll write examinations at the end of June. Brigid used her contacts at a nearby school run by the Sisters of Mercy. They've kindly agreed to make the necessary arrangements and administer the exams. No need for you to send my old textbooks. I'll have my diploma in hand before they arrive. You may be saying, "Don't count your fish till they're in your net." Between the school's and the public library, I have what's needed. The rest is up to me. Brigid's helping me with language and literature. She graduated first in her class and can recite Shakespeare to suit the occasion as she did the other day when I advised her to wear a raincoat. "So foul a sky clears not without a storm," she said. If I didn't know better, I'd think the quote referred to the war.

The American base is indeed a fort. Minimum qualifications and maximum acquaintances (references), not talent or ability, are what's required. At first, I admit, I felt knocked off my feet. Since then, and with T.'s advice, I'm concentrating on obtaining references and earning money for my board.

For now, picture me as a shopgirl at the Royal Stores. My boss, Ida, is head of ladies' wear while the real head, a man, serves overseas. She wants to be a clothing designer though she hasn't yet sold anything. Think of women with spare time, wondering what to wear next. Rolling your eyes? "You'll be tops in Nfld," I said to Ida. "The whole world," she said. Regarding being a forecaster, she said they should name a hurricane after me, that I'd blow them away with my skills.

Crag Point. Nfld spring is around the corner—a season in a class of its own. Before you know it, the tamaracks will be sprouting aqua-coloured needles, snowshoe hares will shed their winter whites, and flower buds will appear on the berry bushes. Teo may learn to appreciate Crag Point, perhaps not so much as the place deserves, yet enough that he won't be dying to flee. Tell him I'm willing to make inquiries regarding factories or stores where he might find work. On the other hand, please advise whether I should write to the authorities to alert them that the light station is, for all intents and purposes, unmanned. Mariners beware! By the way, I left behind a handkerchief he gave me. It's on the desk in Vati's room. Do whatever you want with it.

Yours till the ice ages,
Violet
PS: When you see Fred, ask about my Pine H. visit, his son Thomas and his sister Rose. One thing's for certain—Vati made the right decision not to send me there to live and attend school.

MOVIE REVIEW

Imagine winds wailing, trees soaring past like kites, houses spinning round in the cyclone. Your head spins along with them, heart skips beats, jaw clenches, hands grip the armrests. Your eyes bulge at the sight of the Emerald City, yellow brick road, and ruby slippers. You're seeing colours that make the real world appear black and white. The speakers are blaring, the music's like nothing you ever heard, and you're wishing you knew the words to sing along. When it's over and you catch your breath, you want to see *The Wizard of Oz* all over again.

26

n the last week of June, the winds shifted to the northeast, capelin rolled onto beaches in biblical proportions, and with them came miserable capelin-scull weather. Fog mixed with chimney smoke shrouded the city, so damp it penetrated the bones, so dense it clouded the mind, so persistent it weakened the spirit. A faint easterly breeze waltzed it around city streets, creating mirages and prompting citizens to greet each other, eyebrows raised as if to say, "Ever seen the likes of it?" It crept in through the Narrows, then travelled uphill past Chapel Street to Military Road. There, for five days, I wrote examinations in a school office surrounded by pictures of Jesus and the Pope, their eyes on me, a look of pity combined with compassion.

The office belonged to a soft-spoken Sister Bernadette of whom I saw only face and hands, the rest hidden under a white cap and guimpe with a black veil. Not even her ankles were visible under her tunic, drawn in at the waist with a leather belt, a crucifix dangling from the end of rosary beads. She wished me success and proposed that, upon graduation, I consider a career in teaching. In September, attendance would be free and compulsory from the age of seven to fourteen. Outport schools would be desperate for teachers, especially those who could teach arithmetic.

"I'd take her advice as a compliment, Violet," Theresa said when I told her what Sister Bernadette had said. "You already got Ellen saying she's good at math. You'd make a top-notch teacher."

Tutoring Ellen had given me a taste of the satisfaction teachers must feel when their efforts pay off. She was advancing quickly in her understanding of mathematics, appreciating as I did its value as a tool.

"Here's a better compliment," Noreen said. "You'd make a top-notch weather forecaster. It would put the Americans in their place to have a Newfoundlander, a woman at that, telling them whether it's safe to fly their planes or sail their boats."

"Learn a lesson from Noreen. She's smarter than the men at the factory and they still won't promote her. No one's going to hire a woman forecaster."

"If every woman gave up so easily," Noreen said, "you'd be in a maid's uniform instead of at the switchboard."

"In America," Brigid said, "men and women are self-made. That idea hasn't caught on here yet."

"Self-made only works for men," Noreen said. "Women need a collective voice if they want anyone to listen. That's the point of unions."

"Money, not unions, is what women need to move up in this world."

"Not anymore, Theresa. The Depression proved the failure of capitalism. The war proved women can be equal workers. Newfoundland is changing. Power is shifting in our favour. Curse the merchants and the elite!"

Brigid spoke almost before Noreen had finished. "See? I knew she was a commie. Wait till I tell Danny."

EXAMINATION REGULATIONS

June 22 will mark the beginning of examinations for grade 11 academic and commercial. Students may choose from among twenty academic subjects, including navigation, physiology and hygiene, botany, and economics. A pass diploma requires a minimum score of 50 per cent on English language and literature along with four other subjects like those chosen by Miss Violet: German language, mathematics, physics, and history. Candidates for commercial may choose from among fourteen subjects including penmanship, dictation and spelling, bookkeeping, shorthand, typewriting, and commercial law.

Philip invited me to celebrate the end of examinations with dinner and dancing at the Newfoundland Hotel. He came to Chapel Street in a taxi to get me. I invited him in to meet Mrs. Doyle and Theresa.

"You sound exactly like Father Phil," Mrs. Doyle said. "He was Irish too. Used to be right strict with his penance. God bless his soul."

"I'm not a Cath—"

"True that is," Theresa said. "You're not a cabman. Your driver will be honking his horn any minute, making a racket like that mister brought Violet to us back in April. Say toodle-oo and be on your merry way."

"Come again for a chat, Father Phil," Mrs. Doyle said. "That's what we'll call you. Don't keep her out late, Father Phil. Don't let her go on about the weather either."

Theresa herded us through the front door, no "Goodnight" or "Have fun."

"What was that?" Philip said, opening the taxi door for me. "Is she the same how-now-brown-cow Theresa giggling over my accent at the Caribou Hut? Father Phil! There's another person assuming all Irishmen are Catholic. My roots are in the Scottish Lowlands. The only religion in my family's history is Presbyterian."

We sat hip to hip in the back seat. I was wearing a dress Ida had lent me, of her own design, in rayon—figure-enhancing, cocoon rather than bell-shaped. "Don't mind Theresa. I was scared of her at first too." I leaned closer to him. "Tell me you missed me."

"And that smell. It's awful. What the blazes is it?"

"Wintergreen oil. It helps with Mrs. Doyle's rheumatism." I glanced at the driver's rear-view mirror to make sure he wasn't watching when I kissed Philip on the neck.

He sniffed, then pinched his nose. "I can smell it off you."

"Wintergreen?"

He laughed. "You're remarkably easy to tease."

The taxi hit a pothole. We laughed together, bouncing on the seats, grabbing hold of each other and the door handles.

I breathed in the scent of his cologne with its hints of a forest. "You smell absolutely divine."

He reached his arm around me. "Are you happy, darling?" he said. "Can I call you darling? Not too soon after only two months together?"

"As long as I can call you that in return, darling." I turned to kiss him.

"You still haven't answered. Happy?"

"Ecstatic. I earned my diploma. I've finally accomplished something."

"I'll tell you what you accomplished. Making me lonely on my short stay in the city. Not free for dancing, too busy studying. I hope you're planning to make up for it."

DREAM DESTINATION

Whether you're an adventurous tourist visiting "The Norway of the New World," a captain of the skies, or a woman new to the city, the Newfoundland Hotel is sure to delight. Erected on the site of a former British fort, the modern, fireproof building has been in operation since 1926. The hotel's dining room caters to locals and visitors seeking quality service in an elegant setting. After your meal, join us in the ballroom for an evening of dancing with a live orchestra. Consider the hotel for that special date with the man or woman you long for in your dreams.

When we arrived, the hotel porter opened the taxi door and we entered the majestic lobby, my arm in Philip's. In the dining room, a waiter in a white dinner jacket held out my chair and placed a white linen napkin in my lap. We ordered the cowboy's special with steaks the size of our plates.

While we waited for our food, Philip laid a jewellery case in front of me. Its black velvet cover shimmered against the white tablecloth. "Here's something to celebrate this milestone. You're an attractive and original woman. I think my gift captures both."

I opened the case slowly. Inside was a Rolex wristwatch in rose gold with roman numerals.

He removed my old watch, the crack visible on its face, then fastened the new one on my wrist. "My darling girl, let it be a reminder of the fond moments we've shared together, of how fortunate I am to have met you that day on the train."

"No one's ever given me anything this lovely. Thank you." I couldn't wait to show it to Rose, proof that Philip was serious, that she'd been wrong to brand him as purely self-interested. Theresa had been critical of him ever since she'd found out he was divorced. I was tired of hearing her say, "You're asking for trouble." What would she say now?

"In exchange could you have a photograph taken for me?" he said. "I'll stare at it when I'm up in the clouds, something to take my mind off the mission."

Later, in the ballroom, we danced, my left hand resting on his chest, showing off his gift. He requested a tune we'd danced to at the Caribou Hut, "Moonlight Serenade."

"This could be our song," he said. He leaned in close, holding me tightly, not hiding his desire.

27

Despite the war, or perhaps to spite it, life carried on. Nothing could stop the change in the seasons, the return of the warm south-westerly breezes, the reappearance of wildflowers, wispy Queen Anne's lace, purple lupins, and rhodora. July's headlines reported that prospects were good for both the cod and salmon fishery, while the classifieds featured announcements of upcoming weddings, sports days, and openings of playgrounds and pools.

The balmy breezes had Americans and Canadians breathing a sigh, realizing the island really did experience summer after all—the period of hibernation had come to an end. Some considered their prayers answered, others merely thanked the warm southwesterlies for tenaciously hanging on. Music and voices normally contained inside buildings and houses travelled out into the streets through open windows. Similarly, outdoor sounds, like the howls and barking of Pete and his canine conspirators, travelled inside.

The shift in the seasons was accompanied by a positive shift in moods at home. The decision had been made to hold an evening celebration for Mrs. Doyle's June and Brigid's July birthdays.

"Invite Father Phil," Mrs. Doyle said to me.

I was happy for the opportunity to introduce him to Danny and Brigid, Noreen and Ellen too. I imagined Theresa singing, Danny and Brigid waltzing, and Philip and I joining in.

"Let's go to a club instead," Philip said when I invited him. "I'm heading to central Newfoundland in a day, crossing the Atlantic this weekend, and don't fancy spending one of my last nights pretending to be someone I'm not—Father Phil or anyone."

I couldn't disappoint Mrs. Doyle. In addition, this was a step forward in our relationship, bringing him home to meet the closest I had to family in the city. "There'll be singing and dancing. We'll leave early, I promise."

"If you insist. What do I get for the sacrifice?"

"My eternal worship and affection."

"Can you throw in something else?"

On the evening of the celebration, the others were in the kitchen while I waited in the hall, listening for Philip's knock on the door. I wore a light cotton dress with buttons from collar to waist and easily undone. I made good use of my new watch, checking it every minute. When at last I heard the squeal of the taxi's brakes, I rushed outside and raised my hands to his cheeks to pull him close, not caring who might be watching out their window. I didn't ask where he'd been, why he was an hour late, or mention I smelled alcohol off his breath. I took him by the hand to guide him into the kitchen where we stood facing the others.

He squeezed my hand when Mrs. Doyle welcomed Father Phil.

I squeezed it back when Theresa spoke.

"Well, he couldn't be a father now, could he?" she said. "Priests don't date. Not unless they break their vow of celibacy. That would be like dating while you're still married."

If I could have caught her attention, I would have let her know that I didn't appreciate the comment.

Danny reached out to shake Philip's hand and introduced himself. "Glad there's at least one other man here," he said, chuckling.

I served Philip a glass of gin and he quickly fell into a lively conversation with Danny about friends and acquaintances in common at the base.

At the table, Ellen said the only reason she went to Mass was because the priest was so good-looking. Brigid talked about two sisters who'd left the convent to marry.

"They would have been better off single," Noreen said.

"How would you know if you've never been married?" Brigid said.

Their conversation continued while Danny and Philip stood, leaning against the wall.

Philip was on his third glass of gin and Danny had been drinking beer for the last hour. They stood near the kitchen doorway talking about the Americans' production of bombers.

"Newfoundlanders should be grateful the Americans are here," Philip said. "You'd agree with me on that wouldn't you, Violet?"

I looked at Noreen, across from me at the table and could tell by her scowl that trouble was brewing.

"Grateful for what?" she said. "A ninety-nine-year lease for fifty rickety destroyers? Is that all we're worth? Tell me—"

"Grateful for being generous caretakers," I said, "building roads, hospitals, and employing local people." I glanced at Philip but he was watching Noreen.

She shook her head. "Caretakers? We're not foundlings anymore. We're lending millions to Britain these days, not the other way round. The tables have turned."

"Regardless how much money Newfoundland has," Philip said, "it could never afford what America produces. Wouldn't you say that's true, Daniel?"

Danny nodded and clinked his glass against Philip's. "It sure is. We're churning out a new B-24 bomber every hour. By next year, we'll have installed five hundred miles of cable and twenty thousand poles from St. John's to our air force base in Stephenville."

"The Americans are here to defend us," Brigid said.

"Who gave you that idea?" Noreen said. "They're not here for your or my sake. 'Move aside, goofy Newfies,' they say. They're no different than the Brits. You could all do with a bit of reading on colonialism and anti-imperialism."

"What gibberish!" Philip said. "Newfoundlanders should get down on their knees and thank the US for its help, and Britain should be thankful to have Newfoundland off its teat."

I cringed at the comment.

"Why's everyone so quiet?" Mrs. Doyle said. "When's the singsong going to start?"

"It's started," Noreen said. "We've heard those old, worn-out refrains too often already. Time for another tune."

If I could have, I would have nudged Noreen from under the table.

"Aye, and what would that be?"

"A ballad called 'We shall overcome. We have overpaid.'"

"What's that one, Noreen?" Mrs. Doyle said.

"It's a heartfelt tune about a neglected orphan who grows up, breaks away, and ends up lending money to the self-appointed guardians who used and abused her most of her life."

"Ha ha. Violet, you didn't tell me your friend had such an imagination. If it wasn't for Britain's generosity and for the enterprising spirit and capital of people like my friend the late John Barrow, the entire lot of Newfoundlanders would be on the dole, living off a handout from government of six cents a day."

Ellen stood up and I expected her to say the Barrows were her employer. I hadn't told Philip in case he preferred not to fraternize with his friends' servants.

"I know the maids used to work for him," Ellen said. "Guess why they nicknamed him Smacker." She reached her hand behind and smacked her bottom. "That's why."

The smack had Mrs. Doyle tutting, Theresa shaking her head, and Brigid telling Theresa to control Ellen.

"John Barrow's enterprising spirit was matched by his integrity, and I'll listen to no one who insults—"

"Britain's generosity?" Noreen said. "Keeping us indebted and dependent? Treating us like we're lazy, codfish-simple slaves? Making us fight their wars? Is that what you call generosity?"

"It's called a democracy."

Noreen stood up from the table, hands on her hips. "We don't have that here. We have a codocracy. Serfs and ruling lords. Merchants give fishermen credit, no cash, for their catch."

"Last I heard, you had a Commission of Government."

She pretended to laugh. "Right-o. You mean those six dictators in top hats? The ones ready to lease us to China for ninety-nine years if they thought they could turn a profit and be rid of us in one shot?"

"Who's force-feeding you this propaganda? Catholic priests? There's your ruling lords." Philip laid his empty glass on the counter. "I'd say that's enough singsongs for one evening. Happy birthday, Mrs. Doyle and Brigid. May the road rise up to meet you and all that. Good evening."

Brigid and Danny said goodbye to him as he left the kitchen. I followed behind, relieved to be out of that situation, mad at him, but not wanting to make matters worse by accusing him of provoking Noreen. She was as much to blame. Her allegiance to her political views obviously trumped any loyalty to me and our friendship.

I grabbed my coat off the rack in the hall.

Philip raised his hand to stop me. "It's been a long day, darling. I'm not in the mood for dancing, for arguing either. I'll be in touch when I'm back from overseas. Wish me luck."

LETTER TO THE EDITOR

Dear Sir: Allow me to take up my pen to join recent debates in your most esteemed paper regarding the future of our great nation, Newfoundland. America's eastern Alaska, Canada's tenth province, or an elected responsible government? Don't these questions of choice risk dividing and distracting us while the enemy takes aim? Rather than blame the Empire for its wrongs, can we not move forward in a spirit of co-operation and mutual benefit? Can we be independent without loss of our heritage and roots? Can we be friends though we share opposing views? Respectfully, Mr. Victor Morgen.

28

July 25, 1942

Dear Maryanne,

Happy 70th! Watch for a gift of Moirs Pot of Gold chocolates. Save the box to store my letters and keep them smelling of caramel and cocoa. Don't open the treats in front of Fred. He'll say, "One more" until they're gone. Enjoy them for yourself.

Sincere apologies for not having written since May. June was a busy month for studying and examinations, special events and celebrations too, including St. John's Day, the centenary of the arrival of the Sisters of Mercy in Nfld, and Memorial Services for members of the Royal Newfoundland Regiment (Mrs. D.'s Timmy). It's been so hot this month, I barely have the energy to write. I never felt such temperatures at Crag Point, not with a constant flow of air near the cliff's and water's edge. My bedroom might as well have a stove on full blast, its oven door open. At least in winter, I'll be able to pile on blankets. These days, what can I do other than open two windows that offer no cross-draft?

<u>Work</u>. I've been a shopgirl for two months already. My boss, Ida, said I should know by now, women shop to relax, to escape their worries, forget about the war, and therefore didn't want to listen to my arguments in favour of cancelling May or June's air-raid tests. Everyone was complaining about them, so I fail to see how I could have avoided discussing them with customers. The actual practice at 11 p.m. left many citizens with lingering nightmares (e.g., Ellen). The Luftwaffe wouldn't risk losing an expensive bomber and experienced pilot knowing the RCAF patrols would spot them before they reached our shores. There are other threats far more worrisome. Similar

rules at home—no mention of U-boats, torpedoes, sinking ships, drownings, bombs, air raids, fires, etc. Ellen asked what was the point of doing grade 10 if we're going to die, burned in our beds or shot in the street? T. said that the only fire Ellen needs to worry about is hell, that she'll end up there if she doesn't stop talking back.

Chapel St. We finally had a lock installed on the front door, a necessary defence in the new St. John's. Noreen negotiated a deal on a bathtub, missing two rear feet and mounted on two uneven blocks of wood. T. reminded us that the water doesn't get hot by itself, but costs money. If we want more than one bath per week, it will have to be a cold one. Even one is a delightful luxury.

I saw my first parade last month, United Nations Flag Day, with civil defence workers and armed forces members. My heart beat along with the rhythms of drums and troops marching in unison. Noreen and I went together. Although she can be annoyingly extreme with her political opinions, she's fun to be with and generous with intelligent advice. On her recommendation, I plan to set aside a small portion of my salary for war certificates. Who needs to buy a new summer frock when the money could help win the war? As the slogan goes: "Eat it up. Wear it out. Make it do. Do without." Noreen said if things don't work out between me and Philip, she'd happily be my girlfriend—one who kisses and whatever else goes with that. I hope she finds a woman to fill that role, but I'm content to be merely a good friend. Anyway, I don't see why it wouldn't go well with P. I simply need to get used to him being away so often and stop worrying that something will go wrong.

Hear ye! Hear ye! Dec. 26, Mass of holy matrimony for Brigid and Danny at the RC Cathedral. He proposed on her birthday. We all like Danny, including Noreen, though she'd never admit feeling anything but resentment for the Americans in Nfld. He's very attentive to Brigid, always making sure she's served before him, pulls out her chair, and keeps an arm over her shoulder. It's a happily-ever-after story. In the new year, she'll go live with his parents in Montana. I wish her every happiness, although I wonder how she'll cope with living in a landlocked state where winter temperatures make Nfld seem tropical.

I went with them to the base for a scaled-back American Independence Day celebration on July 4. Philip had a prior commitment. The fireworks were limited because of the wartime shortage and blackout rules. What a thrilling spectacle all the same. Imagine fresh spruce resin and birch sap popping in a bonfire, with sparks shooting up into the air. My favourite part was the hundreds of voices singing "The Star-Spangled Banner" and "God Bless America" accompanied by the US Army Regimental Band. Newfoundlanders sang the "Ode to Newfoundland," a love song to the island's weather—tempests and blinding storm gusts, windswept frozen lands, sunrays, spindrift, and wild waves. At a dance that night, the orchestra played Glenn Miller hits. Ask me the name of any song. There's no mood like the Miller mood! I made sure not to dance with any individual man more than once. "I have a boyfriend," I said. Usual reply: "Where's he tonight?"

Philip. Falling in love, like dancing, is good for morale, and what could be more important during a war than maintaining morale? If only he wasn't away so often and didn't have to be so secretive. There's nothing secretive about my feelings. I miss him terribly. I'll ask where he'll be while away, and he'll say, "In central." Sounds like something out of a spy movie. No telegrams or even telephone calls. The Ferry Command isn't a secret otherwise he wouldn't be wearing his RAF Ferry Command badge. However, the location of its air base is supposed to be. The censors call it "airport N.," Nfld Airport, I assume.

In the fall, training will be over and he'll only be visiting St. John's while on short leaves. He'll be air-ferrying bombers full-time across 2,000 miles of water from Nfld to Britain. The bombers are built in Canada and the US and designed to destroy German cities—the magnificent cities I imagined I'd one day visit with Vati. It takes a brave man to fly during a war, over the North Atlantic, and with a devilishly difficult climate. He promised, after the war, he'll fly me overseas. Take off one day, arrive the next. "Dear war, please, please end soon."

Crag Point. Libraries will soon be expanded to communities outside of St. John's (in addition to the travelling library). Why not consider moving somewhere less remote or nearer your daughter? Neither you nor I owe allegiance to Teo or Crag Point. I'm fortunate to have lived there, equally fortunate something bad (Vati's death) forced me to leave. The city's where I belong. Noisy, crowded, dusty, rough, and dirty in places, yes. But it's *intensely alive, bustling with activity, with foreigners and locals, each of us on our own paths, towed along with the momentum.*

I think of you often, while drinking tea, reading the paper, or counting foxes (ha ha) while falling asleep. Think of me, please, not just when you see the light flash or a storm strikes without warning. Skim a rock over the water at low tide. Try to beat my record of fourteen skips. Once the blueberries are ripe, pick a gallon for me.

Best wishes for a fall without leaks, winter without shovelling, and spring without blackflies. May you live to be one hundred!

Yours till your birthday comes round again (& again),

Violet

PS: I'm including a recent photograph. I gave one to P. He said I had the look of a gypsy, meant as a compliment.

POT OF GOLD

Buy a box of Moirs Pot of Gold chocolates to support the 1,000 workers at a confectionery plant that serves as the largest employer of women in Halifax, Canada. The candies are made by men, then individually hand-dipped and swirled in chocolate by women. The swirl gives each chocolate its original top pattern. The female dippers are paid piece-meal and require up to two years of training and practice to learn the skill. Although supply of the chocolates has suffered during this difficult period, demand has never been higher. Share them with loved ones.

29

Spotless skies, balmy evenings, and soothing breezes—August was generous with its fine weather. The drab, monochrome city that greeted me in April had turned magically into a spectrum of blue and green. In the calm oasis of nearby Bannerman Park, children played marbles or hide-and-seek, while mothers in their snappy sports dresses fanned themselves. Fathers rested in the shade of tall beech trees, complaining about the scorching temperatures, debating whether the heat had to do with the war, with God's will, or was the world simply getting warmer and how much more could they tolerate? Shopkeepers like Mrs. Clarke, working in cramped spaces, encouraged customers to pray for a period of good old rain, drizzle, and fog.

Theresa had taken a short holiday, the first in a year, to care for her bedridden mother on Bell Island. She invited me to accompany Ellen to the Island to meet Ellen's mother, Lucy, and for Sunday supper. I didn't want to go if it meant missing a day with Philip.

"I can't figure out what you see in him besides his looks," she said. "Find yourself an honest sailor, one who's not already married."

I made excuses for his behaviour at Mrs. Doyle's and Brigid's party, that he'd had too much to drink and had been under pressure before his upcoming mission. "I'd rather not go if he can't."

"All right. But tell him if he insults us again, he'll have to deal with me."

THE ISLE OF IRON

Come visit Bell Island, the place that supplied Germany with iron ore from 1935 to 1939. The subsea mine is owned by and exports its ore to the Dominion Steel and Coal Corporation in Sydney, Nova Scotia. Containing up to 60 per cent iron, it is considered the most valuable ore in the Empire and is the only source for Sydney's steel production. Steel is needed for everything from helmets to tanks, aircraft, and ships. The Island's coastal defence battery with its searchlights and quick-firing guns, operated by the Newfoundland Militia, is designed to protect the mines from an enemy attack. Fear not for your safety while visiting Bell Island.

The ferry ride in Conception Bay waters was so smooth, I could close my eyes and imagine I was on land. I didn't need a sweater over my pastel green dress with its white collar and three white buttons.

"Your ears will be sore from listening to men's whistles," Ida had said when she loaned it to me.

Philip reached his arm around my shoulder and stroked the bare skin below my sleeve. More than anything, I wanted to be somewhere alone with him, to make up for having been apart. We leaned on the railing, I on one side of him, Ellen on the other, our attentions fixed on the island up ahead, playing I spy. Ellen spied a massive sea monster, Philip, Ireland's Cliffs of Moher.

If I admitted what I really thought, I'd upset Ellen, then Theresa would be angry with me. The U-boats were hiding in those waters, sniffing out targets, and didn't need spies to inform them that vessels filled with iron ore destined for the Allies were docked in clear sight on Bell Island's doorstep. "I spy a huge flat boulder, two miles wide, three times as long, rising one hundred feet up out of the water at low tide."

Once we arrived at their home, Ellen went to see her grandmother. Theresa had invited an uncle for the meal, and Philip stopped to talk to him.

I went to the kitchen where I found Theresa chopping up a head of cabbage. I offered to help.

"Go say hello to my sister, Lucy. Tell her Ellen's off to school in a couple of weeks. She'll get her diploma, and, one day, please God, find a good man to marry, not the first bucko with an offer of a kiss and a plea for a squeeze. That's what Lucy needs to hear. A scrap of good news for a change. Heaven knows she deserves it."

Lucy sat on a wool blanket on the grass, looking like a slightly older version of Theresa, with the same red hair and pale freckled skin. With an arm raised over her forehead to block the sun, she made me think of Mrs. Doyle's reaction to my opening curtains in the morning. "You must be Violet. Have a seat. Welcome. Where's Ellen? I'm dying to see my girl."

I pointed at the house. "Delivering a tin of Milady toffee to your mother. There's one for you too, bought out of her own savings."

"You're the one deserves the toffee. I heard you're making her smart with numbers. That true?"

As Ellen's tutor, the person responsible for saving her from a life in service, I'd been anxious about meeting Lucy. Ellen hadn't yet begun school, which meant I couldn't be sure how she'd fare in a mathematics classroom. "She's already up to where they'll be in the syllabus by October. She learns quickly."

"She's a quick one for sure. Too bad she couldn't wait till the war's won to be living in the city. It's not safe."

I brushed a horsefly off my leg, glad to have something to talk about besides tutoring Ellen. "It's safer than here, especially anywhere close to the piers and shoreline. Even then."

"Sailors and longshoremen? Is that what you're on about?" Lucy said. "Theresa tells me St. John's is maggoty with young, randy men."

"I meant safe from an attack. The U-boats are out there, roaming with the whales, squid, tuna, and other giants." I reached my arm forward and fixed my gaze on my fingertips, pretending they were the tip of a rifle. "Their *Kapitänleutnant* caught scent of those iron-ore carriers ages ago. They're a perfect target, worth a torpedo for certain."

"Kappie tin what?" Lucy stood and stretched. "Theresa told me you were an odd one, going on about wind and fire. I suppose it's not your fault, living in a tower on the edge of a cliff up north, not fit for gulls, your Pop gone mad."

I was disappointed to realize I couldn't trust Theresa with details about my life. She and Lucy had it wrong. If my father hadn't fallen on the stairwell and hit his head, we'd be happily living, not in the tower but in our cozy, comfortable, happy home—by a cliff's edge, yes, but with an inland pond, forests, vast skies, clean air, peace, and calm. As for gulls, there were black-backed, ring-billed, slaty-backed, and even rarer ivory gulls.

"Nice meeting you, Violet. Thanks a million for helping Ellen. That handsome fellah yours?"

"Am I interrupting?" Philip said, standing so tall, he made Lucy seem like a child. "Pleased to meet you. I'm Philip."

"Lucy. See you at supper." She looked my way. "Not a peep to Ellen about any Krappi Krauts or torpedoes. All right?"

I nodded even though I hadn't planned to say anything to Ellen. I reached up, grabbed Philip's hand, and tugged on it for him to join me on the blanket.

He bent down, hands on knees for support. "What the blazes were you talking about? Don't you realize what people are thinking when they hear you say those things?"

I was surprised at his tone, the anger over a few words about the war. "What things? All I said was those piers and ships we saw from the ferry are a perfect target. The *Kriegsmarine* surely has its eye on—"

"Shush." He lowered his voice though there was no one nearby to hear. "You could be reported for talking like that. German words? Are you showing off, or are you simply lacking common sense?"

"Common sense, exactly. If we want to defeat our enemy, we need to think like them. How else can we anticipate their next move?"

He stood up straight. "For crying out loud. I don't plan on anticipating anyone's moves besides my own. Speaking of those moves, have you forgotten I'm flying across the Atlantic soon?"

"I didn't say anything about an attack by air. The *Luftwaffe* wouldn't come this close with the RCAF watching and the observers—"

He frowned, jaw clenched. "Do you have even the teeniest inkling of the dangers I face crossing the Atlantic?"

"Of course I do. You're a different person before each flight. I wish you could be happy like you are while dan—"

"Sometimes, you seem positively heartless. Either that or oblivious. And you're a fool talking about the war, especially on an outing that's supposed to help us forget it."

I was considering what to add in my defence when he told me he was going to get a drink, preferably something stronger than a Coca-Cola after listening to me.

At day's end, under a cloudy sky, we boarded the ferry and sat indoors, Ellen on one side of Philip, I on the other. She rested her head on his shoulder. I tried to do the same, but he shrugged to brush me off. A baby squealed, the sound amplified in the hollow space, so loud compared to the blaring silence between us. An apology wouldn't change that I'd spoiled our let's-forget-the-war outing. He regretted his decision to volunteer to serve with the RAF. Who could blame him? Courage had its limits, even in a war. I hated myself for ruining the day. Heartless? Oblivious? A fool? How disappointing he should see me that way. Even more disappointing to think he may have been right.

WATCH-LISTEN-REPORT

Enemy bombers can quickly overwhelm even the most sophisticated defences, including anti-aircraft gunners, air-raid wardens, and the RCAF fighter squadrons. Let us be thankful for the 1,500 volunteer observers and spotters of the Newfoundland Aircraft Detection Corps, including lighthouse operators, fishermen, lumberjacks, housewives, and other ordinary civilians who watch the skies for enemy aircraft. The role of the ADC has recently expanded to include observation of the sea for U-boats and the land for suspicious persons making suspicious comments. Follow the Corps' motto: Watch-Listen-Report.

30

August 24, 1942

Dear Maryanne,

This is letter #4. Have you received #s 2 & 3?

Work. *"Welcome to the Royal Stores. I'm Miss Morgen. How can I help you, madam? We have every style from oxfords to wedges to no-toe slingback sandals. Care for our promenade pumps with a crocodile insert, currently in stock and last season's bestseller? Needing practical footwear? Our rubber boots are on sale. Stock up prior to the deluge. What's your size? I'd say you're a seven. Have a seat, please." After eight hours per day, I am repeating those lines in my sleep.*

Ida insists once the real head of ladies' wear returns from the war, she won't go back to working the floor. I don't blame her. She wants to see her clothing designs on women, not merely on paper. I'm helping her determine how much she'll have to borrow to pay for fabrics, hire seamstresses, etc. Who'll lend her the money is anybody's guess. She says she'll start small, with three or four dresses organized into a collection. She'll deal with the fabric shortage by relying on higher hems and simpler styles. Apparently, Japan has completely cut off supplies of silk. Wool is hard to get because it's needed for uniforms.

T. says it's too soon to ask Ida for a reference, and she thinks the office-girl positions have been filled. Brigid's right in saying I need to be more patient with myself. She promised to have Danny keep eyes and ears open in case something comes up for me at the base. Sister Bernadette offered to give me a school reference (pending receipt of positive exam results). The name check for the civilian unsuitability list shouldn't be a problem.

THE WEATHER DIVINER · 149

Philip. Remember your advice? "Don't end up pregnant until you're happily married." Noreen says there's an epidemic of unmarried women getting pregnant, not solely at the factory. They lose their job, reputation, and often family and friends too. Brigid claims she didn't do anything too intimate until she was engaged and even then, not without protection. I told P. that. He said he wasn't planning on proposing to me or anyone. I hadn't meant to hint at an engagement.

Too bad I don't have the courage to ask him about his former wife. Why did they marry? Why did they divorce? He doesn't care to talk about his life in Ireland. He's fond of saying, "Let's leave it at that" or "There's nothing to be said." Though he won't admit it, I can tell by his change in moods that he's terrified of taking to the sky in wartime. Ferrying a bomber across the Atlantic is nothing like the luxurious, leisurely travel he was used to before he joined the RAF.

I have a million questions I want to ask him about aviation and wind, but he says I sound pedantic when I talk about weather. I told him, finally, that I want to be a forecaster. He said while he didn't doubt my skill, I'd have a better chance at becoming a princess. The chief meteorologist, McTaggart-Cowan (nicknamed McFog), at the Gander air base is a Canadian Rhodes Scholar with Memorial University College graduates working under him and an American weather unit alongside them. "Do you have a college degree to go with your forecasts?" P. said, aware I didn't. I told Noreen about his reaction, then had to endure a lecture on paternalism, chauvinism, and misogynism.

Chapel St. Annual garden parties are happening across the island, with the largest, the St. John's Regatta, taking place the first Wed. of Aug. Thanks to the weather for its co-operation! T., Ellen, and I went together. They were adorable, strolling arm in arm, joking and giggling until Ellen unfastened the top buttons of her blouse while flirting with a champion rower. T. told her to button up and stop pushing out her bust. Ellen said, "I'm not going to hide something I'm proud of," then pushed it out even more. There's a lesson for me, not regarding busty confidence, but self-advocacy. Ellen said, "You're not my mother." I never said that to you, though I do recall, as a child, asking if you were my mother. Remember your response? "I'll be whatever you need me to be."

On Sundays, I go with T. and Ellen to Mass at the Cathedral (5 min. walk). Built of local limestone and Irish granite almost a century ago, it stands with its two towers on the hill, dominating the city's skyline, facing the Narrows. The immense interior features magnificent stained glass windows and vaulted ceilings that look like they're decorated in gold. I love listening to the organ and feeling the sound resonate in my chest, then standing outside on the landing with bells chiming joy and cheer. Although I don't understand Latin, I do leave there hopeful divine forces are on our side. Victory to those who are righteous! Am I naïve? Victory to those who are ruthless (e.g., the Nazis)? Oh the horror!

Crag Point. Garden progress? Pesky fox playing hide-and-seek? Leaks in pantry window? # gallons of berries picked? Granddaughter have her baby? Boy? Girl? Say hello to Teo and Fred. Still at odds with each other?

As the world turns,

Princess Violet

PS: Forgot to mention—I had a patch test for TB. All clear. No X-ray required.

FAITH & FIGHTING THE FÜHRER

Today's homily calls on Christians to rally divine faith at the front and at home. Do not desire your own good, instead give yourself to others, your family, community, country, and the Almighty who reigns over us and over those with whom we do battle. The loathsome Führer cannot conquer the hearts and souls of those who fight evil in their everyday lives. Lasting peace comes at a cost of selfless service to and love for others.

31

da stared at my shirtwaist dress. "You want to borrow any old outfit for a posh party? Bet you didn't have too many of those back at your Lighthouse Point." She took a measuring tape off a hook on the wall.

"Crag Point. It doesn't need to be a cocktail dress specifically. I can't afford anything tailor-made."

She measured my bust while I stood, arms outstretched, eyebrows raised. "This event commands tailor-made. You'll have it for free in return for modeling my Fitz Original design to ladies who can afford quality and originality. Ladies like your hostess, Mrs. Barrow. This is a once-in-a-lifetime opportunity for me, Violet."

I hadn't expected such a generous offer. "For me too. I'm flattered. Thank you. But what did you have in mind exactly?"

"It won't be a factory-made war special that says style-rationing on the tag. That's for sure." She stared at the ceiling. "Maybe a modern version of Coco Chanel's little black dress. An LBD designed to flatter a woman's fine features, her curves." She wrapped the tape around my waist, grabbed a pencil, and scribbled the measurements directly on the wooden table.

"Are you sure I'm the right person for this LBD?"

"Aren't you the girl who bragged when I first met her that she wanted to be a weather forecaster? The girl saying V for victory? Where's she now?"

I laughed though I didn't find the comment funny. "She's a shopgirl, remember?"

"That's what she does, not who she is."

"Sounds like you want me to model more than a dress."

"In a way, I do, yes. Wear it with confidence, with the attitude of a woman who recognizes her worth and knows her power."

"Can that woman tap her heels together to get what she wants?"

"I forgot you have a sense of humour. Let me check those measurements again. It needs to fit tight as a peel."

I didn't care how it fit or even what it looked like. I simply wanted something to make Philip proud of his girlfriend. We'd gone to clubs and movies together, but this was my first invitation as his guest at a party and at the home of Mrs. Barrow, of all people. I told the others about the dress and the invitation, hoping they'd congratulate me.

"Ida made me a dress when I was seventeen—first piece of clothing I wore that wasn't a hand-me-down from Lucy or Mom," Theresa said. "Didn't charge me a penny. Skimpy though."

Ellen swayed her hips and pretended to be blowing kisses. "Sounds like a Betty Boop dress. I'll wear an outfit like that one of these days. Don't take my boop-oop-a-doop away!"

"There's no room for cocktail parties in the world I live in," Brigid said. "Not with sailors seasick, homesick, war-sick, body parts blown off by torpedoes or frostbitten."

"It's not just sailors suffering," Noreen said. "There are children begging in the streets—bare feet, rotted teeth, and empty bellies. Why? Because the city's merchants are controlling the prices, driving them up. Call it a let's-profit-from-the-war party."

Ellen sat up, facing me. "Tell Mrs. Barrow, it's true I spilled coal on the carpet. Who needs ten fireplaces anyway? I forgot to open the chimney damper before I set the fire in the grate. I fooled up, but I'm no fool. I'm starting school soon."

I hadn't planned to tell Mrs. Barrow anything, and I refrained from mentioning Brigid's elaborate wedding plans. When I asked Philip about Noreen's accusations, he scoffed.

"Tell your radical friend to stop reading letters to the editor. Public Health and Welfare are in charge of price controls. Gwen, Mrs. Barrow, is not a local merchant. Her money's her grandfather's. He made his fortune in the steel industry, buying ore from Sweden and Bell Island. There's a German connection there somewhere."

Noreen could call it what she wanted. For me, it was a meet-Philip's-girlfriend party. I pictured him introducing me to his friends, saying,

"I wish I had her for a co-pilot." They'd want to learn my secret for making accurate forecasts. I'd push out my chest like Ellen, stand confident like Noreen, polished like Brigid, in control of everything and everyone like Theresa, and with Mrs. Doyle's do-as-I-say attitude. I'd tell them, "It has nothing to do with secrets. It involves observing and interpreting signs and patterns, measuring, calculating, and reasoning."

They'd say, "Tell us more."

Eventually, Philip would announce, "Enough chatter! They're playing our song. Let's dance."

After, he'd invite me to his hotel room. I'd make sure to arrive home by midnight. No one on Chapel Street would ever know where I'd been and what I'd done.

YOU'RE INVITED

Mrs. G. Barrow of Circular Manor will host a cocktail party, September 4, in honour of Captain Philip Campbell. The much-admired and respected Captain is returning to dedicated RAF service in central Newfoundland. Those curious about who else may be in attendance need merely to think of the names of the city's elite. On the arm of this great man will be the ravishing Violet Morgen with a dress and an attitude designed to turn heads.

I left Chapel Street in a taxi, alongside Philip, proud to be the hero's girlfriend, his guest at a cocktail party in one of the city's finest manors. I leaned in closer to him, longing for his attention, his respect and approval too. "In case you're wondering. I won't utter a peep about you-know-what."

"What exactly?"

"Torpedoes and U-boats. Remember Lucy and Bell Island?"

"Aye, I do. Apology accepted." He put his arm around me and kissed my forehead.

I rested my head on his shoulder, thinking how lucky I'd been to have met him. Did it matter to him that we would soon be seeing much less of each other? Once the war ended, would he return overseas? Would that be it for our relationship? What was our relationship? "Will I see you next month?"

"If I make it back from overseas."

I wished he wouldn't talk that way. "Of course you will. Please mark the twenty-sixth in your calendar for the wedding. They'd love to see—"

"We don't need to talk about that now, do we, Violet?" He turned away from me to gaze through the window.

"No, darling," I said. He obviously had something on his mind, something that wasn't about me—or was it?

At Circular Manor, a man in a black, double-breasted coat opened the taxi's door. We walked single file up the front steps, Philip ahead of me. I went immediately to the bathroom because the sleeveless and strapless dress with its built-in bra felt like it had fallen below my chest. Ida hadn't warned me I'd need to constantly tug up on it. Little black dress indeed. No wonder Theresa hadn't let me show it to Mrs. Doyle or Ellen.

In the bathroom, though I couldn't find a bathtub, I was impressed by the porcelain cross handles on the sink, even more impressed when I turned the one marked *H* and the water gushed out, steaming.

Someone knocked. "Can I get you anything in there, miss?" the voice said.

To myself I said, "Yes, I'll have one of these bathrooms for our Chapel Street shack." I opened the door to a mature woman in a black uniform with white apron, cuffs, and collar.

She took the raglan out of my hands. "Mr. Philip—the Captain, I mean—he's in the main room," she said and walked away.

In her place was a waiter wearing a white jacket with black buttons and bow tie. He held a tray in front of me. I peered at the drinks in shades of red and brown with garnishes of decorative cherries, slices of lime, and flower petals.

He pointed to a cocktail. "Care for a Downtown Daiquiri?"

The glass's etched floral pattern suited the elegance of my elbow-length gloves in shiny black satin. However, its inverted cone shape made it too shallow to satisfy my thirst. I drank it in a gulp, then followed with a Heart's Content.

"Like the Grand Hall, do you?" the waiter said. I'd been admiring the staircase's balustrade, its bottom post shaped into a horse's head. "A master carver from Harbour Grace did that," he said. "Rugs come from Persia, wherever that is. The chandeliers get their glitter from France."

"Where does the cocktail's glitter come from?"

"From me. I'm Robert. Lay your empty glass on the tray. That's the Muddy Mary. Try one of each, then tell me which one's the best."

If the guests were anything like Robert, they would keep me good company. When I told him I lived with Ellen, he asked how she was doing.

"She's doing perfectly." The drinks tasted perfect. The setting was perfect. The evening was going to be perfect.

COCKTAIL MENU

Downtown Daiquiri: Demerara rum, sea salt, & molasses. Smoky.

Heart's Content: Jamaican light rum, rhubarb, & plums. Smooth.

Muddy Mary: Dogberry & apple wines. Sour.

Stephenville Sling: Gin, partridgeberry juice, & brown sugar. Sweet.

32

Philip reappeared at last, debonair in his RAF summer service dress jacket. He held his visor cap under his arm, badge visible, gold wings and crown with "RAF Ferry Command" on black felt.

I stood on my toes to kiss him. "I'd love to dance with you."

He fidgeted with his tie like it irritated his neck. He'd been doing it ever since I joined him in the taxi. "What happened? I thought you were behind me."

I tugged up on my dress and laid my empty glass on the waiter's tray, then took a Stephenville Sling, something sweet to mask the sour taste of the Muddy Mary. "I was solving a problem with my dress."

He reached his hand around my waist, then let go. "Aye. Do you have anything to cover up?"

"You don't like it?"

"I told you this is a formal event. That's strapless, sleeveless, short, and, frankly—" he paused, "shocking."

"I thought you'd prefer that." I leaned in closer to him just as a woman reached out to shake my hand.

"Delighted to meet Philip's friend at last. He's told me so much about you, Violet. I hear you have a barometer." She laughed, tilting back her head. "Gwendolyn Barrow. Please call me Gwen."

I looked up at Philip and smiled, flattered that he'd talked about me. As for Gwen, after listening to Ellen's tales of the haughty and wicked Mrs. Barrow, I'd expected horns and hooves. Instead, she had an attractiveness that distinguished her from most women I'd served at the Royal Stores. I'd never seen her there or on Water Street. Her maids would have done most of the shopping and likely took care of everything else—served her meals, prepared her bath, made her bed, and curled her shoulder-length blond hair. She seemed young for a widow. Ellen had said she was thirty-four. Perhaps class and money compensated for the normal wear and tear of aging.

"Pleased to meet you, Gwen," I said, my lips tripping over the words.

She laid her hand on my waist. "Well, I say I've never seen anything like it." Her laugh was a high-pitched staccato that made me want to plug my ears. "A daaling dress, nonetheless. Daaling girl too," she said. She laughed again and held her smile so long, I suspected she wanted me to notice her perfect teeth. "Come join the others." She waved to the waiter. "Robert, tend to the Captain's guest. Serve her another cocktail."

VIOLET'S ADVENTURES IN NEWFYJOHN*

Oh, this is the place where the innocent gather,
With black dress and gloves, and tight fit all around;
All sights on her figure, with eyes growing bigger,
She'll bedazzle them all, her confidence found.
Sung to the tune of "The Squid-Jiggin' Ground"

I'd met the hostess and, aside from the way she smiled and laughed, I liked her. How would I explain that to Ellen? I entered the living room with another Stephenville Sling, sucking on a cherry, my arm linked into Philip's. In an instant, we were swarmed by people wanting to shake the hero's hand. Someone said, "Bring us back a bottle of Irish whiskey," someone else, "Scotch." The conversation revolved around Philip, which revolved around flying, with guests revolving around him. The only person who seemed to want to revolve around me was the waiter. No sooner had I emptied my glass than he'd served me another cocktail.

The chatter of so many voices and the bright lights made my head spin. No ladies fanned themselves, yet the room felt terribly hot. I thought my legs might leave me stranded. I squirmed out from the crowd and headed to the room's edge. I had to steady myself twice on the floor's unevenness. What a relief to find an empty armchair in the corner, away from the traffic and noise.

I hadn't been there for long when a man sat in the chair beside me. He'd unfastened the top button in his olive-coloured gabardine jacket with medals adorning its lapels. I sympathized with him. My dress felt uncomfortable too. I had to be constantly tugging up on it.

"Taking a break?" he said.

I winked.

"I've no idea how I get roped into these events," he said. "At least their Scotch is good. Wish I could afford to stock it at home. Not on a Canadian salary, I can't. We aren't paid like the Yanks. There's a reason their boots shine bright as their smiles. I should introduce myself. I'm Major Ingles." He stretched out his hand to shake mine.

I raised my glass. "Violet."

"That's quite the dress you're wearing, Violet. Very daring. Here with someone?"

I asked myself the same question. "Are you one of Rose's officers?"

"Who?"

My glass was empty, my thirst finally quenched, taste buds overstimulated. "Never mind."

"You don't seem like a local girl. From Montreal by any chance?"

"*Ooh là là.*"

"Bingo! I knew I was right. What I meant regarding the dress is that I find you quite attractive. Women from Montreal usually are. Speak French?"

We were an odd pair, he attentive to the woman beside him, she scanning the guests, wondering why there was two of everyone.

"*Ich spreche Deutsch.*" The words required too much effort. Was I losing my ability to speak German?

"That doesn't sound French. You still haven't told me who you're here with. As you may have guessed from my uniform, I'm with the RCAF, stationed at our new air base in Torbay."

I imagined sitting on Signal Hill instead of in a stuffy place with stuffy people. I'd gaze in the distance at that base. "Royal Canadian Air Fog. Worst site ever for an airport." I made a ha-ha sound. "Too foggy even for gulls. The Germans are laughing at the Canadians."

"I doubt the—"

I expected him to say Germans weren't known for their sense of humour. He should have met my father. They would have been about the same age. He didn't get to finish because Mrs. Barrow appeared, cutting off the conversation and my view, blurry though it was.

"There she is. This is the second time I've had to search for you, Violet." She sounded displeased, like it was the tenth time.

I touched her dress to move her aside. The silk felt smooth, a rare fabric during a war—one better reserved for parachutes.

She brushed my hand away. "This is Dr. Matthews and his wife from Nova Scotia. My goodness, dear, pull up your dress."

Ida had told me to model it with confidence, and I wouldn't disappoint her. "You're the big blue boss, blue gloves to match, camouflaged for a fine day. Order your pianist to play 'Moonlight Serenade.'"

As if she hadn't heard a word, she continued talking. "Violet's father comes from Whitney Pier, Nova Scotia."

"Ah yes," said the man. "Steel mills and coal mines."

I gazed up at the bottoms of their chins and nostrils. They seemed funny from that angle, but I wasn't amused. I spoke up so she'd be sure to hear me. "Whitney Pier has no air. Sooty coal dust in your hair. Vati's from Germany. Like you, Mrs. Blue. German blood in your veins. Blood made of steel. Steel made of Bell Island ore."

With the armrests for balance, I tried to stand, but fell back into the chair. "Party's a bore." I swung forward, bent over, and out came the sour Muddy Mary. "I'm feeling much better now."

Philip appeared in an instant, attentive to Mrs. Barrow's shriek, the other guests pausing in the middle of sentences to gasp.

"Why's everyone staring?" I said. "How rude. What are you doing, Philip?"

"Your dress, Violet. Help me pull it up over your chest."

I reached an arm around his waist while he pulled up on my dress. "I missed you. Can I have this dance?"

The dancing felt awkward, he on one side, Mrs. Barrow on the other, leading me to the Grand Hall. "I'm so sorry, Philip, daaling," Gwen said. "How dreadfully embarrassing."

"Don't call him daaling," I said. "And by the way, Ellen's no fool. She understands equations. Bet you don't know how to solve for x —"

"Robert," she said, "help the Captain while I get someone to clean up the mess. Dear God."

Philip grabbed my raglan from the maid and twisted my arm into it. I jerked it loose.

"Co-operate, Violet, please."

"You mean, don't say, 'Torpedo, torpedo, torpedo'?"

"Bad enough that you've shamed yourself. You're shaming me and the hostess."

The front door opened, and I felt an invigorating blast of cold air, a perfect temperature for dancing. "Are we going to a club or to your hotel?"

The waiter and Philip walked me down the front steps, then stuffed me into a taxi like I was an oversized piece of luggage.

"Goodbye, Violet," Philip said, then shut the door.

The taxi jerked forward. I looked back but he was already out of sight.

By my side was Robert, no tray, cocktails, or glitter. "Sorry, Violet. I blame Barrow for nagging me to quench your thirst. What happens when you drink normally?"

"I don't drink normally or abnormally. You were my first cocktail ever." I rested my head on his shoulder, wishing it was Philip's. "Down the trough. Up to the crest. Life's so bumpy. You think you got it figured out and there's fog, fog, fog."

TRAVEL: WHITNEY PIER

United Empire Loyalists, Scottish Highlanders, German Jews—Whitney Pier hosts them all. Our largest group of immigrants comes from Newfoundland. While at the Pier, visit one of its many houses of worship, including a Russian Orthodox church and a Hebrew synagogue. Listen for the squeal of trains on rails and horns marking the time of day. Feel the coal dust against your skin. Breathe in the sulphur. Witness the molten slag flowing like lava into the harbour. Let Whitney Pier appeal to your senses. Book your trip today.

33

September 21, 1942

Dear Maryanne,

I've been thinking a lot about Vati's death lately (one year ago this month). An insignificant misstep destroyed him along with the life we had together. Maybe there's a reason it had to happen. Ellen told me she was sorry I'd lost my father but that my loss was her gain. Without me, she wouldn't be in school.

War. At Crag Point we could have pretended there wasn't a war. Forget trying to pretend in the city. Earlier this month, two steamships filled with iron ore, waiting on a convoy, were torpedoed off nearby Bell Island with twenty-nine sailors killed. T. spent last weekend over there comforting her mother and sister. If you believe the newspapers, RAF bombers recently struck 500 German factories and industrial sites. Revenge is in the air. Everyone's saying we (St. John's) are next. Anti-torpedo baffles have been installed across the Narrows. They're supposed to offer protection from torpedoes like those rumoured to have hit close to the harbour's entrance in March. I have a feeling we'll need a lot more than baffles to keep us safe.

Cards were sent to households advising what to do in the event of an incendiary bomb attack. Officials are making plans for a potential evacuation of women and children to the city's outskirts. Insurance companies are warning of a conflagration. We're supposed to keep baths and sinks filled. Meanwhile, the city's water pressure is below normal due to the hot weather and drought (49 days without rain). Noreen blames the American base for consuming so much of our water. The last fire to ravage the city took place in the month of July with the same dry conditions as now. To make matters worse, there's a lack of firefighting equipment, personnel, gas masks, etc. Free sand is available from fire halls, but you need a vehicle to pick it up.

Work. Good news first. Congratulations to me on successful completion of my examinations. Results received shortly after my last letter. Overall average 78%, which qualifies me for a diploma though not for much else—not even to work at the Royal Stores. Bad news next. Ida let me go, though nothing to do with my exam results. Only temporarily, I hope. We had a falling out. I won't trouble you with details (cocktail party, skimpy dress, muddy mind).

Philip. It's over. Kaputt. Before heading overseas, he telephoned. "It's a matter of suitability," he said in an official voice like someone explaining why I didn't qualify for work. "The age difference, in particular, background too." When I asked what he meant, he said the fact that I had to ask further reinforced his point. ARGH! I offered to return a watch he gave me in June. "Sober up, Violet," he said. In the end, I gave it to Ellen. I am now wearing my old watch.

Surprisingly, though T. had warned me not to date him, there was no I-told-you-so. She said if he showed up on our doorstep, she'd call the paddy wagon to take him away, that he didn't deserve me. Noreen wouldn't let me off easy. She said to avoid people who colonize me, who make me feel inferior or less worthy. Brigid's been kindly inviting me to go to movies or dances with her and Danny. I'm not in the mood and dread the thought that P. might be in the city and I'd run into him.

Chapel St. Yes, we now have a telephone. Catapulted into the future. Four to a line, and two ring no less than once per hour. You could be waiting that long to reach the operator. Last month, T. took the receiver from me in the middle of a conversation with P. "If it's the operator listening, I'll make sure you lose your job." Noreen spilled raspberry jam on the phone directory's cover. T. said she'd be its caretaker from then on. Now we can never find it. Ellen accused T. of being "too cheap" to pay for a private instead of a party line. The argument ended with T. warning her she was in for a rude awakening and Ellen saying T. should join the convent.

Noreen and Brigid don't need a reason to argue, but the telephone gave them one. Noreen was annoyed with Brigid talking on the phone, swooning over Danny. She grabbed the handset from Brigid and hung it up. "You find it annoying too, don't you, Violet?" Noreen said. Actually, I do but couldn't *admit it any more than I could tell Noreen to stop putting me in the middle of their disputes. Modern technology changes people's personal lives. How they behave too. Here's to the good old days.*

That sums up the past month with its record-breaking low moods. Speaking of records, summer is over calendar-wise, though you wouldn't know it given the scorching temperatures. Seventy-two yesterday. At least one hundred in my bedroom. Mrs. D. was right, the third floor's not fit for habitation.

Crag Point. You may have guessed it by now, the change in the weather that supposedly forced my early departure was a lie—a necessary one. Looking back, I wish I'd handled the situation differently so that our last moments together weren't spent arguing. I also wish I'd written to the authorities the instant I realized there was a problem with Teo. They would have sent him back to Toronto. Women don't earn the same as men, but surely the authorities would have compensated me at least until the station was decommissioned. I wouldn't need much money except for books and subscriptions. Growing our own vegetables, preserving berries, keeping hens, eating lots of fish—none of that costs a penny. Here's wishing for a pair of silver shoes or ruby slippers to take me back!

Soberly yours,

Violet

PS: I did visit Goose Hill to see if you'd sent mail there. I left a forwarding address. The owner says hello to your granddaughter.

TELEPHONE GUIDE

Instructions: Using equipment provided and installed by the telephone company, take the receiver off its hook. For outgoing calls, hold the mouthpiece near your lips and carefully pronounce numbers for operator. For incoming calls, listen to your ring cadence (e.g., short-long-short). *Advisory*: Party-line subscribers must not answer or listen to the calls of other parties. Conversations should last no more than five to eight minutes. Defence services take precedence over those of civilians and may result in delays. Complaints related to abuse of rules and infringement of privacy should be made promptly to the Chief Operator. *Cost*: $24.00 per annum for four-party-line service, payable to the Avalon Telephone Company, Ltd.

34

I t never rains but it pours" proved itself true at the start of October and not merely because of the easterly gale that, in one day, brought double the total rainfall for August and September combined. City workers scrambled to deal with flooded streets while residents complained of water funnelling into their basements. Small streams became raging rivers, rivers became ponds, ponds swelled to the size of lakes, and lakes to what seemed like the size of the sea. The basement didn't flood at Chapel Street though the excess water gave the mice an excuse to make themselves at home in the kitchen once everyone but I had gone to work.

Each morning, I stared through the window at a dreary, black-and-white landscape under grey skies. I wished the world could be more forgiving and wondered what my life would be like if there hadn't been cocktails in it.

Noreen had lent me money for October's board. Along with it came advice. "That's enough lazing in front of the window. Enough brooding too. Before long, you'll be cooing like a pigeon. Your pilot's gone. Pick yourself up and get back to work."

"It's more complicated than that."

"Not if you don't see it that way," Noreen said.

"Maybe it all happened for a reason."

"Who put that idea into your head? Things happen and we deal with them. Tell your boss, employees' personal lives have no bearing on their work."

It had been one month since I'd last heard from Ida. She'd called two days after the party to tell me she'd heard about what happened. My excuses had upset her even more.

"Don't blame anything on the dress," she'd said. "The dress didn't get drunk, throw up on the carpet, and insult the hostess."

The conversation ended with Ida shouting into the phone, saying if I couldn't admit my wrongs, she couldn't employ me and not to bother coming into work. She'd hung up in the middle of my apology. I hadn't meant to blame the dress, though it wasn't my fault it kept falling so low or that Philip didn't like it. If anything deserved blame, it was the cocktails. Why had Mrs. Barrow encouraged the waiter to ensure I always had one in hand?

When I finally mustered the courage to visit the Royal Stores, I found Ida unpacking, sorting, and storing new inventory. While I helped her move ladies' winter coats from the boxes to hangers, I apologized for not being an ideal employee and promised to never again do anything that would soil my, her, or the store's reputation. "I learned my lesson. There's Del Monte fruit cocktail and cocktails with a whole lot more. Both have sweet and sour tastes. Only one will make you do and say things you'll regret."

She continued unpacking boxes, paying attention to the contents rather than to me. "I had high hopes for the dress, even paid the seamstress overtime to make it, spent hours at the sewing machine myself. You were supposed to be free advertising. You were advertising, all right."

"Please let me make up for it. I have an idea. The Victory Woman collection. A percentage of sales of fashion items could go toward the purchase of Victory Bonds and war certificates. 'Women helping women' could be the slogan. My friend Noreen works in a clothing factory. She says the future's in synthetics. She knows seamstresses interested in taking on work on the side."

"Thanks, but for once I haven't got clothing designs on my mind. I'm off to Halifax in a week. A friend's hitching up with a sailor, and guess who's the maid of honour. I'll be the first in my family to visit Canada, travelling on the *Caribou*. Can't wait to get away from this place—the store, the city, the island, my dull life. God, I wish the war would end so we could get on with our lives. You're the expert on U-boats. Should I be worried, bring my own torpedo netting or a German dictionary for the ferry ride?"

I forced a laugh, wondering if I should bluntly ask for my job back. "You'll be sailing on the Cabot Strait on a passenger ferry. The Nazis are chasing merchant ships, freighters, and military targets in the St. Lawrence. I seriously doubt they'd waste a torpedo on a civilian target when they could kill as many with a box of matches."

She stood, hands on her hips, head cocked to the side like the possibility of such an attack hadn't occurred to her. "You with your matches and fires. Why do they sail with lights off?"

"Blackout rules. Seasickness, not torpedoes, may be your biggest worry."

"Glad I booked a cabin in that case." She flipped through her calendar. "Pop by when I'm back. Ask your friend where the factory gets its synthetic fabrics. How much do its best seamstresses charge for work on the side? Is their rate any better than what the Royal Stores clothing factory charges? Gather some information for me while I'm gone. Theresa said you were looking to redeem yourself. This might be a place to start."

WOLVES IN DARK WATERS

Hiding in our waters are 220-foot-long creatures made of steel, prowling in packs, chasing convoys and merchant ships as they deliver much-needed resources to our overseas Allies. In the past six months, these ruthless predators have been hunting in the St. Lawrence and have preyed on British, Dutch, Greek, and Canadian vessels, with a particular appetite for freighters. Fortunately, the wolves have shown no appetite for passenger vessels sailing in the Cabot Strait.

I trudged back to Chapel Street, one minute thinking about redemption and the next worrying about how to convince Mrs. Doyle to allow me to postpone paying November's board. That meant lying again about why I wasn't working. The last time, she'd glared at me like she didn't believe my story about sales slowing down after the summer and employees let go temporarily. This time, I'd need to be better prepared. I stopped by Mrs. Clarke's store for a loaf of factory-made bread and a package of easy-to-chew Purity Factory Jam Jams, Mrs. Doyle's favourite.

I stood at the counter while she tidied the shelves, humming a tune that resembled nothing I'd ever heard. "Should I leave the money with you, Mrs. Clarke?" She didn't reply, so I said it again and louder.

She came to the counter, squeezed the bread out of shape and crushed the Jam Jams when she stuffed them into the bag. "You're looking nice and dry, today. I'd say you were nice and dry during the storm too."

I decided against asking for credit, laid one dollar on the counter, then waited for my change. "Fortunately, yes. We certainly dodged a bullet there."

"You could have warned me," she said. "I heard you got a keen nose for weather. I've been on the phone every day, fighting for Mayor Carnell's ear. It's too late now for him to do anything. My coal's soaking in a pool of water."

The signs had indeed pointed to a storm—a quick change in wind direction, the black cumulonimbus clouds, a radical drop in barometric pressure, and the telltale scent of a charge in the air, the ground readying to satisfy thirst. "We needed the rain, but I'm sorry it had to flood your basement."

"And sorry you should be. You must have seen it coming, and you kept quiet, no warning. Radio's useless, never tells us anything. No forecast of a storm in the *Evening Telegram* either. We know more about the goings-on in Russia. If the *Daily News* wants to forewarn us about storms, they ought to do it on the front page, not hidden in the ads."

"As you know, since the war began, they've cut back on radio reports of weather. We don't want the enemy picking up the transmission, do we? If I warn you, I'd have to do it for others in the neighbourhood. I could end up in trouble."

"There's no enemies, trouble, or transmission in this neighbourhood. We're a hard-working bunch making the best of a soggy situation. Once upon a civilized time, we knew what to expect. The weather's not how it used to be. Why? Anything to do with the bombing and fires overseas heating everything up?"

She was right. Summer temperatures had left the city parched. So much dust blew around, I could imagine I was in the Sahara. "I don't understand it any better than you, Mrs. Clarke." I shrugged. "Maybe we should blame it on the war's increased factory production and the hot air spewing out of their smokestacks."

"At this rate, if the Nazis don't burn us alive, the sun will. Either that or we'll be drowned by floods in our homes. Start building the ark."

35

October 9, 1942

Dear Maryanne

NOTICE: *Return address is on envelope. Please return to sender if letters are undeliverable. Are you reading this letter, Maryanne, or is the postal clerk? Is it you, Thomas?*

Work. *Ida is away, back Oct. 14. Fingers crossed she'll rehire me. Without any references, who else would employ me? In the meantime, I've taken into consideration an interesting proposition made by a local store owner, Mrs. Clarke, to alert her to upcoming storms—alerts she will pass on to customers, such as those with leaky roofs. Good way to start building my reputation? Next thing you know, people will be saying, "That Chapel Street girl is the east coast's version of Lauchie McDougall, a proper weather diviner." Either that or the authorities will be banging on my door accusing me of contravening regulations.*

Chapel St. *Everyone except Violet is busy. Busiest is Brigid. Each week, there's a concert to fund the Caribou Hut's operating expenses. Lately, she's been volunteering with the Red Cross, helping victims of vessels hit by torpedoes. Many are dying from infected wounds, pneumonia too. Last month's news mentioned a new treatment, penicillin, but it isn't yet available here. When not at the factory, Noreen's attending or organizing meetings. About what?* ~~Overthrowing the Commission of Government.~~ *Union, trades, and labour council meetings, I think. I miss having her around to chat with.*

T.'s working overtime to earn extra money for Christmas. Ellen says what T. needs is a boyfriend and claims to know just the man. If her attempts to play Cupid are successful, she'll have more freedom because T. will be distracted. Freedom to do what? Almost one-quarter of the population are servicemen, and she's a busty sixteen-year-old dying to have an adoring boyfriend. Under other circumstances, in a safer world, I'd wish her the very best.

Philip. I was tempted to send a note to invite him to be my guest at Brigid's wedding. You'd probably tell me the same as everyone—forget him. I'm trying. T. brought home a half-dozen cans of soup from the base and popular with the Americans. After she stored them in the cupboard, I turned them around to avoid seeing the label with the name in bold red: Campbell's. Are the classified ads for the upcoming Halloween balls and dances designed to frustrate me? Why, when I listen to Mrs. D.'s radio, do they play "Moonlight Serenade" (our song)? The other day, I caught myself scribbling on a blank page of my commonplace book, "Captain Philip Campbell." Next, I wrote "Violet loves Philip." Then I wrote "Violet Campbell" and promptly tore the page out of the fine notebook. While reading the news of a plane crash in Nfld this week, I almost hoped to see his name among the crew. Shameful of me, I know, but I feel so horribly bitter I can taste it.

In the end, I couldn't invite P. regardless. Brigid doesn't want ex-boyfriends in attendance because they could bring bad luck. She imagines every possible failure (torpedo attack on the city, snowstorm, fire, air raid, change of mind—Danny's). We'll be relieved once the day arrives (Dec. 26). She's invited one of Danny's Ping-Pong pals to make up the eighth person at our table—Benjamin Dion, RCAF ground staff. She claims we have something in common. She wouldn't say what, except that we were sure to have plenty to talk about.

Travels and whereabouts. Someday I'll venture across the island, board the SS Caribou, and sail through the Cabot Strait to Nova Scotia. I'll visit Whitney Pier where Vati worked and the port of Halifax where he and Mutti first set foot on this continent. I'll retrace their voyage in reverse across the Atlantic, battling the same currents and winds in the opposite direction. First Rotterdam, then Berlin, or what remains of those cities once the last bombs have fallen, flames are doused, the dead buried and mourned.

Yours forever,
Violet

PS: Recently, half-awake, alone in the kitchen, I poured two cups of tea and laid one opposite me on the table. Half a year apart and I'm still not used to being away from you.

SLEEK AND SPLENDID *CARIBOU*

Built in 1925, the SS *Caribou* serves on the Cabot Strait between Newfoundland and Nova Scotia, having made 1,600 round trips transporting freight, railcars, and passengers. The hull's thick steel means the vessel can take on heavy ice and dense sea conditions. The first-class decks host a dining room, smoking saloon, and social hall with amenities including writing tables and a piano. The smoke billowing from its stack comes from coal-fired boilers that power the vessel and produce sufficient steam to ensure heat for passengers' cabins, all of which are equipped with electric lights. Remember the *Caribou* when making your travel plans.

36

Autumn seemed pitifully drab compared to the technicolour summer when I was proudly earning a salary and, most importantly, was happily in love. Now I was shamefully unemployed and unhappily in love with nothing, not even the sun, to brighten my mood.

When the telephone rang that morning, with our short-long-short ring cadence, I wished it could be Ida calling to rehire me, but I knew she'd still be on the train from Port aux Basques.

I answered, curious who could be calling while everyone was at work.

"It's me, Theresa." She sniffled, then blew her nose, the noise echoing into the receiver and my ear. "The *Caribou*'s gone. A torpedo hit her earlier this morning. I'm sick to my stomach, thinking of Ida in those waters."

Judging by how I felt, the sickness must have been contagious. I pictured the last time I'd seen Ida and I'd insisted the *Kriegsmarine* wouldn't waste a torpedo on a civilian vessel, overly self-confident, wanting to impress her, to win her respect—anything to convince her to rehire me.

"Ellen's right," Theresa said. "What's the point of being worked to the bone if you could be wiped off the face of this earth one breath to the next?" Her tone shifted from sad to mad. "I've decided to take a day's leave tomorrow, spend a couple of hours listening in on other callers." She hung up as did I and the eavesdropping party-line subscribers.

Stories emerged of loss of innocent life, of a sailor, *Mother* tattooed on his arm, a Nova Scotian bride, a mother with three children, the captain and his two sons, a new graduate coming to visit his parents, and a corporal on leave to marry his sweetheart. The slow, solemn peal of the Cathedral's bells rang out over the city. People walked the streets, heads down, without exchanging glances.

Theresa stayed up late, downing cup after cup of tea and shouting at the phone, cursing the party line. The hint of her reflection in the windowpane showed a bowed head, arms and elbows resting on the table. She was the first person I'd witnessed crying other than Vati in the final weeks when his headaches worsened, and Maryanne when he died. I was too shocked to cry, incredulous to think I could have lost a friend, and terrified of what this ruthless attack meant for the war. The Nazis were willing to kill defenceless women and children. No wonder they were winning.

Theresa wiped her nose with a handkerchief and fidgeted with it. "Growing up on Bell Island, I'd be struggling to make ends meet, picking berries and selling tarts to the miners, getting by on fish and potatoes. I had to hold everything together because if I flapping didn't, who would? Dad was gone, rest in peace, Mom with a bad stomach, Lucy with a broken heart, Ellen in diapers. What was Ida up to while I was playing Mom and Pop? Hanging outside the store on Bell Island like she owned the place or at her grandmother's playing with the sewing machine. Grand life at home, father a clerk in an office, no soot under the nails or in his lungs, no ten-hour shifts, six days a week, risking his life in tunnels two and three miles out under the sea. Her uncle got her the job at the Royal Stores. Did I have an uncle, aunt, or daddy to find me work? You bet I didn't. It's a tough world out there. You got to be tough back at it to survive."

The world was not only tough but arbitrary. Vati's fall had proved that. He should have lived another quarter of a century. Tough, arbitrary, and unpredictable too, with a war that licensed random attacks on innocent victims. Millions were dying, including people like Ida, a woman with drive, ambition, and so much to offer the world. That she could be gone forever seemed unimaginable. She'd talked about her future as if it was simply a map to follow to get to the other end of the city. Along the way, she'd take advantage of every opportunity.

"I wouldn't have got through school without her," Theresa said. "Where could I scrounge up an hour or two for homework or to study? Ida always let me copy off her, let me cheat on tests too. I never said thank you. Didn't know how because I grew up with nothing to be thankful for." She put a handkerchief over her mouth to mute her sobbing, then ran upstairs.

In the morning, she seemed even more tired than me, eyes half-closed, hunched over, feet shuffling. If I'd had a barometer to measure her mood, its needle would be limp. Did she realize her skirt's hem was off in places and she had a run in her stocking?

For breakfast, she'd prepared a mix of reheated and fresh porridge, molasses already added and rationed by her. "There's a shortage, in case you haven't heard."

Brigid pushed aside her bowl. "When I'm married, I'll serve eggs and bacon with coffee, fresh orange juice, and milk."

Theresa laid down the kettle and sat at the table. "That's grand, Brigid. Make it for your breakfast from now on, for us too. Fruit cocktail on the side. Tea, not coffee. If I think of anything else, I'll let you know before I place my order."

"Good job putting Miss Bourgeois in her place," Noreen said, "making gourmet breakfasts for Yankee Danny because nothing we do in Newfoundland could ever meet her American standards."

Theresa pointed her spoon at Noreen. "I don't see you getting up a half-hour early to make tea and porridge for us. Where's the equality in that arrangement?"

Noreen shook her head. "No one asked you to. You do it because of Ellen."

"In the US, freedom's more important than equality," Brigid said.

"Good luck down there in freedom land where I hear certain people still want the right to own slaves. They'd enslave us if we gave them the chance. You'll be back here in two or three years, wishing you never left."

"Stop arguing, the two of you."

"I can't get through to her, anyway," Noreen said. "No loyalty to her roots, no understanding of the history of this place, the centuries of control and power by outsiders—"

"Tyranny at the hands of the big bad wolf. Merchants oppressing the hard-working fishermen. It's an exaggerated view of the world, a story you create to suit your commie fantasy. I've had my fill. Consider these my last words to you."

Noreen clapped. "Yippee!"

"Enough!" Theresa shouted.

"What about me? Who'll make my breakfast?" Ellen said.

Theresa stood, hand on one hip. "You? Careful or you'll turn out like me, wasting your life, waiting on everyone else."

"How come you said nothing to Violet?"

Theresa rolled her eyes. "Breakfast doesn't matter for Miss Queen of Sheba, fired from her job, mourning that pompous pilot she never should have got tangled up with in the first place. She can sleep in till noon, eat breakfast at dinnertime, then be off to play with her barometer, loiter at the Gosling Library, or go for a stroll in Bannerman Park. Grand life. Wish it was mine."

I didn't bother to defend myself. What could I say? Theresa was right. My life was pointless, and I was going nowhere.

TRAGEDY BY THE NUMBERS

Time of strike: ~03:40.

Date: October 14, 1942.

Location: ~20 nautical miles south of Port aux Basques, Nfld.

Conditions: ~50°F, 20 mph winds.

Lost lives: 57 military personnel, 31 crew, 49 civilians.

Lost mail: 84 bags of letters, 170 of parcels, 891 of newspapers & prints.

37

With Theresa hovering over me, I searched the newspaper's list of survivors and those missing. Ida's name wasn't there. Theresa said she wouldn't trust the papers to tell the truth, still angry that the September attacks on Bell Island had been hushed up by the censors. "One of these nights we'll be killed in our sleep, and no one will hear tell of it. Since morale's more important, let's pretend nothing bad ever happens. Well, it does."

Friday's papers reported that an additional thirty bodies had been found, along with three unidentified women.

"She's one of the unidentified, I bet," Theresa said. By Saturday, she was talking about the funeral, whether it would be on Bell Island or in St. John's, whether the store would give any employees leave to attend. "I don't have any days left. I'll have to take it without pay if I want to go to another one. I at least owe Ida that."

I had yet to lose anyone in the war and didn't want Ida to be the first. "Don't give up hope too soon, Theresa. I'll go to the Royal Stores Monday morning. They're sure to know something."

Once the day came, I hurried downtown, trying not to imagine the unwelcome news I might hear at the store—shopgirls talking about Ida in the past tense—"She was a better boss than Mr. Russell."

The first thing I saw when I entered the store was one of the shopgirls sobbing, two others comforting her. I assumed the worst until I noticed everyone else going about their business, serving customers as though Ida was simply upstairs sorting through new inventory. As it turned out, the girl was mourning the loss of her nephew. Before long, I was heading back to Chapel Street to give Theresa good news.

"They better be right," she said after I told her.

"I couldn't believe it either until one of the girls showed me a telegram Ida had sent to the store. 'Return delayed. Oct 21.'"

"Be there bright and early to see her for yourself. Call me at the base and let me know."

I should have given Ida time to settle back into work before I went to see her, but I selfishly needed to confess my mistake, to hear her say it didn't matter and that she would rehire me. I was glad to find her alone and not have anyone else see me crying. I hadn't expected to be abruptly overwhelmed by my bottled-up emotions. I felt sorry for myself as someone who'd lost all those close to her—parents, partner, Maryanne, to a large degree, and nearly Ida.

She stood behind an ironing board waiting for the iron to heat up, a pleated skirt laid out in front of her.

I went behind the board and wrapped my arms around her, my head resting on her shoulder.

"Good to see you, Violet. Gracious. Are those tears for me?"

I stood back and lowered my head. "Sorry. I'm like this sometimes when I'm overtired." I wiped my eyes. "I stupidly pretended to know what those U-boat captains were thinking. If anything had happened, I would have—"

"Don't think any more about it. Keep playing with your barometer. Leave the war to the generals to figure out." She unplugged the iron, set it aside, and grabbed some hangers.

"I thought you were gone." I sniffled.

"Glad to know I'd be missed."

"You were lucky."

"Lucky's not the word. If I hadn't met Frank. If I hadn't changed my ticket at the last minute to spend a couple of days with him in Halifax, so many ifs, makes me think I drew an ace instead of a joker for a change. Either that or God's giving me a break, payback for all those prayers I said up until I was twelve. Thank you, God. Thank you, SS *Burgeo*. If I'm ever married and have a kid, I'm naming him or her Burgeo in honour of the ship that got me home safe and sound."

"Did you cross in daylight?"

She nodded. "You'd think it'd be safer at night."

"The *Caribou* proved that wrong."

"You should have seen me, on deck the whole trip, first in line for the life raft, a life belt over every scrap of clothing I'd taken with me. I was frozen, but I didn't dare go inside. I'll be having nightmares for the rest of my life, picturing passengers clinging to rafts with holes in the bottom, women crying, babes screeching."

"I underestimated the value of a passenger vessel as a target. Freight, mail, plenty of servicemen and women. No wonder they—"

"Underestimated is right, but you're not the only one assumed the Nazis wouldn't target a passenger vessel in these waters. No more talk of the tragedy for now. I'm so glad to be back in St. John's. The war's got Halifax standing on its head. Glad to be back at work too. Can't believe I'm saying that. I feel so alive. I don't know if it's Frank, dodging that torpedo, or a combination of both." She eyed the ceiling. "I'm like Earhart at the wheel or whatever it is she used to steer her planes. I've got a great idea for a collection of clothing."

"The Victory Woman?" I paused, hoping she might say yes. "Remember? I proposed it last time I saw you."

"I remember. But victory for what? The war? What happens when it's over? Women's lives shouldn't have to revolve around the war, or their work. Show me a woman with her own ideas, her own talents, building her own life, spending her own money. That's the kind of woman I want to design for. Understand what I'm saying?"

"Of course, yes. Does it relate at all to the Victory Woman?"

"It's what victory gives us that matters—freedom. The war's offered women a taste, showed us opportunities we never had during the Depression or before, choices we didn't know existed, skills and smarts we didn't know we had."

"Speaking of opportunity, do you need a shopgirl by any chance? I'm sorry for everything—for having suggested what happened at the party had to do with the dress. Sorry for filling customers' ears with war and weather talk. Sorry for giving you the wrong advice—"

"Let's put all that behind us. And yes, I could use a hand to help gear up for the Christmas rush. Sales are already up throughout the store. Monday to Thursday for now. Interested?"

"Very. I'll be a model employee, I promise."

"Change the subject, please. What did Theresa say when she thought I'd gone down with the ship?"

"She said she wouldn't get over losing you."

"Haven't seen her in ages. I miss the girl. We used to be best friends. Seems like we're so busy, we never see each other anymore. There's a dance at the USO, the American GI's home away from home. Let's go together, the three of us, this Saturday. There'll be no shortage of good dancers to choose from. You're a single woman now that your pilot's flown the coop. Not to worry—they don't serve cocktails."

V FOR VARIETY ENTERTAINMENT

To bolster troop morale, US military bases on the island can expect visits from some of America's top performers, including Bob Hope, Frank Sinatra, and ventriloquist Edgar Bergen. At the United Service Organization (USO), the American oasis in St. John's, watch out for performances by soldiers including trumpeter Leo (Leopoldo) Sandoval and pianist Ralph Walker. No entertainment would be complete without a song by the young crooner Donald Jamieson, Newfoundland's own Bing Crosby. Enjoy an entertaining evening at the USO with friends, old and new.

The streets seemed eerily dark as Theresa and I walked to the USO, flashlights in hand. A dog followed us until she said, "Go away, Blackie. Get on home."

A man tipped his hat at us. "Grand evening, ladies." A truck drove past. We smiled at the compliment in the driver's whistle.

My nose was running, my breath visible in clouds. The wind blew through my woollen coat and mitts. I told Theresa about an idea I wanted to share with Ida. "I wonder what she'd think of women's outerwear designed for protection against severe weather. Freedom from the extremes."

"Weather's the last thing on her or anyone's mind," she said, "unless it's clothing that keeps you cozy in the icy water after your ship's been torpedoed."

When we arrived at the USO, Theresa led the way through the crowds until she spotted Ida, waved, and called her name.

Ida continued dancing until the song ended, then joined us.

Theresa wrapped her arms around her.

Ida looked at me, grinning. "You'd never guess that a woman who wears clothing size extra, extra small could squeeze the wind out of you."

Theresa let go of her. "I reserve those hugs for special occasions, like when a friend who's dear as a sister turns out to be alive, not gone forever."

Ida held Theresa's hand. "Like I said to Violet the other day, glad to know I would've been missed."

"Missed?" Theresa said, then told her about the prayers she'd recited, requests for the Holy Ghost to intercede, and supplications made on her knees in a pew at the Cathedral.

"Did you know, Violet, when Theresa and I were growing up on Bell Island, she was a little squirt sticking out her tongue and throwing rocks at boys?"

Theresa wagged her finger at Ida. "I'd be throwing rocks while you flipped up your skirt for them."

"I was only showing off my designs," Ida said.

They laughed, then continued reminiscing and telling funny anecdotes from their childhood.

"We're boring Violet," Ida said.

"You're not bored, are you, Violet?" Theresa said.

More distracted than bored, realizing how I'd missed the excitement of these evenings, dancing with Philip, his cheek against mine, his hand on my back, his breath on my neck. I even missed the anticipation of the taxi arriving outside, and of course, those first kisses after being apart, he saying "darling," telling me he missed me, that I was Violet, a rare and beautiful flower.

"It's her first night out in over a month," Theresa said. "She's been hiding at home, praying for her job and her boyfriend back. She got one of them at least."

Ida pointed to the far corner. "Speak of the devil. Her Captain Campbell is over there somewhere. I'm sure I saw him while I was dancing."

I stood on my toes, hand on my heart. Last I'd seen him had been from the rear seat of a taxi leaving Circular Manor. Since then, whenever I heard a plane overhead, read about one, or saw a couple kissing, I longed for him. If the orchestra played "Moonlight Serenade," would I dare ask him to dance? Would he give me a second chance? Ida had been upset with me and gotten over it. Mightn't he do the same?

Theresa tapped her foot to the music. "Get out on the dance floor, Violet. Show him what fun you're having with a friend resurrected from a watery grave."

We didn't need to wait for invitations. The American servicemen were lined up and ready. I accepted an offer to dance. The movements felt awkward, my partner and I apologizing for stepping on each other's feet, my fault for steering him to the other side of the room. The song had almost ended when I caught a quick glimpse of Philip. My hands were trembling so much, my partner asked if I was a nervous dancer.

"Yes," I said, just as I spotted him again.

The song ended and the soldier asked for a second dance.

I stood on my toes, searching for Theresa and Ida. "Another time."

"Aw. Give me your name, at least."

"Victoria."

"Nice. You got a telephone number, Vicky?"

"Sorry, no." I edged my way through the crowd of dancers twirling around and bumping into me.

"Small town," Theresa said when I told her I was going home. "Bound to happen. You'll get over him."

"No, I won't, Theresa. Thanks anyway. Tell Ida I'm sorry I had to leave."

"Don't worry about her. She can take care of herself. You're another story. We'll chat later tonight if you wait up for me. Don't walk home by yourself. Got a dollar for the ride?"

I waved goodbye. "Thanks, yes."

A taxi was dropping off passengers as I left the building. I sat in the back seat and told the driver my destination.

He eyed me through the rear-view mirror. "Remember me? I picked you up at the train station around Easter."

"Hello again, Andy. I won't need you to pound on the door tonight."

He laughed. The wheeze in his chest reminded me of Mrs. Doyle's breathing. "You're leaving the USO awfully early. My daughter, Heather, is with her boyfriend at the K of C. That's the hot spot to be on a Saturday evening if you don't mind tight crowds. A nice-looking girl like you must have a boyfriend. Get him to take you there. Where's he tonight?"

"He" was chatting with men in US Air Corps uniforms, his arm around a familiar woman's waist, a woman named Gwen Barrow with everything I lacked—breeding, wealth, class, property, along with privilege and power to command. Who was I if not simply a girl from nowhere, living in a rundown boarding house, selling shoes, wishing she'd never left home?

"Boyfriend? Gone," I said. Forever.

38

November 9, 1942

Dear Maryanne,

The post office has experienced disruptions, but only with international mail. Injured your hand and don't want to dictate correspondence to Teo? You mistakenly wrote 8 or 10 Chapel St. on the envelope? Forgot the stamp? I've written to Fred and am hoping for a prompt and simple explanation.

Chapel St. With zealous censors at work, I doubt you heard about this second Bell Island attack. Destruction of a loading pier, two ships, forty men dead, five from Nfld—proof the war has effectively landed on our doorstep. Not that we needed proof after the Caribou. Poor Ellen's having terrible nightmares. She swears she won't take the ferry again to B.I. until the war ends. Are the Nazis plotting a final pounce before winter storms force them to head for safe ports? Do they have a new land-based strategy? Are they mingling among us at dance halls, concerts, movies, or in stores? These last months of 1942 could prove the deadliest.

T. took a day off to attend the funeral on B.I. The mine was shut for the event and the procession a mile long. She went over Friday past, back last night. The tragedy has hit B.I. hard. Labour shortages and difficulties with shipping mean the mine's not doing well. When it suffers, the whole island is affected. The force of the explosion was felt in the Power household though without physical injury. However, her mother and sister are very much on edge, fearful of another attack.

In happier Chapel St. news, Brigid asked T. to sing at her reception. I'm fairly certain she did it because she knows T. needs a distraction, that she was ready to snap. Now, she practices in the kitchen, hallway, bathroom. At least twice I've had "Over the Rainbow" as background music for my dreams.

Work. I am once again Miss Morgen in ladies' footwear, Royal Stores, where we currently have a special promotion on military and dress oxfords, square toe, leather heel, while supplies last. I'm part-time, as if Ida only partly forgave me. From now on, I plan to be a model employee, one deserving of a glowing reference. Ida's more determined than ever to have her designs made by seamstresses and sold at prices that reflect their high quality. Her new collection is centred around stylish slacks, "designed for versatility, practicality, functionality, and freedom." No Rosie the Riveter overalls. No cinched waists or girdles either. Slacks are much better suited to this climate. Wind turns skirts into weathervanes. Bare legs, even under a coat, are at the mercy of every draft.

City news. Absentee landlords, dilapidated houses with destitute families living in deplorable conditions—welcome to the new St. John's. We applied a fresh coat of whitewash on our house every year, but whitewash wouldn't work in St. John's, not with so much chimney soot. Meanwhile, prices are rising. Imagine paying one dollar for a brace of rabbits! Twelve cents for a pound of sugar and up to $1.20 for a dozen eggs! If the Crag Point hens find out, they'll go on strike.

Children behave like strays. "Got any gum, lady?" Substitute chocolate or cigarettes. They sell the cigarettes for money to buy candy. If this is prosperity, what were they like before the war brought so much cash to the city? Every time I pick up the paper, I find a report of a child drowned in the harbour or run over by a truck. There are juveniles before the courts and gangs of boys stealing old women's handbags in broad daylight, smashing windows, robbing cars and houses. Drunkenness is rampant. I suppose I'd be drinking too if I had to confront the same horrors of war. Every one of them deserves a medal for their service.

Crag Point. This fall, T. and I picked partridgeberries on the hill next to the base. Including the marshberries in our tally, we came away with a bounty of six gallons. She said, had she realized I was a champion picker, she'd have taken me out while the blueberries were ripe. How many gallons have you picked and preserved? Root cellar jammed with potatoes, carrots, turnips, beets, and parsnips? Is Teo enjoying the upstairs rooms in the house? We had a storm surge with gale-force winds last month. Was he on watch?

Relax with a pot of tea, take out paper and pen, and write. Write a to-do list. Write *"This is what I did today."* Write *"Here are the answers to questions in your letters."* Anything will do.

Desperately yours,

Violet

PS: Please let me know if you want me to restart the newspaper subscriptions.

WHAT ARE WE FIGHTING FOR?

Introducing the Fitz Freedom Collection designed for a woman with an appetite for choice. Freedom to wear her moods, realize her dreams, speak her soul. Freedom to stand out in a crowd, to say, "This is who I am. This is what I believe. This is what I want." Freedom to choose comfort over style and admit her curves. Freedom to fly a plane, build a bridge, run a country, drive a taxi. Freedom to be a famous designer or female forecaster. What are we fighting for, if not freedom?

39

blamed myself along with Mrs. Clarke for neighbours coming to the house, expecting Miss Violet to tell them whether, for example, a particular day would be good for hanging out clothes or tarring the roof. Others dropped by to say the trees in their gardens were full of dogberries and asked if it might be a sign of a harsh winter following the spectacular summer. And didn't a girl knock on the door early one Sunday morning, convinced she saw the face of Jesus in a cloud and wanting to know was it a sign of good or foul weather, punishment or reward?

Mrs. Doyle insisted the best way to stop these individuals coming to the house was to punish them with a lie. "If it's calling for rain, tell them we're in for grand weather. 'Hang out your wash, sheets and eiderdowns too.' If you see blue skies in your binoculars—I mean the other thing…"

"Barometer."

"—warn them a flood's around the corner. Say, 'Get out your rubber boots and your buckets.' That will teach them to stop banging on my door."

My approach didn't require a lie. I simply ignored the knocking and hoped they'd go away. I was doing exactly that, reading the paper and enjoying a pot of tea in the kitchen when someone knocked persistently. Mrs. Doyle banged her shovel on the coal bucket, something I couldn't ignore.

I opened the door to peep outside and saw a man in a khaki US Army uniform, size extra big, tall, and official. "I'll save you trouble right away, sir. I swear I don't give out forecasts anymore. It was a mistake and I've learned from it."

"I'm not here for the forecast, though I wouldn't mind finding out when it's gonna warm up." He stepped closer. "Richard Furlong, Private, first class, US Army, here to see Miss Violet Morgen used to live at Crag Point and left this forwarding address at a Goose Hill residence. That you, miss?"

"Yes, but if you're not here for the forecast, then—"

"Did you visit Bell Island in August?"

"It's Theresa you need. She's on the switchboard at the base. And how did you know I visited there?"

"It's mighty miserable out, miss. Lemme in and I'll explain."

"Miserable? Fifty degrees in the middle of November? Sixty degrees two days ago. The normal high is around forty. These temperatures are record-breaking, something I haven't observed in all my years of forecasting. Call the weather police. If this continues, there'll be spring cleaning in February and trading wool coats for raglans, raglans for short sleeves. Of course, there'll be substantial savings on coal."

He glared at me, frowning like he hadn't understood. "It's tropical if that's how you see it, miss. Can you lemme in out of this heat? I got a question or two about your visit to the Island before the September attack."

With the Private standing in the hall, the space seemed suddenly much smaller. His hands were even larger than Fred's, not weather-worn. Nothing about Private Furlong seemed worn. He fit Ida's description of men from the US: "So tall, filled out, and healthy-looking, you wonder whether they had the Depression where they grew up."

Mrs. Doyle banged on her coal bucket. "Who's there, Victoria? Did he come with the coal?"

I called out over her coughing. "It's for me, Mrs. Doyle."

"Come in, come in, or run back home to your mother."

I squeezed around the Private and opened her door.

He ducked to avoid hitting his head.

Mrs. Doyle shielded her eyes with her forearm when I opened the curtains. "Glory be. Who are you? How'd you get so tall? Did Ellen do something wrong?"

"It's nothing, Mrs. Doyle. He's here with a couple of questions for me."

Her bed wasn't made and she was still in her nightgown. "What kinda questions? Do you want to go on a date? Better not be expecting the forecast. You'll get more than you bargained for. She should start charging for it. We could use the money. Everything costs a fortune since you people arrived."

He held his hand over his nose, likely to block the overpowering odour of wintergreen oil, then sneezed.

"Ges—" I caught myself before I said gesundheit. "The kitchen's at the end of the hall. Take a seat there, please, Private. I'll be with you shortly."

I combed Mrs. Doyle's hair and helped her into her housecoat.

"I knew this day would come," she said. "If you were an English girl in Germany, they'd be beating down your door, ready to lock you up and hide the keys."

"I'm not German, my father was naturalized before the war, and the Private is here with questions about my visit to Bell Island."

"That's what you think. Don't be trusting what the Americans say. They're not our people. Run down to Clarke's. Put a couple of beer on my account. We'll soften him up, squeeze the truth out of him, then tell him to go play baseball. Hurry. I can walk to the kitchen by myself."

TROJAN HORSES

Beware of men or women operating surreptitiously alongside us, aiding and abetting the enemy. Do not share information these traitors might use to sabotage our war effort. Do not sell or provide strangers with fuel. Report any suspicious, traitorous, or unpatriotic behaviour. Watch for hidden or camouflaged equipment that might be used to transmit or measure weather phenomena. Be on guard against subversion, sabotage, and espionage. Keep your eyes and ears open for spies and saboteurs from Japan, Germany, or Italy.

It wasn't my fault that Mrs. Clarke wanted to know who'd be drinking the beer and wouldn't serve me until I divulged every detail with a commitment to update her later.

"What took you so long?" Mrs. Doyle said, sitting alongside the Private at the table. "Give this big boy a beer, and while you're at it, heat up the leftover fish cakes for him."

He sat chest out like he'd been called to attention by Mrs. Doyle herself. "I appreciate your hospitality, ma'am. Newfoundland people are the nicest. They remind me of folks in my home state. But I don't have time for refreshments right now. Maybe one day when I'm off duty." He caught my eye, and I wondered if he was expecting an invitation.

Mrs. Doyle tutted. "You'd think they'd teach you to say the name right. Say *Newfin* the way you'd say *bluefin*, then heavy on the *land*. Understand?"

He nodded. "Yes, ma'am."

"Before it slips my mind," she said, "I got a husband in America, the Boston docks, last I heard. Haven't laid eyes on the fellah in so long, I forget what he looks like. Know any Charlie Doyles?"

"No, ma'am. Sorry, ma'am."

"You're here about Bell Island," I said. "Go ahead, please."

Mrs. Doyle tapped on his arm. "Don't be minding Victoria. I'll fire off a litany of questions if I feel like it. Tell me. There's Furlongs up on Queen's Road and a bunch over on Lemarchant. Are you family with either lot?"

He opened his file folder halfway and used the cover to shield its contents from Mrs. Doyle's eyes. I might have told him she could barely see a hand in front of her, let alone the fine print in his file.

"No, ma'am. I'm from Texas." He glanced at his watch.

"Carry on with what you're at," she said. "So many torpedoes are going astray these days, next thing you know, you'll have to dart off with unfinished business."

Private Furlong paused to read the file. "I've come to talk to a Miss Violet Morgen, not Victoria. That *is* you, is it, miss?"

"She's more of a Victoria than a Violet," Mrs. Doyle said. "But seeing as how you're so important in that uniform, go ahead and call her Violet. Richard? Is that your name?"

"Yes, ma'am."

"When you've been around these parts long enough, you'll see there's no Richards, only Dicks or Dickies, Richie or Rich. A big, strong fellah like you? I'd say you're a Richie. Get on with what you're at, Richie." She tutted. "You haven't got forever, have you? You must be run off your big American feet chasing the bad guys. God help us." She made the sign of the cross.

He coughed to clear his throat, hand in a fist over his mouth. "Like I was saying, I need to ask about your visit to Bell Island, Miss Morgen. After, I'll report to my superior. He'll lemme know what action to take."

Mrs. Doyle tapped her fingers on his arm again. "If you're chatting with this superior fellah, tell him Victoria's a superior boarder in Mrs. Doyle's superior boarding house. She's the only one lends an ear to Noreen, and she made Ellen sharp as a crackie with numbers." She paused to take a deep breath. "Tell him to contact us any time. Victoria will give him the forecast, no charge. She's superior at that. I'm not bad at it either. My rheumatism tells me when rain's on the way. Wind before rain, canvas remain. Wind in the west, fishing's best. Wind in the east, not fit for a beast. Ever hear tell of Sheila's Brush in March?" She patted his hand. "Never mind. You've had your fill of words today, and Victoria hasn't started yet."

The Private's shoulders rose as he took a deep breath. "The American Army is aiding the Royal Canadian Navy's investigation of the Bell Island attacks. We're going through files opened this past year. I was assigned to yours."

"I don't understand."

He closed the file and rested his hands on top. "It was opened in April, notes about some of our men out of commission after eating sandwiches you sold them. Also, your father was listed in the Registry of Aliens."

"I never tasted her sandwiches," Mrs. Doyle said. "Theresa does the cooking. What odds about her father as long as he's not one of them Nazis? My Timmy was gunned down by Germans in the Great War. That didn't stop me from welcoming Victoria into my home. First night I laid eyes on the strange girl, thinking she'd come from the last century, I found out everything, country and religion. She wouldn't be under my roof if either bothered me. Queen Victoria's mother was a German princess and her hus—" She coughed. The talking, plus walking to the kitchen, had stirred up phlegm, which she expelled into her handkerchief.

He held one hand over his mouth like he was feeling ill, my file in the other. "Mind if I use your restroom, ladies?"

I pointed to the ceiling. "It's directly above us here." If I'd known we'd have a guest I would have removed our undergarments hanging on a line from one end of the bathroom to the other.

"He's got a crush on you," Mrs. Doyle said. "If you can't see it, there's no hope for you. Show him a smile for a change."

Perhaps if he'd been more like Philip, I would have welcomed her advice. "The Private's not my type."

"I'm not saying to marry the man. Humour him. Get him on your side. Didn't they teach you anything back at that crag?"

We heard sounds from overhead—the toilet flushing, water gushing through pipes, a creak in the floorboards, feet on the stairs. He re-entered the kitchen holding the file to his chest and ducking in the doorway.

"You're refreshed after visiting our bathroom, bath and all. I told you it was superior."

"Thank you, ma'am."

"Please, tell me more about my file. Could I look at it myself?"

"Sorry, no. But that's about it except that the former keeper at your last place of residence, Mr. Russo, has Italian ancestry, and you were his assistant."

"Former?" I said. "You're going too fast. Where's Teo? Do you know anything about Maryanne? I haven't heard from her in—"

"Let the man have his say, Victoria. Don't be tying him up. He's dying to be on his way."

He turned his attention from her to me. "Your father was a Mr. Heinrich Morgenstern. So in fact, you are Violet Morgenstern, not Morgen. Why did you change your last name?"

"I didn't. My father changed it on the passenger ship that brought him across the Atlantic more than twenty years ago. He wanted a fair and fresh start. Things we take for granted, like religious beliefs or a surname, can make people targets for discrimination, even violence."

Private Furlong wrote something in the file. "Any contacts with people of German ancestry in St. John's?"

"Contacts?" Mrs. Doyle said. "If she had them, I'd be the first to know. No one goes in, out, up, or down in this house without me catching them. Theresa keeps me well informed of the goings-on. What she doesn't tell me, the neighbours will. They're the eye on the outside. Any ruckus and their ears are itching. Victoria only goes to the Cathedral and the library. No talking or contacting in either place."

She'd said it better than I could, and I had nothing to add.

"Regarding the library, Miss Morgen, did you ever communicate with anyone besides staff?"

"You got a queer way of talking," Mrs. Doyle said. "Do all hands where you're from—your parents, neighbours—do they talk slow same as you?"

He smiled. "We got a bit of a drawl in Texas. Miss Morgen, please answer my question about the library."

"No, Private. I met with no one." I decided against telling him that if I really was a collaborator, I could insert forecasts into particular volumes for spies to telegraph them to the enemy. They depended on forecasts as much as did our side.

He opened my file and skimmed the page. "You dated a Captain Campbell. That right?"

Mrs. Doyle leaned closer to him, tugging on his sleeve. "They're not all Catholics over there in Ireland, in case you didn't know." She whispered, "He's divorced." She shook her head. "Catholics don't allow it. We don't even like saying the word." She tutted. "They're not all salt of the earth either. I've no patience for his highfalutin, hoity-toity kind, telling us we're—"

"May I ask what my relationship with him, or any man, has to do with this questioning?"

Private Furlong sat up straight, as if he'd suddenly realized he'd come to ask questions of Violet Morgen, not to be distracted by the house's owner. "You visited Bell Island together in August, a month before the first attack." He opened the file, read something, then closed it. "While over there, you told folks the iron-ore carriers were a perfect target. Do you—"

"That's not fair." I sighed, frustrated to have my comments taken out of context. "How did that remark end up in my file? Lucy Power claimed Bell Island was safer than St. John's. I told her she was wrong. I was simply stating facts."

"Facts?"

"Those vessels were bait, well worth a few torpedoes no matter their cost in Deutschmarks."

His smile puzzled me. Was it a tactic designed to distract me or was he pleased with my facts?

"Why's a young gal living in this little house got torpedoes on her mind? Where do your loyalties lie exactly, Miss Violet Morgenstern?"

"What's little about my house? I got two floors above this one. I told Victoria when she first came here, I said, 'The third floor will be grand for your bedroom.' She got it fixed up so nice, I should raise her board."

Maybe Mrs. Doyle wanted to stall him to give me an opportunity to formulate the best possible answers to his questions, but my response came easily. "Torpedoes are on my mind because, frankly, at this point in the war, with the Nazis controlling most of the west coast of Europe, I sincerely believe our side is losing. What kind of world will we be forced to live in if the Nazis win? A world my father warned about, one he struggled to shelter his family from. At least he died not knowing that they'd get this close. Please don't bother questioning my loyalty. You can be one hundred per cent certain it rests with the Allies."

That last comment, delivered with my voice quivering, brought an end to the questioning. I asked about Teo. The Private knew nothing and wouldn't have been able to share such information anyway. He left Chapel Street assured of my innocence and allegiance, carrying an unopened bottle of beer and three fish cakes wrapped in brown paper.

"Come again sometime, Richie," Mrs. Doyle said, fingers crossed behind her back.

WEATHERGRAM

15 NOV 42
SOUTHWEST OF ICELAND, 47.56° N 52.70° W
WIND NORTHEAST, NEAR GALE FORCE
HIGH TIDE 2300H, SWELLS 13FT
TEMP 51°
BAROMETER FALLING, LOW VISIBILITY
RAIN & FREEZING RAIN

40

December 3, 1942

Dear Maryanne,

'Tis the season to be jolly. I'd be far jollier with news from you. Noreen receives regular letters from Corner Brook, Ellen from Bell Island, Danny from the US. Why not me? Eight months and only one reply. I wrote Fred to say if I don't hear from either of you by next week, I'll ask Ida for leave and head to Pine Harbour (Crag Point if necessary). I can't believe you'd deliberately remain silent simply because, as you wrote in your brief May missive, you have no news to report.

On the other hand, excuse my worrying if the problem simply has to do with censorship. I've seen the notice in the paper regarding "Matters That Cannot be Mentioned in Letters," including, "The landing of survivors from ships wrecked or lost through enemy action." I did write to you about Brigid helping injured sailors. Everyone knows they're being cared for at the Red Cross. I assumed censorship only applies to overseas correspondence and to those serving. Danny has to follow the Nfld Base Command rules regarding correspondence—no mention of weather, nothing about the barracks' location either. Letters must be unsealed, and he's not permitted to use postal services outside of the base.

Work. Since I'm on the topic of censorship, Ida's given me notice—any more talk of wind and fire, I'll be out of a job she dismissed me from once already. I explained to some of the shopgirls how, in 1892, all it took was a pipe, hay, and northwest gusts. Today, a box of flammable materials, a match or two on a blustery day, and voilà—St. John's is reduced to ashes and chimneys. One of them accused me of giving her nightmares. I apologized for having talked about being snug under the covers while flankers swarm the sky like flaming insects. Does Ida expect me to ignore customers when they mention the fires that destroyed Canadian Army barracks on Signal Hill on Tuesday and US Army barracks on Sunday? Everyone's talking about them.

Chapel St. Ellen followed through on her plan to find a boyfriend for T. She is now dating someone Ellen worked with, Robert. As it happens, we met before. He was the waiter at a Sept. cocktail party I attended with Philip. T. met Robert briefly the night he accompanied me home in a taxi from the party. Less than six weeks together and they can't seem to be apart. He's a regular at Chapel St. I can't help picturing him holding a tray of cocktails, the hostess urging him to serve me another.

Brigid and Danny have invited me to the base for Christmas Eve celebrations. T. has decided she'll stay here for Christmas, B.I. for Near Year's Day. She's invited Robert and is cooking duck for our meal. I've been placed in charge of peeling vegetables and of the cleanup. Apparently, Mrs. D. makes the trifle each year. Noreen's promised to treat us to homemade bull's-eyes candies and fudge. Robert's going to help T. make one dark and one light Christmas cake. I'll miss your pudding, but I'm looking forward to tasting the cake. I'll send you a piece in the mail. Did you receive the chocolates?

Brigid and Noreen are now talking to each other. At last! The tension was suffocating.

"Violet, please tell Noreen I don't want to listen to her complaints about working conditions for Nfld labourers on the base."

"Violet, please tell Brigid her overworked pinkie's gonna fall off if she doesn't stop sticking it out."

Noreen deserves credit for doing Brigid a valuable favour. She claims she did it to spare us "Brigid's whining," but I think it was because we all, including her, wish the loving couple well. So many women are getting married these days, Brigid couldn't find anyone, not even on the base, to take in her dress around the waist. Noreen works with many of the best seamstresses in the city. They're quite happy to do her favours. She arranged to have the waistline altered and also enhanced with a lace sash. They've been remarkably civil with each other ever since. Brigid's toned down her praise for the Americans. Noreen realizes criticizing Brigid's personal choices is inconsistent with her ideas about women's rights.

T. announced she can't sing at Brigid's reception because she's terrified to perform for an audience, especially one with her new beau in it. "I'm a no-good pipsqueak singer," she said. Brigid didn't seem to mind, I guess because there'll be a full orchestra for the evening anyway. Mrs. D. minded. I too. Even Ellen was disappointed. In the end, Ida came to the rescue with an offer T. couldn't turn down. Ida will make her a special performance gown. T.'s supposed to tell people it's a Fitz Original. In T.'s place, I'd ask to see the gown well in advance.

War. Blackout tomorrow, 5:38 p.m.–8:04 a.m. Ugh. Compare that to late June (10:30–5:30). In the paper this week, I saw a familiar name in the casualty report. R.I.P. Edward Cuff (17) from Gull Cove, killed when a torpedo hit the merchant vessel he served on. I knew him only briefly but instantly recognized his sincere earnestness. He was so eager to be of service to passengers. He glowed with enthusiasm about his future. We see names and statistics every day about men and women with their lives cut short because of the war. Names on paper are one thing, knowing the person, another. May his loss be a sacrifice that will ultimately bring us closer to peace.

Crag Point. If it isn't too windy or wet, I enjoy hiking up Signal Hill (when it's not burning). Troops occupy the area with their barracks, recreation, and dining facilities, etc., primarily on the Hill's west side. I go by way of a route used by civilians on the east side. It feels good to escape the city's grime and frantic traffic. With winter setting in, I may not be able to do it for much longer.

From the hilltop, I can pretend I'm in the tower at Crag Point, looking out over an expanse of water and sky, eyes fixed on the horizon. I imagine walking back to the house through the passageway and finding you in the kitchen, knitting to the steady rhythm of the clock's tick-tock. On the table is a steaming pot of tea and two servings of your boiled pudding, fresh from the cookstove where the spruce junks crackle, and the heat rises through the floor vent into my bedroom.

Heartfelt wishes for a peaceful season. Crossing my fingers in the hope of seeing you in person in 1943.

Yours longingly,
Violet

PS: On the beach you said, "Don't waste your pennies sending letters to me." It's not a waste!

A CITY ON GUARD

Standing atop Signal Hill, one can appreciate why it has served for centuries like a citadel defending the city. At the Hill's highest lookout point, an enemy approaching by sea could be spotted well before it reached the Narrows. Today, the US Army's strategically positioned anti-aircraft guns defend against aerial attack, while the Royal Canadian Artillery operates nearby coastal defence batteries at Cape Spear, Fort Amherst, and Chain Rock. On your next visit to the Hill, bring your binoculars, watch for periscopes and planes, or simply marvel at the great expanse.

41

December was less than a week old yet already hinted at trouble with more chills than comfort, more greys than blues, more gusts than breezes. We ate breakfast and supper with curtains closed. We rose and went to bed with them closed. Meanwhile, volunteer air-raid wardens patrolled neighbourhoods, ready to impose a fine on offenders. I remembered Teo's descriptions of Toronto at Christmas, the city aglow with lights. I wouldn't see that in St. John's this year. The proclamation had been made. There could be no modification of rules to permit outdoor illumination on any property, residential or commercial. The blackout would remain in effect for the remainder of the war.

Winter would soon be upon us—my first in the continent's most easterly city, a reputation paid for in extremes of snowiest and windiest. I was preparing to go outside to shovel the slush before it froze in front of the house when I heard a knock on the door. I opened it, hoping to see the postman with a stack of letters, saying, "These are for you" and apologizing for not getting Maryanne's mail to me sooner. It wasn't the postman. It was Thomas Peckford, my brief boyfriend and interceptor of packages sent to Crag Point.

I invited him into the narrow hallway where we stood awkwardly close together, I spewing nervous chatter, "Hang your coat here. Don't worry about the slush on your boots," he saying, "Are you sure?" as if any of that mattered under the circumstances. Had he come to visit his schoolhouse girlfriend? Should I inform him she was no longer the girl he remembered?

Mrs. Doyle called out and we entered her room.

Thomas introduced himself as a friend "from out Violet's way," as if that summed up our relationship.

He'd barely said hello when she started coughing, gently at first, then almost gagging. I reached over to pat her back, but it was my hand she wanted and grabbed it tightly.

Thomas asked whether there was something wrong and should he come back another time, or not at all, and I pictured the moment the steamer reversed in Pine Harbour and I'd wondered if Fred had been right in saying I knew nothing about people and the world except what I'd read in the papers.

The coughing stopped. She dropped my hand and pointed to the chairs for Thomas and me. "The spitting image of him. That's what you are."

Thomas let out a quick laugh that sounded more tense than amused. "Hope the other fellah's good-looking."

Mrs. Doyle gazed at the embers. "'You'll be the boss of Water Street someday, Timmy,' I said to my boy. 'The boss of the whole town, I'll be, Mom,' he told me. He was only eight when he started selling cod tongues door-to-door. They don't make his kind anymore." She smiled at Thomas. "You're exactly like him. Yellow hair and blue eyes."

He squirmed in the chair, leaning to one side, then the other. "What's Timmy at nowadays? Not at cod tongues, I don't suppose."

"Last I laid eyes on Timmy, he sat right where you are, wearing his uniform like a badge of honour. Last I heard tell of him was in a We-regret-to-inform-you telegram. It's not just the rheumatism made me miserable. The happy Mrs. Doyle is missing too. All's left is a woman with a heart barely beating, so lonely without her boy."

Thomas said he was sorry, then told us about his grandfather who fought in Gallipoli. "We still got the rule in the Harbour—nobody fires a rifle near where he can hear. A quick, hard bang puts him in an awful state."

Mrs. Doyle blew her nose into her handkerchief. "I try not to think of him too much. I get so worked up, I can't breathe. Did you ever hear it said, 'At the going down of the sun and in the morning, we will remember them?' There's not much going up or down here. The closed curtains take care of that. Victoria knows, don't you, Victoria?"

I nodded, unsure of what to say. I'd heard about Timmy from Theresa. His black-and-white studio portrait rested on Mrs. Doyle's side table, his regard expressionless, staring ahead, though not at the camera. She'd been polishing its frame for nearly thirty years, kissing it goodnight and falling asleep with it in her lap. As for the curtains, I wondered if perhaps it wasn't time for her to let the world in again. Yet, who was I to think like that as someone who had so desperately clung to the hope of reuniting with her captain?

"All this remembering stirred up a desert of a thirst. Victoria's not much of a cook, but she makes a decent pot of tea. Hurry up, Victoria."

While the kettle boiled, I ran upstairs to put on lipstick. I was on my way back to the kitchen when I decided to return to the bathroom and wipe off every trace. Thomas might have assumed it meant I wanted him to notice me, to offer the kiss I'd requested in the schoolhouse. Did I still want it? Did he even know how to kiss?

I filled our cups while Mrs. Doyle asked Thomas if he was the kind of man who knew how to fix things, and could he see to the broken flap over the coal chute?

"Yes, Mrs. Doyle. Give me wood, a hammer, some nails, and I'll build you a house." He laughed nervously, and I wondered, was he even the same person? Perspective changed the view, like in Fred's dory when I saw Crag Point from the water and barely recognized it.

"Is your pop delivering the mail? I sent eight letters to Maryanne with only one reply."

Thomas glanced at Mrs. Doyle like he needed her permission to speak. I sensed something was wrong and I felt a chill, like a door had opened, letting in a draft.

She held up her rosary beads dangling from her wrist. "He didn't come this far for courting. He's got news." She made the sign of the cross. "News for you, Victoria."

His eyes centred on the fire, hand combing his hair, wiping his brow, pulling on his shirt collar, combing his hair again. "In early May, Pop picked up your letter and brought it to Crag Point with his regular delivery. He was supposed to head back to Pine Harbour that afternoon except he could tell Maryanne was feeling poorly—"

"What do you mean, poorly?"

He turned to face me. "Pop didn't say too much except that she was having trouble breathing. He stayed the night, had to listen to that Russo fellah complaining about everything from—"

I leaned forward in my chair as if that could help me understand better. "Tell me about him later," I said. "Is Maryanne better now?"

Thomas coughed to clear his throat. "She wrote you a letter that night. Pop sent it off right away in Pine Harbour. You got it, right?"

"I did. Tell him, thank you. But you still haven't—"

Mrs. Doyle waved her handkerchief. "For Pete's sake, get on with the story. I'm dying to know how it ends."

"Yes, Mrs. Doyle," he said. "In the morning, Maryanne could barely get out of bed. She argued with Pop, said she needed a rest, that was all. Pop knew better. He wouldn't leave Crag Point without her. There's a missus in the Harbour who tends to the sick. He convinced Maryanne to go with him, had to argue with Russo, tell him he couldn't take him along. The man was vicious, wouldn't—"

I sighed. "Please, Thomas. Answer my questions about Maryanne."

"Not a whole lot more to say. I'm sorry, Violet. Truly I am."

I clenched my fists so tightly, my nails dug into my palms. "Are you saying what I think you're saying?"

He shook his head and nodded, confusing me. "When they got to Pine Harbour, Pop pulled the hood up off her face and saw every bit of life was gone. He figures her heart gave out. He arranged a real nice funeral, sent word to her daughter too. He found a woman to replace Maryanne and took her to Crag Point. Russo left at the end of summer, said he wasn't putting up with another ten months of winter."

I wanted to tell him to stop using so many words, as Mrs. Doyle often told me. I stood, holding onto the chair to steady myself, then left the room. Outside, standing on the front stoop, I took deep breaths of the cold air. I pictured fragments of my last rushed moments at Crag Point—a purple sky at the horizon, the rumble of swash and backwash, a promise to write, a silhouette in the twilight, she asking what was wrong, and I lying, saying, "Nothing. Hurry, please."

Thomas draped his jacket over my shoulders. "Come inside."

Who was he to comfort me? That was Maryanne's role. I turned around, unable to stop sobbing nor stifle my anger. "Why wait till today? You had my address. You or your father could have written. What did you think she was to me? A servant?"

"Don't be cross, please, Violet. I was planning to tell you that part. She made Pop promise, if anything happened to her, he should leave you be for a year, say nothing, not spoil your plans."

"Spoil my plans? She died, Thomas. Didn't it occur to your father each time he picked up the mail and saw my letters that I was worried? That I needed to know?"

"It's not often I agree with Pop, but I'd say he did the proper thing honouring her dying wish. He changed his mind after he got the letter you sent addressed to him. He told me I should come here, no matter how far. I almost took off when I saw you. Didn't recognize you, new hair, clothes, name—real city girl."

"What would you know?" I said, under my breath, wanting to blame him. Surely, her death was someone's fault. "There must be more. What else did your father say?"

"That's it."

I blew my nose in my handkerchief. "You're making excuses, pretending you did nothing wrong. Have you forgotten how you left me waiting on the steamer?"

"Blame Pop for that. He warned me if I ran off with you, he'd make sure I never laid eyes on Pine Harbour again."

"How could I know that? And if he hadn't received my letter, would you have kept me waiting until April? Would I still be writing to her, thinking she's reading my letters?" I brushed him aside and went indoors, not caring if he answered, angry at him and Fred but mostly at Maryanne.

Mrs. Doyle patted my hand. "It's a shame you only found out today. Imagine how many prayers you could have said for her soul. She'd be on her way to heaven by now. Anyway, all hands will be here tonight to celebrate the start of Christmas season. Brigid's man, Theresa's new man too. You'll join us, Thomas. We'll have a grand Irish wake with a song and a prayer for Maryanne."

LIVES LIVED

Maryanne Pottle (1872–1942) led a life of generous service to others. With her own daughter grown and married, she became a mother to Violet, on whom she bestowed loving and devoted care. Ever so busy, she would often say, "No rest for the Mary" (weary). May their paths cross again. Let it be on a magnificent September afternoon, the two sitting content in a blueberry patch, buckets overflowing with ripe, fat berries, sun on the water, shimmering like a salmon's scales.

42

Maryanne's wake took place that evening in the Chapel Street kitchen, attended by people who were strangers to her, who shed no tears and felt no sense of emptiness or loss now that she was gone. Gone without a real goodbye. They weren't mourning. They were celebrating. Theresa and Robert—six weeks together. Danny and Brigid—the month in which they'd marry. Ellen and Noreen—three weeks to Christmas holidays.

In the hall, Thomas rummaged in his satchel, then handed me the letters I'd sent to Maryanne. I flipped through them to make sure none, apart from the first, had been opened.

He handed me a box of chocolates. "These are for you too."

I held them, more surprised than grateful. The box's lower corner featured the image of a beautiful, smiling woman. She wore a blue gown with matching shoes, holding a box of chocolates, her own image on it. On the same box on the box, below her dress, in miniscule letters, was the message I'd written, *To MP from VM.*

"Thank you," I said.

"Thank Pop. He's the one asked me to give them to you. I got so hungry on the trip here, I almost opened them."

The last time I'd seen Fred at Crag Point, he was arguing with Maryanne about my future. She was convinced I could tap my heels together and be hired by the Americans. What would she say now? That I gave up too easily?

In the kitchen, I introduced Thomas as a friend of my family. "He brought us a box of chocolates," I said, making up for being angry with him earlier.

He smiled shyly when they called out, "Welcome, Tommy."

Theresa served him a beer.

Ellen stood up, chest out, and offered him an egg sandwich. "Made them myself."

Mrs. Doyle, Noreen, and Ellen had chairs to themselves. Theresa sat on Robert's lap, Brigid on Danny's, and since we hadn't enough chairs, I had to sit on Thomas's lap. In April, when we first met, I might have welcomed that arrangement. Now, the intimacy felt awkward and forced.

Mrs. Doyle dabbed her eyes. "It's some nice to have men around the house. I want to hear them sing with the girls. Sing so loud the neighbours will be pounding on the wall, warning us to behave. Don't forget Victoria's Maryanne. Sing 'We'll Meet Again.' Sing it real slow, like Vera Lynn."

Noreen pretended to be directing the choir. Ellen said she didn't want to sing along because the song was boring. Brigid and Danny kissed. Mrs. Doyle smacked Brigid's arm and told her to wait until she was Danny's missus. She said nothing to me, though I barely had the motivation to pantomime. Robert was too busy listening to and admiring Theresa to be able to sing, probably envying Thomas's vocal cords and talent. When the song ended, Brigid said she wished Thomas and Theresa could perform at her wedding reception.

"We'd be the Marjorie Reynolds, Bing Crosby duo," Theresa said.

Mrs. Doyle waved her handkerchief. "Attention Marjorie and Bing, sing 'White Christmas.'"

Brigid groaned. She didn't care if the song was number one on the charts. "Sing anything but that. Snow is the last thing I need for my wedding. I'm counting on you, Violet. Don't take your eye off your barometer."

At eleven, Mrs. Doyle pronounced the wake over. "Maryanne would be a hard woman to please if she wasn't charmed with the grand send-off we gave her. Say your prayers before you go to sleep. Spare one or two for me."

Theresa helped Mrs. Doyle get ready for bed, then joined us in the hall as we passed coats and gaiters overhead.

There were shouts of "Thanks for the chocolates, Thomas."

When Thomas mentioned his plans to head to Scotland, then someday travel the world, Danny encouraged him to visit him in Montana.

"Visit *us*," Brigid said.

Thomas said goodnight and reached forward to kiss me on the lips, but I turned my head and the kiss landed on my cheek.

After the men had left, Theresa said they each wanted to tell me something. Ellen reached a hand around my waist. "I hope she went to heaven. Hell's full of Nazis." She turned to Theresa and put her arms around her neck. "Promise, Aunt Theresa, you won't leave me like her Maryanne did."

Theresa closed her eyes and pulled Ellen toward her. "Before long, you won't need me. Go on to bed and don't be giving yourself nightmares thinking your young aunt is gonna die soon. Heaven's too crowded for now."

Brigid laid her hand on my shoulder. "I don't know if it helps, but I wish I'd had someone important in my life instead of nuns at the orphanage. They took good care of me, but that was it."

Noreen brushed Brigid aside. "Yankee Danny'll make up for your suffering."

"That and more," Brigid said. She marched up the stairs, head raised, chin out, eyes straight ahead, practicing walking down the aisle.

Noreen held me tightly. "I liked you, Violet, the moment I laid eyes on you. Cry on my—"

"Enough, Noreen. Violet's turning violet."

"She likes me better than you, Theresa." She winked at me. "Can't blame her, right Violet?" She whistled "White Christmas" while walking upstairs.

Theresa held my hand. "We can be a mean, miserable bunch, worse than a bout of harsh weather. But we look out for each other. You might not have your Maryanne, but you have us on your side. Wartime or any time, we all need allies." She patted me on the back. "Pop in to see her nibs."

I found Mrs. Doyle in the same chair as that night when I'd first met her, the coal embers brightening one side, the other shadowed. And yet she seemed so different now, more wounded and weary than fierce or hostile.

"I'll offer a week of prayers for Maryanne," she said. "If that doesn't get God's attention, I'll try the next level down with one of the saints. She'll be in heaven before you can say the Hail Mary."

"Maryanne would have appreciated everything you've done for me, not only welcoming me into your home."

"I'll never forget that night, you pounding on my door, riling up the dogs, disturbing our sleep. I asked the Holy Ghost, 'Should I trust Theresa telling me the girl could help Ellen, or should I steer clear of the trouble a stranger, her father a German at that, could bring to my home?' It's not often I bother him. He gave me the go-ahead."

"Lucky me."

"You helped Ellen. That helped Theresa. Helping Theresa helps me. It frees up a lot of prayers. And who else out there will help us if not us crowd? We got to stitch our broken hearts together and hope they make us whole. You're a good girl. Odd at times, I can't deny it, but we're used to you now. Before you go, top up the grate."

I left her room and stood in the hall where I'd been eight months earlier. The bulb hung from the ceiling without a globe, the floral design on the canvas flooring was more faded than when I'd first seen it. That distinctive odour was still noticeable—faint whiffs of fried fish mixed with wintergreen and the acrid stench of damp gaiters. Twelve Chapel Street was no mansion, yet it offered a sense of belonging in palatial proportions.

In my bedroom, I re-read my letters to Maryanne. Except for the first one, she hadn't seen them. Maybe that was for the best. I opened the empty box of chocolates, laid the letters inside, then stored the box in my trunk. I turned off the light and opened the curtains expecting to see the green beam. All I saw were stars, trillions of miles away. I took out my binoculars from my trunk and trained them on the sky until I found Venus. Though its brilliance stung my eyes, I stared, remembering Vati, Mutti, and Maryanne, forever at the centre of my universe.

DON'T KNOW WHERE OR WHEN

One of the most endearing melodies of this second not-so-great war, "We'll Meet Again," resonates at home and in battlefields. Twenty-five-year-old Vera Lynn has become a radio darling with her rendition of the song about sunnier days chasing away dark clouds, and loved ones gone without a real goodbye. Performing since the age of seven, she sometimes sings in London's underground air-raid shelters and in factories. Not surprisingly, she is known as "The Forces' Sweetheart." Let this singer be an inspiration to amateur performers like Theresa Power, preparing their stage debut, and to those longing for loved ones.

43

As Thomas and I walked to the Nickel Theatre, I gazed down at my feet, splashing slush, the print of my boot left to freeze once the temperatures dropped later that evening. In the morning, he'd catch the Sunday express train and head west across the island. He'd get off at the junction, catch the branch line to Lewisporte where he'd board the steamer to Pine Harbour. He had indeed come from far for my sake.

"You said yourself Ellen doesn't need your help with math anymore." He squeezed my hand, making sure I was listening and not simply playing mindlessly with the slush underfoot. "You don't have the right references to get hired at the base, you're sick of selling shoes, and you can't work as a forecaster because no one will take you seriously. What's holding you here? Why not follow me overseas this summer?"

Would Maryanne have encouraged me to follow him, to see the world—something she'd dreamed of doing? Surely not if it meant living in a lumber camp until the conflict ended. "Let's talk after the movie."

Alfred Hitchcock's *Suspicion* was playing. We sat, heads tilted back, in the front row because Thomas didn't want anyone blocking his view on his first visit to a theatre. The lights went out and the screen lit up, our faces with it. The orchestral music set the mood, gay yet mysterious, drawing us into the story. Without warning, a train's horn blew loudly. Thomas turned side to side, searching for the sound's source.

The drama involved a whirlwind courtship followed by a rushed marriage and Lina's growing suspicion about her new husband, the gambling playboy Johnnie. We were so close to the screen, I felt as if I was in the motor car with Johnnie driving, terrified like Lina when the vehicle swerved near the precipice. I closed my eyes to shut out the scene.

I couldn't block the music, the pitch rising, speed accelerating, suspense building to a terrifying climax with tires screeching and Lina screaming. I wanted to scream too. I wouldn't have been the only person in the audience to do so. The credits ended and the white light hit my eyes with a jolt. I bent forward to massage my stiff neck, looked up, dory-dizzy, hot, then cold, nauseous too.

Thomas didn't notice, not when he was so mesmerized by the blank screen.

Outside, in the freezing air, we held hands over our gloves while we walked the short distance to the Knights of Columbus Hostel where we were meeting Theresa and Robert.

Thomas couldn't believe the movie had shown parts of Italy, France, and England. "My best pupil, Jessie, is sixteen. She'll take over in September till they find someone better. My lumberjack contract is for six months. Twelve dollars a week, plus I already saved over a hundred and fifty. Think what we could do together, the places we could visit once the war ends."

I thought of Lina, how I'd been like her, and not simply because of her crown of braids. If she'd been a friend, I would have told her to be suspicious of Johnnie and of herself. I would have cautioned her not to lose herself in him. Maryanne was right—the type of man a woman chooses to love tells tons about her own character. I wouldn't long for Philip anymore. If I saw him again with his darling Gwen, I'd wish them well. As for Thomas, my mind was made up.

COCOANUTS ABLAZE

Picture one thousand revellers crammed into a nightclub with plastic palm trees, cloth-lined ceilings, and leather walls. A single match accidentally ignites decorations. Without warning, a ball of flames shoots through the building. Guests scramble over each other, panicking only to discover doors are locked or jammed because they open inwards. Nearly five hundred are killed while hundreds of others are injured from burns or inhalation of smoke and toxic gases. Let this recent fire in Boston's popular Cocoanut Grove be a warning to similar establishments in Newfoundland.

When we arrived at the K of C for the concert, Thomas went into the recreation room to play Ping-Pong with Robert. I sat with Theresa. She'd been guarding front-row seats.

"I'd feel better if we moved nearer the main exit," I said.

"Come on, Violet. I went to a load of trouble to get four civilian passes for tonight, then came early to be by the stage. Your Maryanne is peeping down this minute, saying, 'Smile. Enjoy yourself.' Do it for her sake."

"Conditions are exactly like last Saturday's fire in Boston. They—"

"We're in St. John's, not Boston. Don't be thinking about fire and," she cupped a hand over her mouth, "Nazis."

"Fires in overcrowded buildings built of spruce and fir with windows boarded up and a single exit don't depend on Nazis."

Thomas and Robert joined us as I was telling Theresa she should believe me, that something simple like a building's faulty wiring, a discarded match or cigarette butt could ignite a catastrophe in an instant.

"The concert is live on radio," Theresa said, like she hadn't been listening to me. "Mrs. Doyle is tuned in. Don't forget to holler and whistle."

Biddy O'Toole's recitation on the lazy husband she was ready to sell for a nickel had Thomas smacking his knee and stomping his foot. When she sang, he held my hand, bouncing it up and down in time to the music.

At last, when the performance ended, all I cared about was getting out of there, but Thomas and the others wanted the performers' autographs.

"I'll meet you outside." I edged my way into a wave of bodies pushing toward the exit. Someone's foot stomped on my toe, and an elbow jabbed me in the ribcage, bone on bone. I felt hands on my back, fingers on my spine, and a force strong as an undertow pushing me forward and backward, the pressure suffocating. The closer I got to the exit, the more the force came from the sides, shoving me to the left, the right. Cold air brushed my cheeks, and I raised my head. I went through the exit like a cork popping from the bottleneck, the pent-up force suddenly released into an open space.

The crowds had dispersed by the time the others joined me. They were in a laughing mood, talking over each other about which performers they liked best and comparing autographs. Theresa pretended to yodel while Robert whistled noisily.

They walked ahead of us, holding hands.

I wrapped my arm in Thomas's, pretending to be listening while he talked about a play his students were preparing, *Christmas in the Harbour*. The damp, frigid air moved through my wool coat, past my sweater and blouse, through my skin to my bones. My teeth chattered. Would there be enough hot water for a bath? If not, did I have the strength to lug kettle after kettle from the kitchen up the stairs?

The walk was a short one to Chapel Street. Robert shook Thomas's hand. "Hope to run into you some blue moon, Thomas. One of these years, I'll head over there to learn how to be a butler."

"Carve my name in the bark of a giant Scottish tree," Theresa said. "Make sure no one chops it down."

They kissed. Robert made a pretend salute, then headed to his boarding house.

"Don't be long. You'll catch your death," Theresa said, then went inside.

Thomas put his arms around me. "I might be back at Easter, for sure by the end of school. You could change your mind by then."

I thanked him for bringing news of Maryanne and invited him to visit me if he came to the city again. I let him hug me for however long he wanted. In times of war or peace, any embrace could be the last.

A SOLDIER'S BEST FRIEND

Leave it to those clever Canucks to invent the "no-after-glow" matches. This feature may be particularly relevant for dealing with the well-known superstition of three lights on one match. The enemy spots the flame lighting the first soldier's cigarette, takes aim on the second, and fires on the third. The Eddy strike-anywhere, no-need-for-brimstone, silent matches serve as convenient tools for soldiers in trenches. A burning match attached to a discarded helmet can make for a simple decoy. When sending supplies to our men, don't forget to include a box of Eddy's matches.

44

Maryanne had warned me about fever dreams. "If you ever see your father or mother, say you're not ready to join them yet."

I encountered everyone except them. In the scariest dream, I was a passenger with Thomas behind the wheel of a motor car without brakes. He squeezed my hand too tightly and repeated, "Are you listening?" while we were about to plunge over the cliff onto a rocky shoreline. Another dream took place in the kitchen with Ellen asking one question after another. "What does the factor y represent in this expression?" Theresa wanted bacon and eggs, but I only had reheated porridge looking like frozen slush. Brigid wept while Noreen sang "White Christmas." Why had I forecast snow for her big day? Mrs. Doyle banged on her coal bucket. She couldn't hear the radio over my coughing and had difficulty breathing because I'd put too many coals on the fire in the grate.

HEALTH WARNING

Pulmonary tuberculosis continues to be a merciless killer in Newfoundland, afflicting mostly those aged 15 to 45. The statistics are not something to be proud of. Except for Chile, we have the highest rate of death from TB in the world and eleven times more cases than in the US. Do not drink unpasteurized milk. Do not spit on the floor or ground. Do not cough without covering your mouth. Stay away from crowds. Start 1943 TB free!

I woke after three days of sickness, my mind sorting between my real life versus my feverish dream. Noreen had been about to call on a friend, a nurse, to check on me. Theresa had skipped Sunday's Mass to care for me and was on number three of nine novenas for healing. She invited me to show appreciation for her devotion to my health by keeping an eye on Ellen during the upcoming holidays. Brigid thought I might have diphtheria or tuberculosis and had gone to stay with a friend. I lay in bed, staring at the underside of the roof. The room was so cold, I hesitated to get out from under the pile of blankets. Though I felt physically weakened, in place of the fog clogging my head was an energized clarity of purpose, a confident sense that I needed to act and follow through on a promise. If things weren't working for me, I had to somehow make them work.

I arrived at Ayre's at the end of the day. Rose was leaving and I offered to walk her partway home.

She kissed me on the cheek and told me she was sorry about Maryanne. "I was a youngster when she and her daughter moved from Pine Harbour to central Newfoundland. I knew she never married, learned that much from tongues wagging. The rest made the gossip headlines."

I hadn't gone to see her to hear about the injustices Maryanne had suffered. "You once said you could get me a date with someone at the base. Could you still do that?"

"Sure, but aren't you in mourning?"

"It's not what you think. I need a date with a Private. Any place will do." Private Furlong had left Chapel Street one month earlier with a wink and a "Hope to see you around." The comment wasn't directed at Mrs. Doyle.

"Why settle for something like a downtown diner if you could be hobnobbing it at the Newfoundland Hotel in satin gloves, your date's wallet stuffed with American dollars?" She listed the names of three different officers wanting company during the holidays. "If you don't want more than a kiss, let him know."

I rested my hand on her arm to get her attention. "His name is Private Richard Furlong. And it has nothing to do with money."

She stopped at the intersection and took out a cigarette. "Don't worry, I wasn't planning to offer you one." She lit it, puffed on it, then blew the smoke up into the air. "Everything comes down to money or the worth of things. You mustn't have been paying attention last time I told you that."

"I want to be a weather forecaster with the Americans."

"I thought you gave up on that idea. Can't say I blame you."

"Private Richard Furlong. Please, Rose."

She pulled my collar tighter around my neck. "I'll check with my contact at the base. Don't expect fine dining. Probably doesn't matter anyway since you'll only be talking about the weather. Take care of yourself. You're too pale. A cigarette would do you the world of good, smooth out that nervous edge. Special deal. Eighty cents a carton in US dollars. Make up your mind soon. Before you know it, the war'll be over and the Yanks gone, every ounce of opportunity along with them."

GET YOUR TICKETS SOON

Grab your Stetson hat and head with your partner to *Uncle Tim's Barn Dance* at the Knights of Columbus Hostel, 10:30 p.m., Saturday. Even with an auditorium capacity of 350 seats, the K of C fills up quickly. Enjoy Biddy O'Toole's recitation "I'm Nobody's Fool." Listen with delight to the amazing Canadian Eddy Adams yodelling "The Moonlight Trail." If you can't leave the comfort of the front room in your Chapel Street home, listen to a live broadcast of the performance on VOCM.

On Saturday, I kept Mrs. Doyle company while she listened to *Uncle Tim's Barn Dance*. I'd seen it in person with Thomas a week earlier, record numbers in attendance, triple the entire population of Pine Harbour, dogs included.

With the radio on full volume, Mrs. Doyle clapped when the audience clapped and said local men could sing better than Canadians. "They don't need to yodel to prove it either. For glory's sake, what's wrong with the radio? Fix it, Victoria."

There were shouts of "Fire!," then the broadcast stopped.

"Where are my girls? Who's at the K of C?" Mrs. Doyle glanced around the room like she expected to find them hiding behind furniture.

"Ellen's in bed. Theresa and Robert went bowling. Brigid's with Danny at the Seagoing Officers' Club."

"Virgin Mary help her. If fire doesn't kill her, she'll die of a broken neck from falling down the club's fifty-nine steps. Call the fire department."

"I can only do that supposing there's a fire."

"There *is* a fire. It's at the K of C."

"They already know that."

"What are you waiting for? Get on the phone."

I went to the kitchen where I waited, pretending to be talking to the operator, warning her of an emergency. When I returned to the front room, Mrs. Doyle was standing with her hand on the chair's back.

She made the sign of the cross. "Dear Lord, don't let this house burn down before Christmas. Save my home and my girls!" She clutched her rosary beads with one hand, her chest with the other. "Say the rosary with me, Victoria. We'll stay at it till they come home."

I recited the prayers earnestly, begging whoever was listening not to harm anyone and to bring an end to the war and its indiscriminate violence. The praying soothed her nerves, and her breathing gradually settled into a regular rhythm. We were on our eighth Hail Mary when I heard stomping in the hall, the door opened, and there stood Theresa. Mrs. Doyle raised her arms in the air, one minute blaming her for staying out late, the next, repeating how relieved she was Theresa hadn't gone to the K of C. Theresa took over patting her back and saying the rosary. We had to wait until midnight for Noreen and Brigid to arrive.

Brigid was crying. "People won't want to come to the wedding. Who'll want to celebrate with death and destruction everywhere around us? Dances scheduled in the city this week are already being cancelled."

"We're in a war," Noreen said. "The killing will carry on. We fight back with life and show them we won't let them destroy our morale. I don't know anyone else's plans, but this Christmas, I'm going to celebrate."

45

By Monday, nothing but ashes remained of the K of C site. On Chapel Street, anxiety smouldered. We discussed how best to protect the house in the event of a fire. We hired a taxi to pick up sand from the fire hall, then placed a bucketful on each floor along with two newly purchased stirrup pumps. People were also listing changes needed for public buildings—exit and entrance doors opening outwards and clear aisles with fastened chairs in auditoriums. At Noreen's factory, they'd held an emergency drill. The entire city was under heightened vigilance. Fire inspections were taking place in Newfoundland and across Canada.

Brigid and Danny were determined the wedding would go ahead, but Benjamin Dion, supposed to be sitting by me, might not make it.

"The Canadians are mourning their men lost in the fire," Brigid said.

Rose telephoned to say Private Furlong was too busy for a date. "No wonder. Whoever dropped that match needs to be caught, tarred, frigging feathered, and set ablaze."

Under other circumstances, I might have been disappointed by the lost opportunity to meet Benjamin, but I was far more concerned about finding someone with connections to the base. I might have called on Danny if he and Brigid weren't so busy preparing for their big day.

Theresa usually raised the pitch of her voice when upset. Had there been any crystal nearby, it would have shattered into pieces. "You want me to help you get into the base to see a Private Furlong to show him your weather journal? That's thirty minutes he could use to figure out who burned down the K of C, murdering a hundred innocent souls. They could have killed us if we'd been there. Some laddie's walking our streets, jiggling a pack of Eddy's, scheming where to strike next. Don't go pestering the Private, Violet. He's got more serious worries, like the rest of us."

"He told Rose he'll be stationed in Argentia in the new year. It's now or never."

"Never is right. Give up this forecaster dream and move on with your life. You're nearly twenty-three."

"If this doesn't work, I'll give up. I promise you."

"Here I am doing you favours again. I cleaned the bathroom twice this month. How often did you do it? Don't bother answering. It's zero. What are you planning to do for me for a change?"

"I'll assume your housecleaning duties for one month. Help me get in to see him, that's all I need."

"Two months. You can't waltz over to the base like in the spring. They've got new rules, guards on gates too. Proper thing these days. The way crime's heading in this city, we won't need a war to get us killed."

On the day of my cancelled date with Private Furlong, I went with Theresa to the base. I listened to the list of housekeeping duties I'd need to assume as part of our deal—the canvas flooring needed waxing, the stairs sweeping, and the bathrooms a Lestoil scrubbing. I should deal with the droppings in the cupboard, then go after the mice.

We passed through the base's guard station where I received my visitor's badge. She headed in one direction, I another.

"Tell them you heard they were looking for anyone with information," she said. "Say you were at the K of C a week earlier. Don't go lying. It's the American Army. They've got these things called lie detectors wired into their brains."

A PILOT'S BEST FRIEND

Both sides in this war rely on meteorological as well as military intelligence. Who more so than aviators? Fog reduces visibility, interferes with anti-submarine patrols, reconnaissance, and tactical movements. Wind affects takeoffs, landings, flight path, choice of runway, allowable weights, and more. Clouds sometimes make for a convenient hiding place even if it means more turbulence. Clear skies make it easier to see the target before dropping a bomb. Not surprisingly, accurate forecasts are a pilot's best friend.

Private Furlong seemed surprised to see me, like I was a missed date come to claim a rain check. "Sure, I remember you, miss. Have a seat for a minute." He glanced at his watch. "Your friend Rose was in touch. Sorry, but they got us working in our sleep. Some of our men were killed in that blaze."

I laid my weather journal on my lap, out of his sight. "I was at the K of C."

He looked at me, eyebrows raised. "The night of?"

"The week before with the Boston nightclub fire fresh in the headlines." I described what I'd experienced—an overflowing auditorium, chairs where there should have been aisles, wood where there should have been windows, exit doors that opened inwards. "I felt lucky to have made it out alive."

He turned the doorknob. "I'm real sorry you had to suffer that experience."

For an instant, I'd forgotten why I'd gone there. "Are you aware of how the wind fed and fanned the 1846 and 1892 fires? If its speed had been any higher during the K of C fire, the loss of life could have been far greater. You've heard of the Chicago fire in 1871? Flames fanned by wind and dry conditions destroyed a large part of the city."

He rubbed the skin on his chin like he was checking for stubble. "Sorry, I don't get it. The weather didn't kill those innocent people at the K of C. I'd say we got a bunch of Krauts on the loose. No offence intended."

"To be honest, I didn't come here about the fire. Let me show you something quickly, please." I laid my open weather journal on his desk, embarrassed by its water stains. I pointed to a forecast for March 16–18, 1941, then turned the page. "As you can see, I predicted that storm accurately." I paused, dismayed to see him check his watch. "This journal is proof of my knowledge of local winds and weather and of my forecasting ability. I'm certain I could be of valuable service to the Americans."

He scratched his head. "Our own trained men do that work."

I thought of my promise to Theresa, to let this be my last try. "Your men know the planetary and periodic winds. Not the local winds. They can bring blizzards, dense fog, intense rainfalls, swells, storm surges, and, as a friend used to say, whatever other mischief they're up to. I guarantee you, I could do as good a job or probably better than any of your men assigned to meteorological duties. If the Americans would simply allow me the—"

He sighed. "Okey-dokey. I heard the Royal Canadian Air Force needs folks at its new Torbay air base. Leave it with me. I'll send it their way. Seeing it's almost Christmas, I'm in the mood to do a good deed for a nice girl."

"Do it for your country, for the Allies, for victory."

46

Mrs. Doyle channelled her shock over the fire into a frenetic push to prepare for Christmas, as if the season's merriment could ward off tragedy. The house had to be scrubbed from top to bottom. Our tree had to be the biggest ever. Noreen warned her, if she put it up too early, the needles would fall off. Mrs. Doyle said if that happened, they'd buy a new one. Noreen said that the tree-sellers would be sold out. "Then you can head up to Bannerman Park, Noreen, and chop one down."

The Water Street shop windows showcased electric train sets, toy airliner models, army doctor/nurse kits, and pull-along dogs. Christmas raffles offered a chance to spin the wheel and try one's luck. Convents held their sales of work, featuring lace-trimmed pillowcases and doilies, fruit cakes, and homemade fudge in four colours and flavours. In keeping with the season's spirit, the classifieds' announcements encouraged customers to spend their newly earned dollars and buy that gift for the special man or woman. "Don't disappoint your loved ones," the ads warned.

The most essential gift to guarantee merriment at 12 Chapel Street wasn't oranges, grapes, nuts, or eggnog. It was tea. We had almost run out, as had everyone else in the city.

"Theresa will be crooked as sin without her morning tea," Mrs. Doyle said. "Noreen and Brigid will be on the warpath. Victoria won't know sleet from sweat. Ellen'll be snoring in class, and I'll be drinking my wintergreen oil."

"In your place," Theresa said to me, "I'd jump at the chance to prove to Mrs. Doyle that you got something to offer. Ellen doesn't need you anymore. Get a couple of tins of tea for her and you'll have her eating out of your barometer."

At Crag Point, the holiday passed us largely unnoticed, so I'd been looking forward to my first Christmas in St. John's. More than anything, I wanted to please Mrs. Doyle, not to win her favour but simply to make her happy. I went to see Don in dry goods at the Royal Stores, certain that he'd help me. He'd offered many times to do me a favour, perhaps hoping for a date in exchange.

"The last box is out back," Don said. "I need my boss's permission to sell it. He'll be at our Grand Falls store till the new year."

Ida could always be counted on to do a favour. I found her in ladies' wear.

"I'm run off my feet," she said. "Short on staff. Long on customers."

I explained about the tea.

"Ignore Don. Free on the twenty-third and fourth? If yes, there'll be a whole box waiting for you after your shift. Ten per cent off at that. Deal?"

I'd been looking forward to accompanying Brigid and Danny to the base on Christmas Eve for the distribution of gifts to needy children. On the day before, we'd planned to head to the Capitol Theatre to see the musical *Holiday Inn* with Bing Crosby and Marjorie Reynolds.

"Deal, yes," I said.

"Excellent. Not a peep to customers about the K of C fire," Ida said. "Be merry."

TEA RATIONING

Threats to transatlantic shipping have resulted in shortages of many household staples including molasses, canned meat, and salt pork. Government has limited price increases of products such as cocoa and is now introducing further measures. Sir J. C. Puddester, Commissioner for Public Health and Welfare, announces the introduction of rationing of tea on an honour system and asks citizens to halve their consumption. Exceptions may be made for individuals such as Mrs. Doyle, for whom a cup of Golden Pheasant Tea is like a dose of medicine.

On Christmas Eve, barely able to see where I stepped or hold onto the flashlight, I lugged the bulky box of tea up the hill from Water to Chapel Street. I scolded myself for having stayed late for staff celebrations with drinks, cake, and mistletoe under which I had to kiss Don from dry goods. I refused three drunk US soldiers and one Canadian sailor who'd offered to help me and arrived home, promising myself I'd never again walk the streets at night.

In the morning, I felt the bed shake.

Ellen's hand gripped my shoulder. "Hurry up. Mrs. Doyle wants her tea." She darted off so quickly, I wondered if I'd been dreaming.

I carried the box downstairs and opened the door to the front room where I stood facing them, smiling proudly.

"If I don't soon get a cup in me," Theresa said, "I'll be tearing out my eyelashes."

"I bought a six-month supply."

"It'll be stale as sawdust come spring," Mrs. Doyle said. "Give me a fresh cup now."

I laid the box on the floor by the tree. Ellen opened it and rummaged through the straw packaging, discarding it over the floor. Theresa told her to stop making a mess, grabbed a handful, and threw it in the fireplace. Flames shot up.

Mrs. Doyle held her rosary beads to her chest, protecting them. "Someone give Theresa a cup of tea before she burns down Christmas."

Ellen held up two tins.

Theresa and Noreen spoke at the same time. "Red Rose Tea."

Brigid examined a tin and read the label. "Made in New Brunswick, Canada. Red Rose Tea is good tea."

Mrs. Doyle waved her handkerchief to get our attention. "Where's my Golden Pheasant Tea?"

Theresa pointed at the floor. "That's your tea. Our tea."

No excuse was going to alter the taste. "Sorry," I said.

"Don't be like old people," Ellen said, pretending to juggle two tins. "Sorry, Mrs. Doyle. Get used to new things—tea, hairstyles, food. A week from tomorrow will be forty-three, not thirty-three. Nothing will ever change if *we* stay the same." She got up to leave the room. "I'm making a pot of Red Rose in case anyone wants a taste."

Ellen returned with the pot and cups, then served us. Theresa and I smiled. I recalled the day Ellen came home from school after her first math test. She'd received a score of ninety-two, and I'd felt optimistic about her future.

Ellen and I sat on the floor, tree needles clinging to the bottoms of our dressing gowns, drinking our tea along with the others. With the radio's volume on low, we waited for King George VI's Christmas address.

"I love Bertie," Mrs. Doyle said. "He tries so hard to be a good king."

"There's no king in the US," Brigid said.

"At least they got that much right," Noreen said.

The King spoke at last, clearly and slowly. We listened attentively while he talked about the Commonwealth citizens overseas in the Empire's outposts.

"Colonial propaganda," Noreen said. "Long may they not rule over us."

The King expressed condolences for those who'd lost loved ones in the war. I missed hearing his next sentence while Mrs. Doyle blew her nose and Theresa rubbed her back repeating, "There, there, we'll get used to the tea."

"They got no sisters over there, or what?" Noreen said, when he encouraged citizens to greet the future, together "in a spirit of brotherhood."

Brigid perked up at the mention of American comrades-in-arms. "This time tomorrow, I'll be walking down the aisle. I'll be—"

"A traitor to your country," Noreen said.

Theresa sang, "Here comes the bride. Here comes the bride."

"God bless you, Theresa," Brigid said.

"God bless us all," Mrs. Doyle said. "And God bless my Timmy, wherever he is."

BEACON IN A STORM

December 1941, two weeks after Japan's attack on Pearl Harbor and following a ten-day journey across the stormy, U-boat-infested Atlantic, Churchill arrived uninvited at the White House, to strengthen the countries' alliance. Churchill's address urged adults to ensure children grew up, not in a "world of storm" but in a free world. Roosevelt's speech referred to the Christmas spirit of brotherhood and dignity—a spirit needed for victory. The two leaders lit the 900 red, white, and blue bulbs on the National Christmas Tree. The tree will not be lit this year, nor again until the war ends.

47

I heard Brigid's snoring when I walked past her door. Had she been awake, she might have checked the weather on this eve of her wedding day. With the blackout curtains open, I stared, mesmerized by the sight of green snowflakes floating in the light beam. Not surprisingly, that night I dreamed in Technicolor, with Brigid's green tears, green wedding cake, and green dress.

I woke in the morning with her hovering over me like a cannon in my face.

"You specifically said not to worry, you'd tell me if we were due for snow."

I looked outside, then pointed to a taxi on Queen's Road. "The roads are passable. You'll walk down the aisle for certain."

The aisle wasn't the problem. As she explained in between her sobs, the couple hired to do the decorations for the reception lived on the city's outskirts. They'd sent word to the Old Colony Club that they couldn't get a taxi to take them there.

"You let me down. You of all people."

"Tell me what you need," I said. "I'll ask Noreen to help. We'll have those decorations up before you can say 'I do.'"

NEWFOUND NUPTIALS

Unions between local women like Brigid Molloy and American service personnel like Daniel O'Brien must comply with the Newfoundland Base Command rules. These are subject to change without notice. Servicemen must receive prior approval from their commanding officer or face pay cuts, jail time, demotion, transfer, and even court martial. A ninety-day waiting period is required following the initial request to marry. The future bride must undergo medical tests including those for

Venereal Disease. Canadian servicemen wishing to marry may do so freely. Soldiers serving in the Newfoundland Militia are not permitted to marry until the age of twenty-one.

That morning, the astringent taste of Red Rose irritating our palates, Noreen and I walked to the Club. We threw snowballs at each other, and I dropped one down her neck. She squealed and chased me around snowbanks. Out of breath, we stopped and lay on our backs to make snow angels.

"Can you keep a secret, Violet?"

"My ears are all yours."

"I met someone special, someone I like a lot. Jill's a nurse at the General Hospital. She drops by the factory once a week to check on the women. Doles out medicine, advice, examinations, for free." Noreen talked about their shared dreams, fighting for better conditions for women and basic rights for workers. "After the war, we'll move to Labrador. Jill's from there."

I listened with envy, wondering if I'd ever feel that way about someone, realizing it involved more than a wish for a kiss in a schoolhouse or the glitter of gifts and compliments. "This certainly is a happily-ever-after day."

"Not for the wedding, it isn't," she said. "Eighty guests. Bit much, don't you think?"

"If the celebration helps morale, it will be worth it."

"Morale?" Noreen said. "Free bar, don't forget. They'll be in a pack-up-your-troubles mood an hour after it starts. Doesn't matter if Danny's footing the bill for the lot. Bit hypocritical after what Brigid said about that cocktail party. I won't miss her. I doubt you'll be crying on your pillow, saying, 'Please come back home, Bridgy.'"

We were arm in arm as we entered the Club, then dropped them by our sides, a puddle of melted snow under our boots. Dangling from the ceiling were hundreds of red, white, and blue streamers left over from a Christmas dance.

Besides what the colours represented for Noreen, the streamers were dangerous. Similar decorations had helped fuel the fire at the K of C and at the Boston nightclub. Hadn't anyone learned a lesson?

Removing them wasn't hard. I merely held the ladder for Noreen, and in less than one hour, they were in the garbage. Brigid had told me where to find her decorations, including small paper American flags for the centre of each table.

"Mind walking home on your own?" Noreen said when I showed her the box of flags. "I officially resign. And on second thought, I think I'll skip the reception tonight."

I admired Noreen's beliefs but wished they didn't have to blind her to other possibilities. Her obsession with the various isms worried me, knowing what Vati had said about one of them in particular—extremism. "What if Jill happened to be an American?"

"Far from it. She's a Labradorian. A proud one too."

"What if?"

"She could be German for all I care."

"Exactly. Nationalism, patriotism, what do they matter if we simply want the same things—freedom, justice, and fairness? The Americans are our Allies, not our conquerors. We need to stand by them or lose this war. Imagine what that might mean for our future, yours and Jill's included. Freedom for women should mean choice. Why shouldn't Brigid be able to choose?"

"You know what, Violet? When I first met you that morning, braids around your head, barometer in your trunk, I said to myself, now there's a girl with her own mind. Later, you showed up, braids chopped off, fancy dress, lipstick. I said, there's another one sold her soul to the herd. Next came that arrogant colonizer, made you feel inferior. Thank your lucky stars you got rid of him, except then your pal Tommy showed up with your future planned. Here you are now, standing your ground, giving me advice, and dead set on putting that barometer to real use, as a forecaster. I say to myself, she could be part of this new crop of women ready to claim what we're owed, willing to fight for a fair and equal place in the world. I hope that's true."

"Ready and willing."

All flags were on the tables when we left the Club. We accepted a ride to Chapel Street from a delivery man headed that way, crammed into the rear of his truck, and arrived with reddened cheeks, our hair pulled stiff.

Mrs. Doyle's door opened and Theresa poked her head out wanting to know if I'd lent Ellen my makeup. "I won't have my niece sitting in a pew wrapped up like a present for a My-name-is-Randy fellah in a uniform. Get her to take it off. And don't forget to sweep down the stairs." She closed the door with a bang.

Mrs. Doyle shouted, "Virgin Mary, get me through this day."

I was walking past Ellen's room when she jumped out in front of me.

"Sorry, didn't mean to scare you. Holy hair!" She laughed. "Did you fly here? Make sure you fix yourself up." She twirled around, then bent over to eye her waist. "Belt or no belt? Any advice?"

"I shouldn't have lent you the makeup. I wasn't thinking."

She trudged noisily on the third-floor steps behind me, making it obvious I'd spoiled her mood. "Don't be a square, Violet. Lots of girls my age wear makeup. This is the forties."

"Theresa doesn't want—"

"Me leaving this house till I'm married."

"She'll be mad at me."

"It's not you, Violet. She's terrified her voice will crack in the middle of 'Over the Rainbow.' She doesn't want a spotlight on her, says she won't be able to sing if she can't see the audience."

"All the more reason to ease the tension."

"Take her side if you want. Just so you know, if I'd failed math, Theresa would have sent you back to your Greg Point."

"Crag Point. I don't believe you."

"Because I got too good at math to fail."

"Do it for my sake, please, for your dedicated tutor."

By the time we arrived at the Cathedral, Ellen was wearing no trace of makeup.

Theresa sat between us. She bit her nails and whispered complaints in my ear, accusing Brigid of not having forewarned her she'd have to use a microphone, and admonishing herself for the choice of songs for a mostly American audience. "I'm no Judy Garland, no Sinatra either. They'll boo me."

When Brigid walked down the aisle, everyone turned to admire her, angelic in her dress made of ivory satin with floating lace panels around the neckline and lace sash. She had declined Mrs. Doyle's offer to lend her a fox-fur stole. Mrs. Doyle herself wore it draped over her shoulders, its beady eyes disproportionately large, a reminder of the creature that had preyed on Maryanne's nerves. "The mister did a grand job on the paws. You'd think I had a real fox around my neck."

Mrs. Clarke waved from across the aisle. Brigid had initially said she wouldn't invite her because she didn't want strangers at her wedding. Mrs. Doyle said if she herself had taken the same attitude toward strangers, she never would have welcomed me into her home. "Pity that'd be."

48

Squalls of confetti showered us as we crowded outside on the Cathedral's landing. Maybe even U-boat crews heard the bells ringing out cheer. The newlyweds kissed while cameras captured perfect moments and onlookers shouted, "Congratulations!" Brigid and Danny drove off in a chauffeured Cadillac limousine with a heart-shaped banner that said *Just Married* and three empty cans of Del Monte fruit cocktail dangling from the bumper. Mrs. Doyle rode in a taxi with Robert, Theresa, and Ellen. Noreen accepted a ride with Brigid's cousin in the front cab of his truck.

I preferred to plow through the snow on foot. I'd done it once in the morning and had an urge to be outside. The barometer had delivered on its promise of a high-pressure system after the snowfall with below-average cold, above-average beautiful, and no wind. Smoke rose straight up from chimneys into a velvety blue sky over a dazzling white landscape. I walked past the fine mansions on Rennies Mill Road, admired the architecture, and remembered the Circular Manor, its Grand Hall, Downtown Daiquiris, Mrs. Barrow's "daaling," and Philip's "Goodbye, Violet."

In the valley, I stopped at the bridge and peered at Rennie's River for signs of overwintering brown trout. I'd seen boys wading in the water in the spring, capturing them with their bare hands. I gazed up at the giant trees that formed a canopy overhead. Without leaves, the branches resembled black filigree. In the brilliance of that winter afternoon, I forgot about those seemingly interminable days of blinding fog, horizontal rain, and hostile winds. On such a spectacular day, I was profoundly in love with life. I'd brave its cycles of loss and gain, hurt and healing like I braved the elements, accepting the worst, rejoicing at the best, adapting to the harshness—taking a lesson from the tuckamore.

When I arrived at the reception, the lobby was overflowing with guests, its air clouded with tobacco smoke.

Brigid was the first person I recognized.

"Congratulations, brilliant Brigid. Brilliant inside and out."

She took hold of my hand. "I'm so sorry for this morning. The snow wasn't your fault. I was so nervous."

"I should have done a better—"

A guest interrupted and pulled her aside.

"See you later," Brigid said.

I headed to the dining hall where I found the others at our house's table—Mrs. Doyle, Mrs. Clarke, Noreen, Ellen, Robert, a seat reserved for Theresa, and by my side, a man in a Canadian uniform.

He stood, then pulled out my chair. "Sergeant Benjamin Dion, RCAF, from Montreal. Friend of the groom."

"Violet Morgen, friend of the bride, from here."

His smile reminded me of Vati's, with squinting eyes and lips shut. Brigid had said we had something in common. I understood what she'd meant when he told me he served at the air base in Torbay. His main duties involved assessing and advising on meteorological conditions before takeoffs and landings. If Maryanne had been there, she would have nudged me to say, "Let him breathe," but I had so many questions. A noisy reception where I had to raise my voice to be heard wasn't the best place to ask for his help. "I want to work there," I said, not skirting around, opening up to him as if he was the last person on earth I could trust, sharing everything from Maryanne's idea of maximum qualifications all the way to Private Furlong's offer to send my weather journal to the RCAF.

"Would you do that?" I said, after Benjamin offered to arrange for me to see his commanding officer at the Torbay base.

"For certain. I'd be doing the RCAF a favour."

SONGS FOR THE SEASON

Ever since the tune played on radio in 1941, Irving Berlin's bestselling "White Christmas" has blown the top off the music charts. Bing Crosby has sung the simple, sincere melody at home and abroad for servicemen and women. They beg him to sing it even though it makes them long for home. The song reminds us that the spirit of Christmas is both optimistic and melancholic, especially for Berlin who lost his infant son to illness on Christmas Day, 1928.

Theresa stood at the front of the room wearing a dress made by Ida—a floor-length, powder-pink, sequin gown that shimmered in the spotlight. Had it not been for Ida's encouragement and Ellen's coaching, she would have been sitting alongside us, ruminating over a missed opportunity.

"Talk first, sing later," Ellen had advised her. "Tell a joke. Shake out the ants in your pants, then open your mouth, shut your eyes, and pretend you're singing in the Cathedral, asking for the Almighty's attention."

The microphone came on with a high-pitched screech that had us plugging our ears. After repeats of "Can you hear me?" followed by congratulations to the newlyweds, she delivered the lines practiced in our kitchen.

"I prayed to St. Jude to have a chance to sing in front of an audience, and here I am. Let's show him our appreciation." Her voice sounded as confident as that night when she'd stood in the doorway, ordering me to go away.

Guests clapped and Robert put four fingers between his lips to whistle. Mrs. Doyle quipped that if there were any dogs within a mile, they'd be crowding around the front entrance, expecting a free bone.

"Thank you," Theresa said. "St. Jude heard you loud and clear. Any more mention of his accomplishments and he'll be needing a holiday."

The audience laughed. Robert whistled again.

Ellen waved her arms in the air. "Go, Theresa!"

"Over the Rainbow" practiced in the Chapel Street house sounded hollow compared to this version with a microphone and accompanied by an orchestra. For a petite woman, Theresa had, as Noreen described it, "the voice of a lion," yet the notes rang out lightly. She started out quickly but sang slowly on the final, "Why, oh why can't I?" She held the last note while the audience stood and applauded.

Robert couldn't have appeared more enthusiastic if he'd been hired for that purpose, especially when she blew him a kiss and the room echoed with whistles from the audience.

She waved a hand in the air to attract our attention, then introduced the orchestra, The Quidi Vidis. "Get ready for the number one hit, 'White Christmas.' Another song about dreams. Many of you are away from home, away from people you love, from the people who know your story. Think of them while you sing along." She held the microphone with one hand and directed the voices with the other.

If the guests sang any louder, the light fixtures would have rattled. They could sing at the top of their lungs and still not disturb Mrs. Doyle. She and Mrs. Clarke swayed side to side, eyes closed. Noreen's voice sounded the strongest of our group, the sincerest too. I liked Benjamin's "White Christmas" voice, in perfect harmony with my own, singing a song about weather, longing for snow.

49

"SHE SERVES THAT MEN MAY FLY"
The RCAF (Women's Division) invites women aged 19 to 41 to join its
ranks. Examples of positions available: waitresses, drivers, hospital
assistants, telephone operators, laundry women, and meteorological
technicians (observers and plotters) with knowledge of mathematics
and physics. Following training, women may be posted to wherever
their services are required. Applicants must pass a relevant trade test,
meet weight guidelines, have completed at minimum grade 8 and be of
good moral character, minimum height five feet. Character reference
required from current employer. Forget Uncle Sam. Serve the Empire
by serving Canada.

The driver gripped the wheel and leaned forward like he was pushing the taxi, not simply steering it. He complained that he'd never driven so far out of the city and wouldn't have agreed to take me to the Torbay air base if he'd known the roads were so treacherous. Besides that, the treads on his tires were worn thin. He wouldn't be buying new ones with tire theft common in the city and rubber in short supply.

"Hold on for your life," he said as we slid down a hill.

On the way up again, I thought I'd need to get out to push.

Once we arrived, he apologized for taking so long to get me there. His last words were, "Buy some grips for your gaiters."

I had Sergeant Benjamin Dion to thank for arranging the meeting with Major Ingles, a name that sounded familiar though I couldn't think why.

Benjamin had promised to make sure my weather journal sent by Private Furlong would end up in the right hands at the RCAF. "We need people with your skills," he'd said.

I followed the directions he'd given me on the phone—two o'clock, December 30. A sign on the door said *Enter*. I stood outside while I caught my breath. Whatever happened, I had to be sure to walk out of there with an offer. That meant making a good first impression, not saying the wrong thing or too much, and acting confident without being argumentative.

"Major Ingles had almost given up on you," a woman said.

She led me into an office where a man sat behind a desk, the Canadian Red Ensign hanging on a flagstaff. I recognized him immediately. He wore the same uniform and had parted his hair to one side, combed over the top to conceal his baldness.

Blood rose to my head like the room was one hundred degrees. My ears felt hot. Did he recognize me in my winter coat rather than a little black dress?

He pointed to a seat. "I received your file and journal from a Private Furlong at Fort Pepperrell. Unfortunately, I haven't had the opportunity to view the journal. However, Sergeant Dion confirmed that it demonstrates the type of knowledge and skills we require. You can thank him for the reference and for making sure both documents were brought to my immediate attention."

"Indeed, I will, Major."

"I don't have much time, Miss Morgen. This war must be waged by land, air, and by sea. RCAF airmen play a vital role in defending Newfoundland. However, the complexity of this war along with labour shortages are placing great demands on our human resources. We're broadening our search for talent and expertise, including among civilians and women for our ground staff. You claim to have an amateur's background in meteorology—self-taught. I'll get to the point. Tell me briefly, how might weather conditions affect aerial patrols this afternoon?"

I turned to face the window, blocking out the memories of that cocktail party, and reminding myself of the depth of my knowledge. "The ceiling appears adequate with minimal cloud cover. However, one hour ago, my thermometer at approximately half this elevation showed thirty-two degrees Fahrenheit, the freezing point of water, as you know. My estimate of offshore winds is thirty miles per hour, making the temperature much cooler. Add high humidity to those conditions. In summary, Major, you have ideal conditions to foster accumulation of ice on aircraft. Ice can affect everything from lift, airspeed, propeller rotation, not to mention that a buildup on the windshield can blind the pilot's—"

"Yes, yes, enough, thank you. We're looking for meteorologists, not mechanics." He gazed out the window, then at me. "I understand from your file, you're fluent in written and spoken German."

I nodded.

"That may be of value to us later. French?"

"No, sir."

"On a different topic, patrols and reconnaissance missions rely on forecasts to plan tactical movements. Those forecasts are part of our arsenal and are encoded prior to transmission to prevent them falling into enemy hands. Need I explain further the importance of secrecy?"

I was glad he'd asked that question. "Those forecasts are our best weapon, forecasters our unsung heroes. I've been saying forever the *Kriegsmarine* is surely attempting to set up its own weather station in a hidden cove along—"

He raised a hand, palm forward, to silence me. "In a military organization, loyalty must be guaranteed, even by civilians. Your father's naturalization records show he served with the Imperial German Navy up until 1918. Are you aware of any recent collaboration between him and the Nazis?"

"My father worked as a naval engineer until the start of the Great War when he began serving with the *Kaiserliche Marine*. His main duty was helping improve the accuracy and range of torpedoes at longer distances. He loved his country, despised the extremists, the fascists, and abhorred any form of violence. He was the last person on earth who'd ever collaborate with the Nazis."

Major Ingles studied me, his eyes framed by thick, black-rimmed glasses. "And *your* loyalty? What of it?"

"I can confirm my loyalty absolutely one hundred per cent. I'm ready to answer Churchill's call—" I lowered my gaze. "Excuse me, sir, I mean, Major."

"Loyalty is required, not merely to the Empire or Allies, but to the organization and one's superiors, under all circumstances, sober or inebriated, on duty, in training, or at a cocktail party. Criticism of any aspect of our operations may not only negatively affect morale, it may encourage the enemy and undermine our efforts. That means no talk of Royal Canadian Air Fog."

I was sure he could see me blushing, and that made me blush even more. "I don't plan to be in that condition ever again and won't utter a syllable related to the problems with an air base at such a high elevation where fog tends—"

He lifted his hand again, palm forward. "You were Captain Campbell's guest that evening. You claimed the Germans are laughing at the Canadians. If it happens again, I'm afraid you'll have to forget any opportunities to serve with us."

"Never. 'Victory to the Allies.' That's what I'll say next time."

"There can be no next time. Speaking of time—enough squandered. Sergeant Dion has vouched for your suitability for the position. His colleague in the US Army, Daniel O'Brien, vouched for your character. I spoke to Captain Philip Campbell on the telephone this morning at our Gander air base. He said you had, and I quote, 'a brilliant sixth sense for predicting weather.' That is quite a reference coming from a man of his skill and experience."

I might have asked what else, if anything, he'd said, but it wasn't the right moment. "Yes, Major. Quite."

"I'm offering you an opportunity to develop that sixth sense. Beginning early in the new year, you'll need to complete an intensive course in meteorology along with a select group of other civilians, all men for now. The course covers the basics of observation, creating weather maps, plotting, and—"

"Forecasting is where I belong. I know my talents. They lie in the analysis and interpretation of patterns and past averages, not the mere observation or collection of information."

"We're in the military. We operate according to protocol and procedures. You'll need to go where you're assigned." He drummed his fingers on the file. "Clear?"

"Thank you, Major. Clear as the bluest sky on a frigid winter morning with a high-pressure system from the north."

He leaned across his desk to shake my hand. "My secretary will fill you in on the details. One final question. Do you go by Morgen or Morgenstern?"

"I prefer the latter, Major. Morgenstern means morning star. When there's water in the air—for example, after a hurricane—the morning star may appear in a violet sky. You see, Major Ingles, I was destined from birth to be passionate about the weather."

I left his office imagining the reaction once I announced my news. On my way down the stairs, I realized I'd forgotten to ask the taxi driver to wait. When I saw his vehicle parked by the side of the building, I told myself this was indeed my lucky day.

He was leaning on the taxi, staring at the runway, a cigarette dangling from his lips, hood up. "First time in my twenty-one years I saw the likes of it," he said. "Two took off and one landed. I could stand here forever watching those planes."

I'd only ever seen airplanes in the sky. I stared at one parked on the runway, expecting any minute for Captain Campbell to emerge from the cockpit in his sheepskin jacket, and say, "I missed you." In return, I'd tell him, "Thanks for the reference and for teaching me to dance."

The driver took one last draw on his cigarette, then threw it onto the ground, still lit. "What I wouldn't give to learn to fly." He cupped his hands and blew air onto them.

"If this war drags on, you might have an opportunity to do exactly that," I said.

He opened the taxi's door. "Right you are, lady. It's not all bad, the war's not. As long as our side wins."

"I'm optimistic."

50

December 31, 1942

Dear Maryanne,

Goodbye to 1942, a record-breaking year. Greetings, 1943. I have ~~high hopes~~ great plans for you. Please don't disappoint.

Work. Who said a woman from an ancient crag can't be taken seriously or that there's no such thing as maximum qualifications? Here I come, RCAF! Even if the war ends tomorrow, airports will continue to need people with my skills. Benjamin says commercial aviation will "take off" at the Torbay Airport and that Gander Airport, the largest in the world when it opened in 1938, will become one of the busiest with transatlantic flights stopping there to refuel. Working for the Canadians will be an honour. Noreen admires their prime minister, Dr. Mackenzie King, and his promotion of social welfare. She likes to remind me that the Canadians came to defend our shores long before the Americans. As for working alongside men only, I plan to wear slacks, Fitz Originals. They're so much more comfortable and practical than a skirt.

Chapel St. For Christmas, Robert gave T. a silver bracelet and heart charm engraved with R. & T. She gave him a wool sweater knit by a friend on Bell Island, a key to our front door in its pocket. T.'s spectacular performance at the reception has already led to two offers to sing at local clubs. Rose will be her manager, and Ida's going to outfit her in stage wear. Ida's given Ellen Saturday shifts in footwear. She finished the first term top of her class in mathematics, top too for talking back to the sisters, telling them their robes are medieval. She hides in my room and from T.'s eyes a tube of Montezuma

Red lipstick, a package of Lucky Strikes, and a silver-plated brass lighter, Brian H. engraved on it.

Brigid is hoping for a little Brigid or Danny by late 1943 or early 1944. Noreen said, for a Yank, Danny was all right. She had fun at the reception and was impressed that, despite the free alcohol, not a single fight broke out the entire evening. However, she doesn't want Brigid to send postcards from the US. She's met a kindred spirit, Jill, a nurse committed to fighting for better conditions for women factory workers. With Brigid now gone, there's an empty bed in the room. Noreen says Jill is considering boarding here. We (esp. Mrs. D.) would welcome a nurse in the house. Mrs. D. offered to say a novena to help Noreen be promoted to forelady. Noreen told her not to bother. Labour shortages mean conditions for strikes have never been better. Recruiting union members is a far more effective use of her talents, spreading awareness of the need for equality a better use of her voice. She says after the war, there'll be no going back to how things were for women. No going back for Nfld either. Hurrah!

Benjamin. Tonight, I have a New Year's Eve date with Benjamin at the Caribou Hut. We got to know each other well at the reception. I showed him how to foxtrot. Soon as ponds freeze over, he'll take me skating and has promised to teach me a few French words. Next week, we're going to see a hockey game at the St. Bon's rink. You'd think we'd been friends forever. He was impressed to learn I'd grown up at a light station and asked a hundred questions. I told him all about you. He walked me home. We stopped on Rennies River bridge to play I spy. I spied a man who, like me, could talk endlessly about weather and winds. He spied a woman confident in her role in the world and place in the universe.

Crag Point. Thomas sent a note to say Teo went to Nova Scotia, seeking work of the non-lighthouse kind. While in Pine Harbour waiting for the steamer, he visited your grave to say a prayer. The new keeper has settled in with his wife and son. He's from a cove on Nfld's Northern Peninsula, population seventeen, and felt the place had become overcrowded.

Looking forward. I bought a notebook for volume two of my commonplace book, with cover and strap ties in lovely brown cowhide leather. Training will occupy me, but I'll aim for one entry per week. No reporting on weather. Nor on the war, which I sincerely hope will end before volume two *does. Lots to write. I'll be meeting plenty of new Canadian civilian and military personnel. Exciting adventures ahead. As someone once told me, my story's not over yet.*

I'll end with, "Till we meet again" rather than "Hope to see you soon."

Auf Wiedersehen,

Violet

EDITOR'S FAREWELL

Farewell to 1942, a most auspicious year, sure to be indelibly etched in our tea leaves. How shall we remember it? As a year of tumult and transformation? Alien invasions, saboteurs, and strangers, or coming of age of a girl and a nation? All honours aside, 1942 is history. Let us welcome 1943 with trumpet fanfare. May it bring following winds and record-breaking comfort, victories great and small, friends merry and bright, just like the ones we used to know, and teapots filled to the brim. Red Rose will do.

EPILOGUE

1944: Weather observations from Newfoundland are taken into consideration by British meteorologist James Stagg in his recommendation to postpone D-Day from June fifth to sixth.

1945: The Allies accept and celebrate Germany's and Japan's surrender.

1946: Fort Pepperrell becomes Pepperrell Air Force Base.

1949: The Dominion of Newfoundland becomes Canada's tenth province.

1961: Pepperrell reverts to its former name, Pleasantville. The 208 buildings are turned over to Canada and Newfoundland.

1977: An automatic *Wetter-Funkgerät Land-26* weather station, code-named Kurt, is discovered on the coast of northern Labrador. Set up by a Nazi U-boat crew in 1943, it is camouflaged with discarded packages of American cigarettes and containers marked as *Canadian Meteor* [sic] *Service*. Kurt's remnants are on display in the Canadian War Museum, Ottawa.

2000: Violet turns eighty.

AUTHOR'S NOTES AND ACKNOWLEDGEMENTS

If it hadn't been for the opportunity to read my mother's diary, this story would never have been told. Her first entry was as follows: *Sitting at our table at Hill Crest. New Year's Day. No snow. Had a dance at Hall tonight.* My mother, eighteen-year-old Maisie, was at home at Branch, Newfoundland, on holiday from her clerk-stenographer position at the Fort Pepperrell base where she worked from 1944 until her marriage in 1949. Maisie's descriptions of life in St. John's featured parties, dances, concerts, movies, sports, and other forms of entertainment—nothing like what I'd expected for wartime.

Curious, I began reading books and articles about the period. What stood out was the positive social and economic transformation of Newfoundland during the Second World War. Before long, I'd imagined a story centred around themes of coming-of-age, development of agency, self-discovery, and determination. Inspiration for the setting came from familiar places. In the 1960s, our family spent summers in Branch in a house on a hill overlooking the ocean, without electricity, indoor plumbing, or many other conveniences. As for Chapel Street, I still picture my dear grandmother Molly by the coal fireplace at number twelve (now torn down), rubbing wintergreen oil on her arthritic joints. For the narrative, I was inspired by L. Frank Baum's *The Wonderful Wizard of Oz*—the tale of a spirited young woman on a quest in a strange land with larger-than-life characters, some helpful, some hindering, a quid pro quo in the balance, and agency at stake.

I began writing, unaware of the challenges of historical fiction. Even simple things like names could be problematic. In 1942, the Basilica was the RC Cathedral; the Crow's Nest, the Seagoing Officers' Club. Gander Airport was initially the Newfoundland Airport. Sources sometimes contradicted each other—for example, regarding on which side of the road vehicles operated on the base and whether or not department stores hired according to religion. In all cases, where possible, I relied on sources Violet, as narrator, would have had access to in 1942.

However, censorship during the war meant she would not have read, though may have heard of, some incidents. For example, a plane crash in the *Evening Telegram* referred to "Somewhere in Newfoundland" instead of "in Botwood." Narrowing the story's scope was another challenge. Though the war lasted six years, I limited my focus to 1942. Yet, as Kevin Major's brilliant *Land Beyond the Sea* showed, whole books could be written about single incidents within that one year. The omission of Labrador had to do with scope, as did the need to gloss over topics like the blackouts and air raids.

Though I've aimed to portray authentically the period and context, *The Weather Diviner* is nonetheless a work of fiction. I took liberty with various details, including the train's times and Violet's single cabin on the SS *Clyde*, which likely had bunks for four. Though the Torbay Airport opened in 1941, the construction of a terminal building may not have been completed until months after Violet's meeting there. In terms of authenticity, I relied extensively on primary sources, in particular on 1942 local newspapers available in microfilm from St. John's Public Libraries or online through Memorial University Libraries. Memorial's Centre for Newfoundland Studies and Digital Archives Initiative offered access to a rich source of 1942 documents, from curriculum guides to telephone directories.

MUN's Research Repository allowed me to consult theses written about the period. Through its library, I accessed journals such as *Newfoundland & Labrador Studies* and *Acadiensis* and various works of non-fiction including Steven High's *Occupied St. John's: A Social History of a City at War, 1939–1945*; Morley Thomas's *Metmen in Wartime: Meteorology in Canada 1939–1945*; and Allan M. Fraser's *History of the Participation by Newfoundland in World War II*. I also accessed books by local authors, including Paul Butler, John Cardoulis, Paul Collins, Jack Fitzgerald, Roderick Goff, Maura Hanrahan, Darrell Hillier, Darrin McGrath, Peter Neary, and Steve

Neary. I found invaluable information from websites of the following: Canadian War Museum, Digital Museums Canada (Community Stories), Environment and Natural Resources Historical Weather Data, Gander Airport Historical Society, Gander Historical Society, Heritage NL, Maritime History Archive (Memorial University), and Newfoundland and Labrador Heritage.

A deep and heartfelt thank you goes to friends and family who, in some cases, read multiple drafts and provided relevant feedback. Thanks to local scholars and experts who responded to questions by email. Kudos to Breakwater Books for the extensive supports they provided and, in general, for the vital and expert role they play in promoting and preserving the culture of the province. Rhonda Molloy is the artistic genius behind the cover and overall design. George Murray is the marketing wizard. Bravo! Sincere thanks to those who completed manuscript reviews and/or editing, in particular, Kate Kennedy, Marianne Ward, and Hélène Crowley. I greatly appreciate your professionalism, keen eyes, attention to detail, and in-depth knowledge of craft. Finally, thank you, dear reader. May Violet's adventures inspire you to discover more about this extraordinary time and place.

Born and raised in Newfoundland, Elizabeth Murphy spent her professional career in a variety of educational roles—as teacher, administrator, and professor. She completed her Ph.D. in Quebec, won awards for her research and writing while working at Memorial University, and served as a visiting professor in Bangkok. Nova Scotia is where she now lazes, reads, writes, and dreams of summer back home on the island and winter far away in Thailand. *The Weather Diviner* is her second novel.